Memento Mori

Margaret Sherlock

Memento Mori

Shorelines  Publishing

First published in 2015
by
Shorelines Publishing
3 St. Marks Drive, Meadfoot, Torquay, Devon.TQ1 2EJ

Copyright © 2015 Margaret Sherlock
ISBN: 978-0-9559710-8-2

Also available as Kindle eBook

Cover artwork tracey.turner@blueyonder.co.uk
Typesetter elainesharples@btinternet.com
Printed by Short Run Press Limited, Exeter

Dedicated to Mum, Dad, Tommy and Billy
Always remembered, always loved

There are mysteries within the soul which no hypothesis
can uncover and no guess can reveal.

Spiritual Sayings by Kahlil Gibran

Introduction

Gold rings can outlive man by hundreds or even thousands of years. These tokens of love which are just as important today, seem to have a life of their own; as if the emotion behind the reasons for fashioning them, is still present within the metal's indestructible fabric.

As the ring passes through the centuries from generation to generation or from stranger to stranger, intrigue grows and curiosity burns. Method and style of manufacture, inscriptions and set gems, all give a clue as to the ring's original intention and sometimes to its original owner, but as time passes, the truth can become harder to find.

This tale contains three sets of characters spanning three hundred years.

But throughout those three centuries, it is the ring that is the binding factor. The ring that takes centre-stage. How its survival and avoidance of the melting pot, makes its mark on the hearts and minds of its three different owners. And dare I say, altering the path of their lives.

PART ONE

The Fashioning

Chapter 1

Cockington – July 1707

Edmund rolled his badly injured body into the dry ditch of the hedgerow, holding back the urge to cry out in pain. The two henchmen were almost upon him. In the dead of night, even a muffled cry would carry on the breeze that was blowing their way. Dawn was almost here and his eyes were alert. As were his pursuers. Heart beating fast but with stayed breath he lay still as a corpse until the two heavily-laden steeds shook the earth and passed. Even then he kept still for a time, breathing deeply of the damp earth beneath his face. When certain he was alone, he shifted his body, turning his head skyward. The movement brought increased pain. The disturbance shaking the hedgerow above him sending droplets of dew to fall upon his face, spots of moisture travelling slowly down his brow and nose. With infinite patience he waited, groaning inwardly as each droplet veered off over his cheeks before reaching his parched lips.

In earnest he'd ridden hard through the night, doubling back in places to outfox his pursuers. It had proved too much for the mare, for she had collapsed beneath him, rolling onto Edmund as she did so. His left arm was done for, bones broken in several places including his wrist. Swelling had already begun, snaking from elbow to fingers, tightening the Memento Mori, as though the ring too throbbed and pulsed with heated anger as it moulded and squeezed to become one with his finger.

Very, very slowly he drew his right hand from under his thigh and reached for a clump of dog rose, its leaves pregnant with dewy mounds. With trembling fingers he tilted the leaves toward his open mouth. The few drops that found their mark were all too quickly gone, leaving a thirst unsatisfied but a lingering taste of the sweetest elixir.

The sky began to lighten and birdsong filled the air, heralding the start of a new day and the easy chance of being seen. Weary with tiredness but mindful of the rogues that still hunted him, he grasped again at the straggly clump of dog rose to make use of its thorns. Ignoring the pricks of pain he tethered long strands of the vine to his clothing, covering the length of his body. Satisfied he could do no more until darkness fell, he closed his eyes.

* * *

A rustling movement around the inner folds of Edmund's tunic dragged him to full alertness and instinctive action. In one fluid movement, his right hand locked onto the handle of the blade held at his waist. Then almost as quickly and in disgust of himself the blade was put away. Long-tailed, four-legged-vermin were the only hunters around and they'd scurried away in fright the moment he'd moved. The track running alongside this part of the ditch, stretching between the Parish Church of Cockington to the Old Abbey at Torre, was little used on days other than the sabbath; even so, he dare not leave this earthy resting place until darkness fell once more.

The sun was higher now and all trace of dew had burned away leaving in its stead the delicate perfume of the dog rose. One such bloom was trapped above Edmund's face – a vision of perfect loveliness. With clenching heart he became mindful of Agnes. Agnes, his one and only love. He'd resisted the indulgence of thinking of her for so long, working overly hard as if a man possessed. He *was* possessed, possessed by guilt. Perhaps the time was ripe for facing his shortcomings. To accept that it was *his* selfishness, *his* weakness that had led to her death. A body racked with pain, was nought compared to the wounds that pierced his heart. He couldn't sleep now, too many phantoms were waiting to steal that pleasure. But still half a day would need to pass before darkness fell. Time enough to face his demons and set the record straight.

Chapter 2

Cockington Court – September 1705

Almost two years had passed since I first laid eyes on Agnes. She was sixteen years old, on the verge of womanhood. I was delivering a consignment of wine and brandy to the Court in readiness for a banquet that very evening. I can't bring to mind what was being celebrated, politics have never interested me and politics seemed to be the only topic of conversation around that time. After making sure my fragile cargo was safely stored, I was taken to the kitchen to deposit the two crates of dried fruit and a linen-lined box of sweet-spice. I was hungry, I recall, and the aroma of boiling fruit, baking pies and roasting meats that mingled and drifted around the place, quickened my step, for I knew from past experience the cook was most generous.

Agnes had her back to me, her arms lost amongst the copper pans that cook insisted she 'scrub until you see that pretty face in 'em'. Her corn-silk hair was secured high on her head, little wisps escaping from the effort of the scrubbing. Although the work was arduous, she laughed merrily as the older woman taunted her about the importance of clean pots, and how as a girl, she often nursed bleeding knuckles at the end of a pan scrubbing session. Cook then softened this remark by bidding the girl to rest awhile, to dry her hands and sit at the kitchen table and sample a slice of one of the apple pies that had just been lifted from the oven. Two slices were cut and placed on a board at the end of the large table – a chair on one side, a three-legged stool on the other. As befitting my station, the chair was mine, but the sight of Agnes' beauty caused rebellion to course through my veins. Insisting that she take the chair, I perched on the tiny stool, chuckling with her at the ridiculous sight I made. For a while neither of us spoke, choosing instead to watch the steam drift up and off toward the open window where it magically disappeared like my rebelliousness. We were shy of each other and as the elder I felt it my duty to bridge the gap of silence, but before I had chance, Agnes reached for the nearer slice of pie saying, 'You may have all day to ponder, kind sir, but I have many more pots awaiting.' The boldness of her remark, impressed me almost as much as her beauty.

From that day forth, I found every excuse to return to Cockington Court. It wasn't difficult, I was the son of a wool merchant of much standing. After each sea voyage to the Near Continent – laden down with the finest bales of wool serge that England could produce – the ship returned with equal measure. Fine wine, linen, tea, silver, silks and spices were in ever increasing demand by the gentry, and especially greedy for these goods was the Squire of Cockington Manor. At this time of year, as many as four trips a month was commonplace. In spite of the age difference of ten years, Agnes and I became close friends, and gradually, without shame or embarrassment, she told of her sorry status.

Her mother had died giving birth to her. Her father, anxious that this bore no guilt on Agnes, gave many reminders that she was so in likeness to the mother she never knew, that for him, it was as though she still lived. He had been the blacksmith of the manor – as his father and grandfather before him – hard-working and respected by all that needed his service. What money came spare he used willingly for his daughter's learning, that she may read, write and prosper in a trade of *her own choosing. For in due time, the smithy would pass to another man's son.*

That time came sooner than expected. In the winter of 1704, Agnes' father fell victim to a vile fever that left his body so weakened it eventually robbed him of the strength to wield a hammer, and in spite of good money spent on doctoring, he had to give up his trade and rely on Agnes for his nursing. The almshouses at Cockington had long since been allowed to fall into disrepair, but as a gesture of goodwill, the Squire allowed a few of the villagers to make one ready as best they could for the ailing blacksmith and his daughter. And, as further help, Cook persuaded the Court housekeeper to employ Agnes by day, allowing her to keep company with her father during the dark hours.

My own father was becoming much impatient with my frequent visits to Cockington. Being the only son in a family of four children, I carried responsibility for one day taking his place and it was expected that I be at his side in all dealings regarding business. But of late, I'd made excuses on many occasion to be elsewhere. He didn't need to ask, anyone that knew me could see I was smitten. My eyes shone, my face wore a constant smile and an inner merriment lightened my step. His first enquiry of the woman who was stealing my affections, was that of status and expectancy of dowry. I responded saying that it was too soon to talk of such things but she was learned enough for reading and writing and her dowry of a true and loving heart would be wealth enough for me.

* * *

It was 31st October, All-Hallows-Eve, an unusually mild, still evening with stars aplenty and a bright moon shining between the sparse cloud. I took it upon myself to wait for Agnes and walk with her across the deer park to the rundown cottage she called home.

At last she emerged holding a cloth covered bowl — a pie or stew or whatever cook had spare and insisting she take for her father. She wouldn't let me carry it and chided my excuse for being there, saying she had no belief in witches and demons being abroad on this night. In truth, my excuse for being there was far more devilish. We were about to make our next sailing. The ship was already half loaded, the weather conditions favourable and it would be the last and most lucrative voyage of this year. Father was adamant I be at his side from dawn till dusk, starting on the morrow. This evening was the only chance I had.

We walked in companionable silence towards the village, Agnes taking pleasure from the evening sky and the hooting of an owl, while I planned my lines with a racing heart. When the almshouses came in sight, I stayed her, took the pot from her hands and placed it securely on the ground.

She smiled, amused. I took both her hands in mine kissing them in turn then in haste said, 'Agnes you must know my feelings'. The smile remained but she said nothing. I stuttered and stumbled through words, opening up my heart and revealing my grandest wish that she become my wife. I was bewitched by her beauty and before I knew it we were tightly embraced, lips pressed so sweetly together.

Nearby voices shattered the spell and we pulled apart, but I knew from that moment, I could never love another. I delved into my waistcoat pocket, pulled out the tiny bundle wrapped in a square of silk and pressed it into her hand. Without shyness she met my eyes saying, 'Dearest Edmund, I understand now the interest you had in my mother's ring'. Her words confused me at first, such was the state of flux I was in. Then I laughed, relieved at her meaning. On my previous visit, as my plan had already taken hold, I paid special attention to the silver band that circled the third finger of her right hand. Playfully I slipped it off and found it nestled snugly on my little finger. On replacing it, and making it seem like a mistake, I gently pushed it onto the third finger of her left hand. She rebelled and I quickly corrected the mistake, already knowing all I needed. The silver band belonged to her mother, Agnes only removed it while doing arduous work. It was my intention to soon put an end to any more arduous work for Agnes.

Her fingers slowly revealed the newly-made gold band I had commissioned from an Exeter Goldsmith who had fashioned many a piece for the family over the years. It was of simple design and highest quality. The bright moon gave access to the five words engraved on its inside, delicate fingers turning it slowly to read its meaning and then even more slowly concealing it again in the silk, without utterance of a single word. I was crestfallen! I felt certain she was refusing me. Then, in her usual bright fashion she spoke, 'I think it only proper that you meet my father.'

On picking up the bowl of food with one hand, taking hold of mine with the other, she lead me to the door of her abode, the height of which fell far short of me. At that moment, I swear before God Almighty, I felt as a mutineer, forced to walk the plank to an unfathomable end.

That night I barely slept a wink. When, from time to time I did slip into unconsciousness, it was fitful and full of nightmarish fancies that couldn't be made sense of, dragging me back into wakefulness time and again clothed in a cold sweat. On the morrow I felt enfeebled, my father drawing conclusion that I'd spent the evening celebrating All-Hallows-Eve at the local ale house. I didn't contest his thoughts. In truth, all I wanted was to be done with this coming sailing, return laden with all the fanciful items that the gentry craved and take for myself the one thing in the world that mattered – my Agnes.

I had promised Agnes' father the betrothal would be of short duration and we could arrange to be wed soon after my return, I also promised

*that once we were man and wife, I would never leave her to go sailing
again. Only after affirming these promises as a gentleman, would he
give his blessing to the joining. Only after sending Agnes out into the
moonlight, on pretence he needed herbs to bring on restful sleep, did he
spill the words explaining his gravest concern for her safety if he should
die before I could take his place as protector. I put most of what he said
down to the condition of his health. A virtual prisoner to his bed must
surely play havoc with imaginings. On Agnes' return, dutifully clutching
a handful of herbage, she was told by her father that the ring from now
on must be worn at all times to show that she be betrothed to another
and soon to be wed. He also warned, on no account must she reveal the
name of her future husband. Again, I felt his firmness of word to his
daughter was the fearful meanderings of his sickness. But I was to be
proved wrong in this matter, as with many others.*

*The next few days kept me tied in body and mind to my father's side.
He was ill-tempered with my secretiveness regarding the ring I'd had
fashioned and the woman to which it had been given; it was not the
time to add to his ill-humour by declaring this would be my final sea
voyage; there would be time enough to speak of it once we'd set sail. In
the meantime, I spoke only of Agnes' fair qualities and of her father's
trade as a blacksmith, falling short of telling of his present state of
health, his circumstances and where they lived. If worse came to worse,
I felt sure I could secure enough of a living for me and my future wife
without dependence on my father's goodwill. The thriving woollen trade
of Exeter, the trading links from the nearby port of Topsham and the
long-standing name of the Rowe Merchants, should be guarantee
enough.*

Chapter 3

7th November 1705 – English Channel

After setting sail on the early morning tide out of Topsham – the schooner packed full with bales of wool serge – there was an air of collective relief, unspoken, but sensed by all onboard. Sailing to the near continent wasn't a long voyage if heading across the channel to France but our course was set for the much further Port of Amsterdam, and at this time of year the weather could change without warning.

The day started dry with light winds. We moved with ease, gracefully cutting through a relatively calm sea. After the much hustle and bustle of the past week, I was in sore need of peace and quiet to reflect on my future as a wedded man. This sorting of mind and emotions and the resting of my aching muscles, was needed before I confided my future plans to my father. He was a forthright man and responded well to the same characteristic; however, if he but sensed the slightest hint of uncertainty, he would scoff and hold back his agreement, whatever the plan.

As noon approached, so did a change in the weather. The wind greatly lessened causing the rising of sea mist to hang in the air and leave a blanket of fine droplets on hair and clothing. The sails sagged and the schooner barely moved. Frustration showed on many of the merchants faces, including my father's, so I put aside once again this opportune time for discussion. Instead, I crouched low, withdrew within, closed my eyes and hoped for sleep to carry me through until the sails billowed forth once more.

I must have slept long and sound, for when I awoke, the sun was near sunk, the air was dry with wind and I could discern land in the distance. Commands hollered from the crew had dragged me from my slumber and much activity was going on around me. Such was the state of my mind, I thought we must be close to our destination. My father appeared at my side and dispelled the remaining confusion with a good shake of my shoulders. After the shaking, I was to learn that one of the merchants, a long-standing Guild member and good friend of the skipper, had arranged to leave ship at Calais, enraging the rest of the merchants; the stopping at a port en route, could mean a whole day lost. Without lowering his voice my father announced that our next sailing would need to be better planned than this. For me, there would be no further sailings, but I had no wish to contradict him at this present time.

To stretch my stiffened legs I walked where possible up and down the deck. My ancestors, originally from Germany, had been merchant seafarers for generations but in truth, I disliked the sea. It bored me when we were becalmed and it griped my guts when the weather was rough. My joy and satisfaction came from the dealing in goods, not the transporting of them over vast distances. I was content buying and selling amongst my own countrymen. I had great respect for the tradesmen and craftsmen alike and counted all as friends. My father was far more ambitious. Gaining ever higher profit is what ruled his life. The Port of Amsterdam, although further to travel, surpassed other European ports in its banking and money-lending, and it was the money lenders that would be our first port-of-call. I decided there and then to delay the discussion of my future plans until our arrival on the shores of The United Netherlands and the necessary finance for the final sailing of this year was secured.

Chapter 4

11th November – The Port of Amsterdam

After many delays, some due to my earlier account of one selfish merchant, and others due to the whim of the weather, we feasted our eyes on the Port of Amsterdam – an enchanting place and the true marketplace of Northern Europe. My father stood beside me, his mood much changed. With arm around my shoulder he bellowed above the surrounding noise, 'My boy, at last we arrive! Come the next year, I plan to seek out greater profit by sailing to The Americas, for there lies the greatest prize of all!'. My response was cowardly. I changed subject and turned my mind to extolling the virtues of this great port for I still couldn't find the words to speak of my future plans.

It was in 1610 the fathers of Amsterdam approved the plan of The Three Canals, a major urban planning project that expanded the city to three-fold its original size. The Plan of the Three Canals, which was the result of cooperation by the Director of City Works and a master mason, carpenter, and sculptor, combined aesthetic appeal, a concern with sanitation, and an interest in the economic function of the city. It called for the digging of three great semi-circular canals, links between them and existing canals with radial canals, the erection of buildings on pilings, sanitary arrangements for each house and a network of drains and sewers, and the construction of merchants' houses with storage facilities on the upper floors and warehouses near the mouth of the Amstel. The city government assumed the responsibility for carrying out this plan. It expropriated the land, dug the canals, and laid out lots for sale to private individuals for housing, thus allowing the government to recoup the cost of building the three canals. Each canal was about seventy-five feet across, which provided space for two-way traffic and a lane for moored boats. The canals were bordered by quays about thirty-three feet wide for loading and unloading, and they were planted with elm trees. I do declare it to be the most beautiful port town I'd ever seen.

My admiration for the Port of Amsterdam's remarkable design and great beauty began to wane when it became clear we'd be held up there much longer than we first thought. On our fifth day ashore, a chain of terrible storms coming off the north sea hit hard the coastline, causing those ships ready to leave, having to stay put in safe harbour. The drinking taverns were filled to overflowing with merrymaking as sailors and merchants alike sought the company of the fair-haired lasses offering their bodies for pleasure. Three more days and all were impatient to leave.

With talk of the storms easing we set sail early the following day. By night fall, we sought shelter at Rotterdam, remaining there for two whole days before it was safe to venture forth. My father had borrowed heavily to secure the extra goods he felt sure would bring abundant return and he wasn't about to risk loosing that cargo to a wild sea. For my part, yearning to be in Agnes' company, to hold her in my arms and taste her sweet mouth was all I cared about. I avoided all talk of future voyages, which meant little conversation passed between me and my father on the homeward voyage.

* * *

It was a great relief to be once again at home. My father too was much more relaxed and even quite jovial as the family – my two sisters, their husbands and three nieces, celebrated our safe return by joining us for dinner. My eldest sister lived miles away from Exeter in the Manor of Wolborough, close to the market town of the new abbots.

At the end of the meal, feeling much bold-spirited from the effect of wine, I announced my betrothal and future plans. This was bad judgement on my part. Even my sisters turned on me, calling it a cowardly and selfish act to keep father in the dark about future changes that affected us all. Before storming out of their presence like a petulant child, I argued, 'Do I not have the right to be wed and raise a family as you? Should I not have the right to choose my own path regarding whether I sail the seas and be away from my family for weeks on end? There's many a sailor who would step in my shoes, while I'm happy working from dawn till dusk on firm ground for all our interests.' Father joined the argument saying he needed a trusted male member of the family at his side for obvious reasons, and I concluded, 'Had he not one, but three sons-in-law that he may consider for the task?'

Chapter 5

Cockington Court – December 1705

It was the first day of December when I finally set forth for Cockington Court, the family carriage laden down with all manner of luxuries. I stopped first at the almshouse, wanting to apologise to Agnes' father for the long time away, but mainly, if she be there, to hold my betrothed in my arms once again. I found the place deserted, nay, abandoned be a better description, for the windows were boarded over and fallen leaves blown high against the door. I made speed and headed straight for the Court. I hurriedly helped the stable lad unhitch the steaming horses before leading them to shelter to recuperate, for I had driven them hard from Exeter without rest or refreshment. I then made haste to the kitchen.

Here too, there was no one around. Disregarding the aroma of baking bread and my empty stomach, I wandered about in rising panic calling out Agnes' name. From a short distance away I heard what sounded like a warning 'hiss', and then words being sharply whispered, 'in here Edmund'.

The words belonged to cook who beckoned me into a small room where game and salted meat hung. She'd been skinning a rabbit and my sudden arrival and shouts had caused her to misjudge the flaying.

Her finger bled profusely, her blood mingling with that of the dead creature. She saw the fear, confusion and the many unspoken questions etched on my face. Laying down her knife, she wrapped a length of clean muslin around her injured finger and guided me to a chair at the table. Taking a jug from the shelf she poured a measure of spirit into a bowl and pushed it to my hand. I drank in one greedy gulp before demanding to know the whereabouts of my wife-to-be. She poured more spirit as an answer. I stood enraged, demanding to know what had taken place. Suddenly, the sound of heavy footfalls descending from the floor above, echoed through the air. With fear-filled eyes cook pressed a finger to her lips stopping my beseeching.

The footfalls halted at the open kitchen door. Framed before me stood a thick-set man of around forty years old. His complexion swarthy, his eyes close-set and as black as coal. On the verge of introducing myself, the fearful look on cook's face and her intruding words, stilled my tongue. At rapid pace she apologised for disturbing him, concocting a tale telling that the lad – nodding toward me – was delivering goods to the kitchen when we came upon vermin in the storehouse. She apologised again most profusely, explaining our excited words were called out in fear of bites from the filthy creature – raising her muslin-wrapped finger as back-up to this lie.

I was dumbfounded. I was no lad. I was a twenty-five year old, well-respected merchant. Who was this fellow in green silk waistcoat, cinnamon-coloured coat and breeches, and atop his head a buttoned-down-tricorne revealing a wig of style better placed in the rich heart of London town? What was his importance here that prevented an honest man revealing his thoughts?

Without speaking, he turned and left us. Before I could utter a single word, cook's finger found her lips and pressed so hard I dare not rebel. When content that he had mounted the steps to the upper floor, she again urged the refilled bowl upon me. I refused the bribe and demanded the whereabouts of my wife-to-be.

With sad deliberation, I was to learn that Agnes' father took a nasty turn for the worse during the first days of November and by the 7th of that month he was dead – on the very day I set sail from Topsham, Agnes was grieving for her beloved father and for more than three weeks she carried this burden alone – shame and guilt were close to rendering me purposeless. I grabbed at the pushed aside liquor and poured it down my throat almost choking on its fiery content. I urged cook to continue. To tell me where I could find my love. Another interruption stalled her before she had chance to say more; Mary, her kitchen maid appeared carrying a tray. In a surly manner she placed it on the table saying, 'she's still refusing food!'

Don't ask me how? But every fibre of my being knew that the maid was referring to Agnes. My eyes sought cook's face and her expression confirmed that knowledge, along with a warning to say nothing. It wasn't necessary to press finger to lips, in a place such as this, the servants knew everything and it was a dangerous gamble to predict where their loyalties lay. As if nothing had passed between us, cook suggested she come to look over the contents of my carriage before I unload to the wine cellar. I sensed the danger afoot for Agnes and that cook may be my only ally, so I played along. Once at the carriage, it was suggested I go about my business as usual, allowing cook to do similar as she had much to do at this hour of the day. She promised to reveal all only when certain she would not be overheard. It was pointless to press her. We arranged to meet behind the chapel at five of the clock, the sky would be darkening and there'd be little chance of being interrupted. She warned me fervently not to talk of Agnes to anyone and to keep silent about the betrothal.

My business as delivery boy – for in truth this is what I had now *become in my father's eyes – was done within the hour. It was a miserable, dank afternoon and I sought refuge in the only place in walking distance, The Church Inn, thankful that at this hour, the Inn was not busy. Even so, I was recognised by Thomas the keeper, for I'd taken refreshment here several times before coming to know Agnes. I was in no mood for his idle gossiping and wary about letting slip Agnes' name. I gave order for stew and coffee and found the most private corner, intent on gathering strength and composure for the cook's coming revelations.*

* * *

Huddled in the west porch of the chapel, protected from the soaking drizzle and a skittish wind that had reared up as light left the sky, I checked again my silver time piece. It was almost five, but I couldn't in all honesty swear that this time was true. My father had presented me with the pocket watch on my twenty first birthday and in spite of the small fortune paid, its accuracy was disappointing. I watched the hand as it moved to five. There was silence all around. Even the wind seemed to abate allowing me chance to hear my own racing heartbeat. Gripped in fear I worried, what if cook's promise was false, just her way to be rid of a nuisance 'lad'. My composure started to unwind. Reckless plans ran through my head of breaking down doors and smashing windows. Then a noise! A rustling of undergrowth. The gasping of breath and the unmistakable shape of cook wrapped in a long cloak, coming toward me. I moved forward to greet her oblivious now of the rain. With my arms as guide, I led her to the most sheltered part of the porch. My beautiful tall, slender mother – dead for many a long year – seemed to be at my side again in the form of a pear-shaped cook.

Giving her time to catch breath, filling that time with words of my sincere gratitude and then stepping outside the porch and looking all about to allay both our fears that we were completely alone, I pressed her to tell all.

She warned me not to interrupt until she was finished and only when I nodded my agreement did she agree to give full account of what had taken place in my absence. She appeared brusk and ill-tempered with me, pressing the point of my long absence, leaving me no doubt that she lay blame at my door.

'Agnes' fate was almost sealed on the eve you first met', she began. At once I was transported back to that beautiful September day when Cockington Court was alive with all manner of activity for the evening celebration. I hadn't bothered to ask the reason for it, my full attention had been on Agnes. Her beauty her…

A sharp dig from cook's elbow, for she knew my mind had wandered, brought back my alertness to her every word. In abruptness, speed and total lack of emotion she passed on the relevance of her knowledge.

'After helping me in the kitchen', cook continued, 'Agnes' services, as expected, were required for waiting on table that evening. Her cheerfulness, and no doubt her other qualities, were greatly admired by, Sir Charles Mannering – good friend to the Squire and reason for the celebration – he'd been newly elected to The House of Lords – a position that could prove most useful for the Manors in the far South West.

Without delay, Mannering requested that Agnes be allowed to transfer to his house in St James London, taking up residence as assistant to his housekeeper. He was informed of her situation regarding her father's illness and how her employment was only of a spasmodic nature therefore out of the Squire's hands. Mannering's response left no argument. He wanted Agnes as part of his staff at his London address and felt sure his friend could easily deal with such a paltry matter.

Unbeknown to Agnes, her father was visited, first by the Court's housekeeper then by the Squire himself, promising help with his nursing and adding to this a sum of money for his agreement to release his daughter into the employ of the politician. The former blacksmith would not give consent and furthermore, made clear that whilst he was alive, Agnes would remain with him unless she chose different.' At this point, cook's voice took on a rasping quality followed by a bout of coughing. I stilled my impatience, allowing her time to spit forth the offending mucus. Without apology she continued.

'On All Hallows Eve, as is my want, I lay a half bowl of stew wrapped in muslin for Agnes to take for her father. I recognise my own wrapping and the knots I use. It stood in the kitchen for no more than an hour. When handing it to Agnes it seemed as though it had been opened and retied. May God forgive me, I gave it no more thought until two days later.' A break in cook's words, as she snivelled into a piece of rag, gave me leave to remember with clarity that very eve. The eve we became betrothed.

With rising dread I bid her continue. She coughed some more and spat at my feet, cursing the devils at work. Was she cursing me? To this day I'll never know. She composed herself and looked ahead, leaving me the strong impression that after this night our friendship would be over. Impatient, I grabbed her by the shoulders, insisting she revealed all. She was silent for a time, her eyes locked on mine. I witnessed in them a flash of irritation at my audacity, but then they softened and lowered as she continued to speak.

'On All Hallows Day, Agnes arrived early for her chores, singing and dancing about the kitchen as though touched by all manner of joy. I saw at once her betrothal ring and assumed you were the reason behind her gaiety, though she held back, even to me, who had won her heart.'

At this I interrupted saying it wasn't I, but her father, who insisted it be kept secret until I return from my last sea voyage. She continued as though I hadn't spoken. 'No matter now, with her father gone they can do as they please.' Frantic, I asked who they were? And what they could do? A harsh laugh passed her lips followed by more of her phlegmy coughing.

'Charles Mannering wants Agnes for himself. He's powerful and very wealthy. You are a nobody, dear Edmund,' there wasn't a hint of kindness in the last two words, just an impression of ridicule. 'But Agnes is independent and strong-willed,' I countered (I wanted to add, that's the reason I love her so, but I wouldn't give cook the chance to ridicule me more) 'even a man in such high status cannot force her will'.

'He can and will. It has been found that Agnes is bewitched. She was seen by two witnesses, gathering herbs on All Hollows Eve and the very next day her father took ill with sickness of the stomach. The stew which I freely gave was found to be contaminated with a concoction that caused him days of foul sickness. On his death, the almshouse was closed to her use. Agnes still refuses to name her husband to be for fear of his murder, (a warning her father pressed on her) and because of this she is threatened with trial for witchcraft and betrothal to the devil himself.'

I was so much in shock at cook's revelations and my own state of mind, I barely noticed the sobs that racked her trembling body. Wrapping my arms about her, not caring that she may well kick me in the shins, I took and gave what comfort I could. After a while I looked her straight in the eye. 'Witch-trials are a thing of the past and a man of his standing wouldn't risk the ridicule of ...'

Pushing from me she interrupted, 'The power and determination of one such as Mannering, coupled with the ignorance, fear, and may I add jealousy of certain country folk, combine to make the perfect mix for his convenience. He need only threaten a trial as excuse to carry her off to London. Once there, she is at his mercy.'

My guilt transformed into rage! I threatened I would not leave

Cockington Court without Agnes, and if that were not possible I'd burn the place down! Cook took this explosion of bravado as of nothing. She was anxious to get back to her chores before the passing of the hour and made no bones about it. Several deep sighs and a little more coughing then a look that gave me hope. I dared to ask for more information, turning cook's face puce with indignation as she fired words of my selfishness causing danger to many livelihoods.

She asked me to check my time piece, anxious to be on her way. Then she offered an ultimatum. If there was to be any chance of rescuing Agnes from the hands of Mannering, I was to swear to carry out her orders to the letter. Feeling desperate and without choice in the matter, I agreed and listened carefully to her commands before heading back to The Church Inn feeling depressed of spirit, her orders fixed deep in my mind. I was to make it well-known to Thomas the landlord that I'd be needing a room for the night with intention of leaving at first light to Exeter; no one in their right mind would ride carriage across open countryside in the hours of darkness; highwaymen were always an unwelcome prospect. I was to consume no beverages that would render me lacking of wit and I was to make no company with the villagers, as the Squire had eyes and ears in all places. After taking some light refreshment, I was then to make haste to my room, resting and gathering strength for what lay ahead. I knew very little of what lay ahead, for I was ordered to make my way to the The Hunters' Lodge, a walk of about fifteen minutes, at the unearthly time of four of the clock and wait there for my carriage. Pressing for more information, I knew, would only rile and set cook against me even more, so I'd stayed my tongue and watched in silence as she wrapped the cloak about her, bowed her head to the wind and scurried away.

Chapter 6

The Church Inn – Cockington Village

Following the orders I'd been given, I left the confines of The Church Inn at a quarter to the hour of four. The wind and rain had abated and fat fingers of thinning cloud covered the moon leaving just enough light to guide my step. Maybe luck was with me on this new day. With stealth and keeping to the darkest of shadow, I made haste toward Hunters' Lodge, home to cook's cousin, Jeremy, gamekeeper to the manor.

As forewarned, a lantern burned in one of the windows – a beacon of light which gave hope and quickened my step. As ordered, I was to wait concealed behind the old oak until my carriage arrived from the stables. This was all I'd been allowed to know and now in the still chill of the early morning, my confidence, in whatever cook had planned, began to seep away. A large section of felled tree trunk lay beneath the oak, thoughtfully put there with me in mind, I thought, until I felt the blanket of damp moss upon its surface. Even so, I was glad of its presence. I perched my backside on the cushioned wood and rested my back against the might of the oak.

Twenty minutes passed and still no sign…of anything. My body grew stiff as the cold and damp seeped into every bone. Dark thoughts swirled around in my head: was this cook's revenge for whatever she though me guilty of? Had Agnes changed her mind in becoming my wife and this tale of witchcraft was concocted to hide her part in wanting to be whisked off to London with Mannering? Driven mad with all manner of negative emotions, I was on the verge of marching up to the Court and beating my fists upon its door when I saw the lantern shift and the sound of a latch lifting. The moon shyly peeped from behind a thinning thread of cloud, giving enough light for me to see Jeremy bidding me forth. I followed him to the back of the cottage. My carriage had arrived. Silently and expertly led by the stable lad. But there was no sign of Agnes. Everything was muffled. The carriage wheels and horses hooves were wrapped around with some manner of cloth that deadened the sound. Even Jeremy hadn't yet spoke a word and as I turned to speak, he pressed finger to lips, just as cook had done. I wanted to call out, Agnes! I was desperate to see her but I sensed that one wrong move could ruin everything. The stable lad, hat pulled down low on his head against the damp chill, gave a curt nod and disappeared around the back end of the carriage. At the same moment Jeremy pressed his mouth close my ear saying. 'Keep the muffles in place until you are well onto the track that leads to The Old Abbey. Then make haste without stopping until daylight, everything then is in God's hands.

I turned to him gripping tight his arms, 'And what of Agnes?' I implored.

His response to my beseeching was only a strong clasp of his hand and the whispered words, 'Have patience!'

The horses, well-rested and with lighter load to pull, were eager to make haste to roads more open and familiar, more so because of the lack of daylight. All my concentration was fixed on steering a safe and as silent a passage as possible, thus preventing my mind thinking of Agnes. The moon was of greater company now and I wasn't sure if this was good or ill; the horses had relaxed their pulling but I became even more wary of being seen. As a consequence of my fear, I left the muffling in place until I spied the dark hulk of Torre Abbey on the horizon. Maybe here, at this once holy place, my love will be waiting? And if not…I refused to think about that.

Taking care that no homesteads were close, I stayed the horses. The muffles on the carriage wheels were already much torn and coming away, needing little time and effort to remove them. The horses however, were less so. I've never been overly inclined to handling the beasts and they sensed this when I took hold of one of their forelegs to lift and make free the cloth. A loud, 'neigh!' rent through the silence causing me, and in turn the horse, much agitation. Considering leaving the damn muffles in place and avoid being kicked, I took a few steps backward, crying out in fright as I felt something behind me! Very close behind me! It was the stable lad, seemingly appearing from nowhere. Still alarmed from the shock, I watched as he moved deftly between each steed, calming them with whisperings in their ears as the muffling was removed. When finished he stood before me, head bowed, face hidden under the pulled down hat. A hat that bore long strands of flaxen hair poking out from it. My heart sang, for I knew at once the nature of cook's plan. I lifted the tattered leather hat and set free Agnes' silken tresses which fell about the shoulders of the coarse tunic. She appeared thinner and frail, but even in grubby breeches, torn stockings and worn out boots, she was the most lovely thing I'd ever set eyes upon. I held her in my arms and promised never again to leave her side.

'Edmund the danger is not yet over' Her words were more chilling than the half hour wait sitting by the tree, not so much for their meaning, for I was in no doubt we were still in close proximity for being discovered, but it was the sadness and hopelessness that carried on the words that rent my heart. I looked into her face, and even without full light it was unmistakable that she was much changed. Apart from her thin and weakened body, her skin held the pallor of sickness and her eyes, her beautiful eyes that always shone with happiness at every undertaking, were dull and almost blank with loss. Yes, it was the great sadness of loss that I detected in her sweet young face. What an idiot! What an unfeeling ass! I at once apologised and gave my condolences on the death of her father and promised again to be her protecter and never leave her side. She gave a wan smile, and touched her lips briefly to my cheek before returning to her hiding place wrapped in a blanket on the floor of the carriage, making any further conversation impossible.

* * *

Dawn arrived, curtains of heavy cloud allowing only glimpses of the shards of light from the east. I felt giddy with excitement and relief. Agnes was safe and soon to be my wife. I decided to head for Wolborough, close to the new town of the Abbots, half the distance to Exeter and home to my eldest sister, Lydia. Here, Agnes would be safe whilst I continued on to Exeter. My father, I knew, would be most displeased with me for staying overnight at Cockington, for the family carriage was always in great demand. No matter, I was my own man now, responsible and committed to another and if this caused him much displeasure, so be it. I was filled with a strength I'd never known before and this strength stayed with me until I reached Newton Abbot.

On entering the town, I was reminded that the day was Wednesday, and I was much thankful for it. A thriving market was held here each week allowing myself and Agnes anonymous movement amongst the throngs of people. Also, Lydia and husband, John – a leatherworker of high repute – would be trading here. I would explain my circumstance and straight away take the shortest route to Exeter, leaving Agnes in their company until my return.

My sister looked well and business was brisk for the leatherworker who was renowned in these parts for producing the softest and most comfortable of gloves. Father had wanted Lydia to settle in Exeter, bringing the skills of John Glover into the family business, but John was having none of it. He valued his independence above all things. Lydia's price for failing to persuade her husband to father's will was that she barely saw the rest of her family. So it was with great patience and understanding that she listened to my predicament and agreed to allow us a room at their home until we were wed. I had money of my own, not a fortune, but enough to rent a small cottage and tide us over until I could find my own niche in a trade that supported the majority of the good people of this county.

I bid Agnes farewell, promising my return the very next day. Before climbing aboard the carriage, she pressed her mouth close to my ear and warned me not to speak her name to anyone – especially not to my father. I looked into her frightened eyes and my heart clenched with sadness. It was tempting to dismiss her fear as part of the poor physical state she was in, but hadn't I made that very mistake with her father? And was I not now paying the consequences? Before leaving her in the care of Lydia, I nodded my agreement, held her tightly and tried my best to reassure her that all would now be well.

* * *

Displeased, was a much underrated word describing my father's mood when I finally stood before him and told of my intentions. His first demand was to know the family name of the woman at the centre, of what he regarded as a 'scandal'. When I refused to give it, his face turned puce with anger, contorting and raging about all manner of recklessness I was bringing upon myself and the family. It was fortunate that I wasn't given the opportunity to speak more fully on the matter – such was his ranting and raving – for I swear to God if I'd mentioned Lydia and John and their offer of kindness, they too would have been completely banished from the family; for the parting gift from my father, was never to set foot in the family home again!

For the remaining hours of that day, I gathered together my belongings and what wealth I could call my own; raising a little more from the landlord of one of the lesser frequented inns by bartering away my best pair of buckled shoes and a fine, blue serge coat in exchange for two gold sovereigns and a bed for the night. My fancy clothes were worn in the main when dinners were held at the Guildhall, and my father had warned me that he'd make sure I'd no longer be welcomed there. My life was in a state of flux, a new path thrust before me, but the very thought of travelling that path holding the hand of Agnes, gave me the iron will that thus far had been lacking in all my endeavours.

That night I slept well and rose early, having been promised a ride on a fellmonger's cart to Newton Abbot. From there I would make my own way to Lydia and John's house and my beloved. And apart from these three, no others would know of my whereabouts.

Chapter 7

Wolborough – April 1706

I will not pretend that the first few months of my new life were a constant of sweetness and light, for there were many pitfalls to overcome. Our first priority was to be married, legally bound together until death, and only death, parted us.

A valid marriage in England and Wales was governed by Canon Law of The Church of England. Banns should be called or a license obtained and the marriage should be celebrated in the parish of at least one of the participants. These requirements were directory, not mandatory, which was most fortunate in our given circumstance. The indispensable requirement, was that the marriage be celebrated by an Anglican clergyman. It was Agnes' insistence for this simpler and quicker way for our joining, and in truth, we had little choice if we were to keep our whereabouts from the broader communities. But it saddened me that we couldn't celebrate and rejoice more on such an important day. And particularly for me, the very fact that I'd not yet secured a place of our own to live, dented my pride as a husband.

Thus we were wedded on the 13th day of December, just a few short winter days after making Wolborough our home. It was a small, very discreet affair, on a bitterly cold day. Lydia and Agnes had collected what they could find amongst the dying, frost-bitten foliage of the garden. Agnes was still a little undernourished and pale in the skin, but her eyes were beginning to take on the shine that reflected her inner goodness.

My sister and brother-in-law were now our only family and we owed them much. I became as younger brother to John, helping where I could with his leatherwork and more importantly, pointing him in the direction of better and cheaper contacts for his hides via Exeter. Lydia became as older sister to Agnes, perhaps even fulfilling the vacant place of Mother to my wife – delighting in her company and tending to her every need. I had always been aware of Lydia and John's longing for children, but for some reason, God saw fit not to satisfy that longing.

By the spring, it was becoming obvious that Agnes was with-child and my sister's fussing increased. Although Lydia insisted we remain in their home until after the birth, I was adamant we now found a place of our own. A tiny two-roomed cottage had recently become available adjacent to a farmhouse two miles from the village. The weaver who had occupied it for over two decades had died and there was no one to take over the loom nor pay the rent – one soul's sad loss is always someone else's gain. And so it was, on the 4th day of April, after much scrubbing and washing down of walls, we carted our few possessions to the cottage and although not strictly appropriate and to much giggling and merriment, I carried Agnes over the threshold of our first home.

That spring and summer were the happiest days of my life. I didn't possess the wealth and standing that my father had planned and instilled were paramount for a fulfilled life. I had a wife that I loved and I was soon to become a father to our child. Who could want for more?

Agnes' appetite grew and so too her belly. By the time August came around, I do declare she was as rotund as an overfed monk! On my reckoning she still had at least a month of carrying the babe and already she was unable to perform such tasks that required bending and lifting. As ever, Lydia was at hand to take on the strain whilst John and I were at our trade. The two women had become very close. So close, I often came upon them speaking in hushed voice, obviously discussing female matters, and to my shame, I would feel a tinge of jealousy that I too couldn't be part of their secret world.

* * *

It was the fifteenth day of August, and I remember it as though it was yesterday. The weather was hot and sultry. Agnes' belly had grown huge, considering the slightness of the rest of her body, making it difficult for her to do anything but the lightest of chores. Also, her ankles and even her fingers were bloated from their usual neat shapeliness. So much so that she could no longer wear her betrothal ring for fear of it binding tightly to her finger; so it was pressed onto my little finger for safe keeping until after the birth. Twice in that week I'd tried persuading her to allow me to seek out a doctor to check her over, but she was having none of it, stating that she was a healthy young woman and giving birth was not an illness.

It was market day and as arranged I would spend most of it helping John whilst Lydia, once her own chores were done, would walk the distance from the market to keep company with Agnes.

I kissed the top of her head and asked if she'd like me to sit with her until Lydia arrived? Playfully, she shooed me away but I couldn't rid myself of concern. With heavy heart I left her sitting on an old milking stool in the shade of the cottage, back against the cool, cob wall and feet propped up on a chunk of wood – her face perspiring from the weight she bore. As I strode purposefully along the well-worn path toward the market, my mind was filled with one thing only, if, in the remaining weeks of her pregnancy the child continued to grow, Agnes would surely burst!

The morning dragged slowly by. Trade was sluggish as were the folks who meandered without purpose around the stalls, lingering in the main at the cider and ale sellers to quench their thirst. By midday, temperatures had risen to uncomfortable levels and again my mind turned to Agnes. Thank the Lord that Lydia was there with her.

Distant bells chimed three, and a restlessness amongst our fellow traders turned into action as though this was the signal they'd been waiting for. Food sellers were the first to start packing – all appetites being dulled in such heat – gradually followed by most others. Even the cider and ale sellers were running short of refreshment, but at least their pockets were full. I shared John's disappointment but we both knew it was pointless to remain. In truth, I was most eager to return to Agnes' side. John insisted I leave immediately, thus when I arrived home, Lydia would know that the marketeers were dispersing early and she could be back at the market in time for the early journey back to Wolborough.

As much as possible I kept to the shade as I made my way back along the path, even so my body was bathed in sweat by the time our home came into view. The cottage garden at this time of day was half shaded and it was here I expected to find the two women taking refreshment and lightheartedly talking. But the garden was empty and the air was quiet. Deathly quiet!

Suddenly, a loud cry rent the air causing resting birds to squawk and scatter from the trees. Then silence again. I ran toward the place of disturbance, our cottage. I stood at the entrance to our bed chamber where Agnes was lying on the bed, her head hidden from view behind the large hump of her belly. Fear rooted my feet to the floor as another cry – hideous and animalistic – filled the tiny room and reverberated around the walls. I found myself at her side, on my knees, gripping a hand that was wet with sweat. After the racking spasm of pain had lessened and her panting breath slowed, Agnes revealed that her waters had broken and the babe was on it's way! These words were as a foreign language, I was a man, inadequate and unknowledgeable of such things. Where the hell was Lydia? Such was my state, I didn't know what I was thinking or saying out loud. But before Agnes could answer, another spasm took hold and another hideous cry assaulted my ears. I felt impotent, at a loss of what to do. I took hold of her hand, allowing her to squeeze the pain into mine, not caring that her nails were drawing blood and our betrothal ring was threatening to embed itself into my skin.

Then Lydia's voice, reassuringly calm.

'I'm here sweetheart, don't worry everything will be fine!'

I was soon to learn the endearment wasn't mine. On catching sight of me, Lydia banished me from the room with the harshest of words, as though I was some stray dog that had happened by. A woman accompanied my sister, heavily built with hands the size of plates, carrying a pile of clean drying cloths on one arm and a bucket of steaming water on the other. Lydia was already at the head of the bed mopping the brow of Agnes when this monster of a woman slammed the door shut on my gawping face. Stunned and feeling utterly useless I wandered out into the searing heat, crossed a fallow field and found refuge in a small stand of trees. And it was here I intended to wallow in self pity until I heard the crying of our child signalling that the nightmare was over.

I quickly became accustomed, and deadened, to the regularity of Agnes' cries, for even here they could be heard. A passing, warped sense of amusement made me wonder if John could hear the cries from the market place. I jumped to my feet in horror, realising that John was in *ignorance of what was happening. He would be waiting, expecting the arrival of Lydia any time soon. Relieved to have at least this purpose, I headed back toward the market as fast as my legs could carry me repeating to myself over and over again, Don't fret so, Agnes is only giving birth to a child.*

* * *

John calmed my nerves and by insisting we tally at the nearest inn to celebrate the early delivery of the child with a jug of ale, calmed me even more. Although childless himself, he appeared to know much of the unnecessary anguish that birthing brought upon the husband. As I marched back in the cooling evening air I felt confident, nay excited, that I could probably now boast, 'I am a father!'

The windows and doors were thrown open when I reached the cottage, even the door to our bed chamber. It was from here I could here three voices hollering. Agnes', weakened from her afternoon of anguished pain, whimpering and speaking my name. The other two, robust and demanding that she 'push' with all her remaining strength. I ran to the open door, halting at the scene before my eyes. Agnes' legs, naked and widely agape with knees bent and brought close to her chest, was an embarrassment to behold. More disturbing was the child's head – half in and half out of her most private part. It had the appearance and size of a coconut, a fruit of the palm tree. The explorer William Dampier had brought back several from the Pacific; covered in dark hair. This one smeared flat with streaks of blood and mucus. My heart bled as she whimpered and moaned for me. Oblivious of my presence, the two women – one on either side of her holding wide her legs, whose only concern was for the delivery of the coconut-headed child – demanded that the pushing be stronger. Agnes caught sight of me and amid the panting I saw the glimmer of a smile. Then the next painful spasm seized her body. A two-pronged verbal attack from the women to 'push harder!' And Agnes turning scarlet from the effort. The larger of the women positioned her massive hand, as if to drag out the babe by the scruff of it's neck but it proved unnecessary. Once the coconut was clear of it's confining walls, it slithered easily onto the waiting cloth – arms and legs scrabbling as though in a hurry to be part of this 'other world'. I ran to Agnes' side and managed to kiss her pale, feeble brow before being caught in the plate-sized grip of the monster woman and pushed from the room. But not before my eyes had cast over the writhing infant. It was a boy! And I was a father!

Chapter 8

Our Cottage – August 1706

I was back in the earlier place amongst the stand of trees. The sun was slipping onto the horizon with remarkable haste, leaving behind colourful bands of pink, orange and purple. With the diminishing light came cooler, fresher air and the promise of a good nights rest for Agnes and myself. And what of the infant? I'd heard the child's first, lusty cries whilst striding across the fallow field and stopped in my tracks in order that the memory of it be held in my mind. Something else resided in that same area of the mind which I hadn't yet queried but pushed aside until I was feeling more at peace.

With back supported against a tree, I closed my eyes and tried to concentrate on bringing relaxation to my weary bones, and calm to my agitated mind. Two unanswerable questions filled me with nagging doubt. It was this doubting that refused to allow peace to manifest.

Why was the babe born weeks earlier than predicted? He appeared to be fully developed and robust.

And why was his hair and skin not of mine and Agnes' colouring?

The Rowe family were of Germanic origin, red hair in the main but sometimes fair and flaxen, as with Agnes. Perhaps when Lydia bathed him, the black hair and olive skin would disappear with the discarded water and banish the doubting from my heart. I pushed aside the fears and doubts, clinging to happier thoughts of our son and how he would grow strong and much loved – being allowed the freedom to follow a path of his own choosing.

I was shaken from my future fancies by the calling of my name from Lydia. I didn't give answer in response. Nor did I make hurry to return, lingering instead on the thoughts that plagued my mind. Besides, I still harboured a measure of peevishness from the way I'd been banished from my own home. Eventually, knowing that the gloom of dusk would soon turn to night I hollered I was on my way and sprinted across the field.

I knew all was not well before I entered our home. Everything seemed silenced, as if the birds, trees and even the cottage itself were holding breath. Waiting for me to open the door and…

The latch lifted, the door opened and there stood Lydia, eyes raw from weeping. She opened her arms to me, mouthing the words, 'I'm so sorry. Edmund'. On pushing past her, I could see Agnes flat on the bed. Her size much diminished, no huge mound hiding her beautiful face – a face that was pale, relaxed, angelic. A face devoid of life! Crooked in her right arm lay our child wrapped in white cloth with just it's tiny face on show. I touched it's soft, pale cheek. Slipped back the cloth from it's head to find it bald apart from a few fine red hairs. It too was in the same unearthly place as Agnes.

Somewhere in the background, Lydia's voice, talking softly, explaining earnestly of what had occurred and what must be done. My head, overloaded with my own questions, my own confusion and my own emotions to pay her any heed. I ran outside, raised my clenched fists to the darkening sky and howled my rage to the God who had allowed this terrible thing!

Chapter 9

Cockington – July 1707

Edmund awoke with a start from a nightmare that had plagued him since the death of Agnes – a coconut-headed infant sprouting horns and coal-black eyes that glowed scarlet in the dark of night.

'Where in God's name am I?' he called aloud, not yet aware that he was half cocooned in a bed of dog rose and it was imperative he remained silent.

He brought a bloodied hand to his face, saw the death ring, almost hidden beneath the bloated flesh of his little finger, and all gradually became clear. He was concealed, hiding in a ditch between Cockington and the old Abbey of Torre, waiting for darkness to fall. The nightmare had caused him to thrash about as he'd tried to push away the child-monster – its fetid breath upon him as its face leered close. This abhorrent closeness, was always the point of Edmund's sweaty awakening. On a soft bed wrapped in blankets, the repeated dream was of nothing. Here, he needed to be more careful, and especially, he needed to remain quiet.

The thrashing about had brought further injury to himself as rose thorns cut deep into flesh. Far from feeling rested, his body felt weaker and much more stiffened. His senses however were sharp. He could tell from the position of the sun, there were still several hours of daylight to pass before he dared to continue on his way. It was tempting, to roll from the confines of the ditch, stumble back to Cockington's Church Inn and quench a thirst that was far more demanding than just his bodily needs – a quenching that could possibly rid him of pain of the body and torture of the heart.

Edmund's finger throbbed as the ring strangulated the blood vessels, as if to remind him, this was not the time for frivolous thoughts. No amount of grog could right the wrongs of this poor soul. No, this mission *must* be carried out. Lives depended on it. Not Edmund's, his life was already on a steady decline into the fires of hell. In the years since meeting Agnes, through marriage, loss and grief, he'd come to know himself very well. He was not the honourable man he once perceived himself to be. He was cowardly. Always had been. Bravery was something he'd regarded as foolhardy – men, fighting to the death for some cause or belief. What purpose could it serve? But now…

Now there was a chance to redeem his cowardly self and make amends to the lives of three innocents.

Edmund took his mind back to the 15th day of August; on recounting the date of an important event, he would ordinarily state, 'In the year of our Lord 1706', but this was no ordinary event and he no longer believed in fanciful religions or the will of Gods. Nevertheless, the date is as stated.

Chapter 10

Our Cottage – 15th August 1706

For the third time on that fateful day, I was back at the stand of trees across the fallow field, escaping from all that I'd just witnessed. In truth, I found it impossible to accept. My young wife gone forever, so too our new-born son. Maybe I was losing my mind, for had I not seen with my own eyes, a healthy boy emerge from her body? A robust child, fully-fleshed with much dark hair and olive-toned skin? Had I not heard his lusty cries as air first filled his lungs? Then, before so short a time, to see him lying dead, much changed in size and colouring. My head ached from agitation and confusion.

Nothing was going to change the fact that I'd lost them both – that too I'd witnessed. Lydia, I recall, had been speaking in earnest, desperate tones to explain something whilst at the same time trying to soften the assault on my feelings. Why hadn't I heeded her words? Paid attention to what she was imparting. Instead, behaving as a young brat sporting a tantrum, I'd run from her presence, venting my anger and disapproval at anything and everything. I'd thought of no one but myself.

I'd sat weeping like a girl in my tree-grove sanctuary until darkness fell. When at length I saw a light flickering in the cottage window, I trudged wearily toward it, my body so spent of emotion, I stumbled several times over the uneven terrain underfoot.

As I neared the cottage door, I'd found it unlatched. Able to enter without disturbing the deafening silence! Three candles were burning. One set at the foot of the bed where Agnes and the babe lay covered by a sheet of linen; protection against marauding insects of the night. Another burned on the hearth, lighting a pot of stew that had been set to cook earlier in the day but as yet had found no takers with appetite enough to eat. The third was at the table where Lydia sat, the fluttering of it casting an unnerving, dancing light on her bowed head as she waited patiently for my return. Even with her head lowered, I could tell she was exhausted – her forthright character, usually reflected in good posture and upright bearing – burdened by the days toll. I sat opposite saying nothing. Apologies for my behaviour should have been voiced but this was no time for unnecessary words.

Lydia slowly raised her head as though emerging from a trance. She looked aged by years. Slowly, she took both my hands in hers, maybe as comfort or maybe to stay my presence. I was going nowhere. Not until all the questions burning in my brain had been answered. She had become Agnes' best friend. Her older sister. Her mother. I had seen them confiding many times. And no matter how heartbreaking, I too needed those confidences imparted to me. My mind was open to receive every detail of what she knew.

Lydia's back straightened and a look of determination crossed her features. In a low, even voice she stated that Agnes' wish was that she, and the child that died within her womb, be laid to rest in the parish of Cockington, alongside her father and long-deceased mother.

She paused, at this point to allow this information to filter into my brain. I was on the point of interrupting, laying claim to the fact that I'd seen the child born and alive, when with one raised finger and a *certain look – a look she often used when I was a boy – my tongue was stilled, allowing her to continue.*

Unbeknown to even Agnes herself, she had been pregnant with twins. Not twins in the usual sense, meaning they were identical, both were male but that was were the similarities ended. The first born was strong and robust having served its full term in the womb. The smaller, weaker boy probably conceived at a later time, but still managing to germinate and grow, was much weakened and was probably injured during the struggle of the larger child's eagerness to be rid of his confinement. Lydia's voice lowered and her hands pressed harder over mine as she recounted.

Agnes' insides were much torn causing internal bleeding. Removing the dead child, which was constricted by the after-birth around its neck, added more complication and resulted in Agnes' death.

The candle between us had highlighted the shock and horror on my face, Lydia's hands squeezing even tighter as tears escaped her eyes. My own eyes wandered over to where the crib had stood waiting for the new arrival. It had vanished. Catching my unspoken question she'd explained how the child had been taken to the farmhouse. The farmhand's wife had given birth a few months ago and she had milk enough to feed two. 'Just for a few days until after the burial', Lydia had added, searching my face for a response on this decision.

I could no longer hold my tongue, blurting out, 'I don't care·a fig about the child'. I'd been supplied with enough information to work out for myself that the surviving child wasn't mine. There was no need to press for more. My eyes had witnessed the stark reality of what must have taken place. Whilst betrothed to me, Agnes had offered herself to another! A man with black hair and swarthy complexion. A man of similar colouring to the distinguished London politician I'd seen at Cockington Court.

Lydia's eyes had moved from me to the cooking pot. It didn't take a reader of minds to follow her train of thought. She was hoping she might delay the inevitable whilst we shared the stew. Hoping the taking in of food would mellow my mood and help me to feel whole again. She was way off the mark. How could a body tolerate food after digesting such unpalatable information? The answer to her ploy was etched on my face and after a deep sigh she'd continued to speak in a low and measured way. Telling how Agnes had confided in her only when she knew her death was close. How it was me, her husband, she really wanted to confess to. And how Lydia had run into the garden seeking me out and calling my name, but...

But she had failed to locate me. I did recall the sound of my name being hollered across the field but I was in no fit mind to respond. I said nothing but somehow indicated that she proceed with Agnes' confession. A blanket of indifference settled about me, there was more pain to follow but I would not allow it to penetrate to my inner core. I dare say Lydia knew of my protection methods – after our mother died I used it many times especially in regard to arguments with my father.

A smile touched her lips and she continued the telling without hesitation and without the caressing of my hands. 'After the death of her father, Agnes had no choice but to move to Cockington Court and share a bed with the kitchen maid. Within a few days the kitchen maid was needed at home to nurse her own father, leaving Agnes alone in the room at night. In spite of cook's quarters being within a short distance, twice in the one night Agnes was overpowered and violated.' Lydia halted, leaving an obvious question suspended in the charged atmosphere.

I waited, my eyes riveted on my sister's face. For lying, was not something I'd ever known her to do.

An almost imperceptible shake of her head. Then she swore to me that Agnes would not reveal who this monster was. That all Agnes would say about the rogue was that he held position and power. A power that was very far-reaching. 'Even as she breathed her last breath,' continued my sister, 'her only concern was for the innocent child and that he be allowed to live a life of love and freedom.'

The story was told with no happy ending for me. Lydia implored me to be mindful that a part of Agnes will live on in the child. To forget what can't be changed and to…

My blanket of indifference slithered to the floor. With anger rising like the pull of the tide, I rose to my feet – the chair scraping loud on the cottage's uneven surface – signalling an end to my listening. I tried hard to hold back words that would shatter the peace both my sister and I were trying to uphold in regard to those lying dead. But to no avail, I let her know in brief and savage manner that I would not be taking on the raising of this bastard!

* * *

Insisting that I walk with her to her home in Wolborough, Lydia snuffed the candles and secured the cottage, feeling discomfort at leaving the dead without light, but not wanting to risk fire breaking out. I cared neither one way nor the other. The indifference was back and the blanket doubled.

Soft light, bleeding through the thin layer of cloud, lighted our way. Our walking was swift, each lost in our own thoughts as the sound of our footfalls filled the silence. Occasionally, the hoot of an owl or the distant bark of a creature, but neither of us commented. When at last we came in sight of Wolborough, Lydia bid me goodnight and urged I return to my own home. Maybe she was thinking I'd seek out an alehouse?

Her last two words stayed with me for most of the walk back. On entering the cottage, I knew with all certainty. Once Agnes was in the ground, I'd never set foot here again.

Chapter 11

Cockington Parish Church – 19th August 1706

As with our wedding, the burial of Agnes was not well attended. The weather had much changed and the violent summer storms that had lashed these regions for the past two days – turning trackways to mud – kept villagers from venturing out, even though Agnes was well-known to many. From Cockington Court, cook was the only presence showing respect and bidding a final farewell to the girl she held dearly in her heart. The pain of loss was evident on her face. So too was the look of disfavour toward me, as though I were at fault for all that had taken place. I'd intended to speak at length with her but after the brief service she scurried away; as if knowing I still had unpalatable questions for her to answer.

Lydia seemed content, she and John were happy to raise the surviving boy as their own, with help promised from the farmhand's nursing wife until weaning took place. She made a point of declaring that the child would be named Percival, Agnes's choice, for this was her father's given name. However, all else concerning the child was to be shrouded in a veil of obsessive secrecy. It sickened me, and her insistence that this was Agnes' choosing, not hers, left me no room to argue the point. We had already exchanged angry words concerning the betrothal ring. Lydia thought it strange that I hadn't placed it back on Agnes' finger so she may be laid to rest as wedded. Agnes lay buried with my son in her arms, would I not want their souls to reach heaven showing her status as married? I kept to myself the thought that grave-diggers were sometimes known for enhancing their lowly pay by the removal of rings from corpses, and, that I didn't care a fig about who may or may not be waiting to welcome my wife and child into a place I no longer believed existed.

As it was still available, Lydia then suggested that she keep it safe until the babe grew to manhood. He could then present the ring to his intended, thus passing it down the line. My response was cruel – a payback for her gain over my loss. I'd turned on her almost spitting out the words that I'd paid good money for the ring, and it was my choosing, not hers, what should be done with it. In truth, the ring was comfort to me, the only thing remaining to show that I'd once had a wife, for on the eve of Agnes' death, I swore to Almighty God, to the devil and to anyone else who was in earshot of my rantings, I would never wed again!

My harsh words put an end to Lydia's constant chatter about the babe, such as, was there a secondary name I would like the child have? How I was welcome to lodge again with them and see him grow. On and on she pressed for me to take notice. To take an interest in the child. But I could not. Over and over I asked myself this question. Can the seed from two men germinate and develop side by side in the same womb? I wasn't educated in such matters and approaching someone who was, would only give rise to Lydia's wrath and a further scolding that Agnes' final wishes had been breached. So as far as the rest of the community was concerned, Agnes died as a result of complications from a still-birth and mother and child were buried together in the same family grave as her parents. In a way this suited me. I was set free of responsibility for anyone else.

As earlier mentioned, I could no longer live at the cottage nor in any close proximity to it, I had no wish to be constantly reminded of all that I had lost. On that very afternoon, I bid farewell to Lydia and allowed John to cart me back to Exeter. Once there I would seek out cheap lodgings and try to carve out a position to suit my meagre abilities. For this is how I viewed myself – meagre and wanting in many respects.

* * *

News of my return, I knew, would soon reach my father's ears. For almost a month I managed to stay clear of him, eking out what little money I had and making profit where I could by trading amongst the cloth makers and fell-mongers in the town of Topsham. I was sharing a hovel with two sailors there who, whilst on land, spent most of their time drinking and whoring away the proceeds from their previous sailing. When at sea, the hovel was still a hovel, but my days were more peaceful. I kept reminding myself that this was only temporary and as soon as I had saved enough, I would move to lodgings more fitting.

It was five weeks after the funeral that I found myself entering the workshop of Nicholas the goldsmith, the craftsman commissioned to make Agnes' betrothal ring. I slipped it off my little finger where it had rested since the 15th of August and placed it in his open palm.

Suddenly, there was a light cough from behind and a firm hand placed upon my shoulder. It was my father. He misunderstood my intention for being there, accusing me of having to sell my dead wife's ring for the price of the gold. His mistake must have shown in my reaction and at once he tried to make light of it; giving condolences I knew were insincere and asking all manner of questions about Agnes that I regarded as none of his business. Nicholas became embarrassed with the exchange, suggesting we take a bowl of refreshment in the adjacent coffee house and iron out our differences before returning with instructions of what was wanted.

What I wanted was to be left in peace. What I wanted, was to discuss with the goldsmith a change of use for the ring from betrothal to memento mori. Everyone has to die, but Agnes' death was far too soon and far too cruel. And I wanted, nay I needed, a constant reminder of that fact. However, my father's wants were always predictably the same. Greed for information. I followed his lead into the crowded atmosphere of the coffee house, the jolly chatter of well-to-do merchants and traders almost deafening and non conducive to my mood. I allowed my invisible protection blanket to fall about me before sitting alongside my father on the only remaining vacant bench. I sensed his scorn as his eyes swept my attire – my circumstance laid bare for all to see. After two bowls of coffee were set down before us on a nearby table, I ventured my first question, enquiring after the business, for I knew this was his favourite subject and would hopefully keep him occupied until the coffee was drunk.

Again, he misjudged my intention. Wearing an all-too-familiar smile that held no warmth, he indicated that I was here in search of employment. In search of his forgiveness relating to the incautious decisions I had made. Someone had been keeping him privy to all my doings. My meagre income, the hovel and the sailors who shared it, and most probably every farthing I'd earned. I drained the last of the coffee, threw a penny onto the table and headed for the door. He called after me, ceasing briefly the room's chatter, 'I am your father, Edmund. I am always here to help, for who else is there?'

Back in the quiet of the goldsmith's workshop and being in the company of one whose skill and artistry forged his livelihood, I found again my own equilibrium. We voiced our thoughts. Mine were those of a man grieving and how I wanted this portrayed in a ring that was *primarily fashioned, so little time ago, for my wife to be. His words, though kind, were filled with practicalities of what was possible on so small an area. His offer of melting the ring and having the gold absorbed into a man-sized version, was promptly dismissed; I'd grown used to it sitting snugly on the little finger of my right hand. I understood his point about the lack of space but I'd never craved the ostentatious in life or in dress and his final suggested design suited me well.*

A skull with crossbones would be carved as a centrepiece under a square-cut crystal. The outer shank, engraved with full skeleton, flora, an hourglass and more crossbones, all emphasized by a background of black enamel. On the inner shank I wanted my original inscription (Absent but for a tyme) left untouched – a reminder that I wasn't there when needed most – leaving only enough room for the obituary. Nicholas stood poised with his pen, to mark in his order book Agnes' initials and the day she died. A flush of panic beset me as Lydia's warnings came to mind and undermined my peace. Would it matter if I changed the detail? Her name and the date of her death were engraved on my heart, why would I care if part of the inscription contained an untruth, throwing into disarray any unscrupulous rogue that cared to pry into the jeweller's pages.

The goldsmith's eyes searched my face. Eventually in a soft, hesitant voice he said he could leave out anything that caused pain or problems. I felt compelled to change one or the other. I would not rob either of us of her name, so A R was agreed upon, and the date, I just plucked the first date that came to mind, the third day in February – my birthday. Nicholas nodded, adding that he presumed the death would reflect six months ago and not five months ahead. No, I answered, let it reflect five months ahead, if I'm to confound, better to confound well.

I left him with my ring, content with his promise that the work could be complete within ten days, or, if I needed more time…I interrupted, assuring him I had the money to pay. I clasped his hand in mine then ventured into the hustle and bustle of the crowded streets, feeling bereft without the ring on my finger.

* * *

I was back to collect the ring ten days later, halting a little way from the workshop to gather my thoughts and present a positive front. I'd agreed to set sail with Flynn and Leary, the sharers of my hovel. We'd be sailing out of Plymouth in two days time and it would be several weeks before I would be able to return to Exeter. My main concern, was not that the ring would be finished – the goldsmith was most definitely a man of his word – but whether I had funds enough to pay him. For all my father's faults, he'd raised me correctly in regard to not being indebted to anyone. As a consequence of his conditioning, I always made sure I carried more than enough coinage to cover anything commissioned or bought. My balance of funds had dwindled somewhat since I was last here. The combination of a sudden drop in trade and the raising of our rent, forced me into accepting Flynn and Leary's offer to join them on their next brief sailing to the near continent. After counting again the coinage in my purse, I marched swiftly onward before my fears took charge of my feet.

Nicholas the goldsmith was perched, head down at his bench, tap tapping away with a tiny-headed hammer as he punched the finishing touches to a silver thimble. He was aware someone had entered his domain but his eyes remained steadfast on the work in hand. I stood watching, lost in the rhythm of the hammer, lost in the tranquility of the moment. I envied his skills. I envied his artistry. But most of all, I envied his independence. Why had I not sought to learn a trade? Earn a living from what I produced rather than making a profit from the labour of others.

The tapping stopped and so too my pointless meanderings of the mind. The goldsmith apologised for keeping me waiting and immediately disappeared behind a cloth curtain, indicating that the ring was indeed finished. In his absence and without conscious awareness, my hand squeezed nervously on the coins contained in the purse strapped to my belt, as though willing them to multiply and ease my concern. The ring was offered to me without pretension, wrapped in a small square of chamois. I unfolded the soft leather and gazed upon the transformation of a plain gold band into a black and gold work of art; the fine detail of the figurative elements that symbolized the passage of life into death. Unwittingly I pushed it onto my finger – its comfortable resting place – then hurriedly removed it, apologizing for not yet having paid my due. Nicholas smiled, bidding me replace the ring back to its rightful place and as to payment, the bill had been settled by my father.

For several moments I wondered if I'd heard him aright; was my fear playing tricks with my hearing? Then anger, rising up within, heat flushing my face. I saw confusion on the face before me and shame mingled with the anger. For the second time, and through no fault of his own, my attitude toward my father had caused this man embarrassment. I wanted to know the extent of my indebtedness. I needed to know how much information my father had wrestled from the man whilst making his impromptu payment. Part of my concern appeared easy to read, for straightaway Nicholas was reassuring me that the rings inner-inscription was hidden under a layer of pitch when my father examined it, and, he added that his order book is never available to the casual onlooker. I nodded my gratitude and he looked relieved. I didn't have the heart to question him further.

As I made my way back to make preparation for the coming journey, I tried to fathom the reasons behind my father's action. Was I being unkind and misjudging his motive? If I had a son who was down on his luck, would I not act in the same way? My mind refused to tread amongst this nest of vipers where all manner of emotions lurked. I crossed the street, where a troop of musicians pranced about and filled the air with a bright melody, allowing myself to be carried along and my mood lifted. Before moving on, I tossed them two coins from my purse but the weight of it seemed even heavier as I made my way back to Topsham.

Chapter 12

Plymouth – October 1st 1706

The carriage swayed gently as it travelled at reasonable speed through the wildness of the Devon countryside heading toward Plymouth. The morning air was mild, a brisk wind, fortunately blowing from behind us, promising to reduce the travel time of the thirty-seven mile journey. I was content to be sharing the carriage with just one other passenger – a lay preacher bound for Plympton – who had fallen asleep soon after the journey began.

Flynn and Leary had insisted on travelling to Plymouth by sea, hitching a lift out of Topsham on one of the many boats that delivered goods to the more southerly dock. It made no sense to me. The roadways were more direct and horses and wheels were not at the mercy of tides, winds and impending storms that caught smaller vessels off-guard around the south Devon peninsular. They'd argued, saying they didn't have money to waste on such luxuries as carriage travel. I offered to pay their share, as a thank you for helping to keep me from the debtors gaol, but their insistence grew stronger, citing my offer as only compounding the waste. In truth, I had no desire to spend more time on the sea than necessary, especially when wind was whipping at its surface. Besides, my father's generosity may as well be put to good use. As the Irish pair had stated many times, their employment was in helping to crew the vessel, my skills as buyer and seller of goods, was in producing as much profit as possible. As a merchant, I should travel in a style befitting that role. So as argument cooled into discussion, it was agreed that we'd meet at The Minerva Inn, Plymouth, as soon after dusk as circumstances allowed.

As the sun climbed higher and the cloud dissipated, warmth filled the carriage and brought about a state of relaxation that had eluded me for weeks. The lay preacher had slumped into his seat, snoring softly, head rocking to the rhythm of the carriage. Before long I too must have dozed off, for a sudden jolt and the sound of a harsh voice brought me and the lay preacher to full consciousness. The driver had stopped on route at an Inn to take refreshment for both himself and the horses which indicated our journey was half over. The harsh voice belonged to a burly-figure of a man, waving his arms and clearly vexed at our early arrival. He was to join us for the remainder of the journey but made it plain to all, he intended to eat his ordered meal first. Adding that he had no intention of bolting down his food.

The appetizing aroma of freshly cooked food, enticed me and the preacher to also take refreshment. After sharing a meal of roasted venison and a jug of ale, we conversed lightheartedly on all manner of subjects from the unseasonably warm weather to the state of politics. Knowing that this might be my only opportunity to speak to him without the burly man listening, I ventured the question that had haunted me since Agnes' death. The preacher listened attentively to my softly spoken words, his eyes moving from mine to the ring when I concluded that my wife had recently died as a consequence of carrying two babes in the womb. He lightly touched my shoulder, an attempt to convey sympathy for my loss, but his answer to my question of whether the seed from two men, could germinate and flourish in one womb, was obliquely answered by stating that he had never come across such a thing. He saw my disappointment and added, 'but the Lord moves in mysterious ways, and so too the devil.'

The second half of the journey was less pleasant, partly because after the lay preacher departed at Plympton, the burly man felt compelled to voice the woes of the world in my direction, and mainly because my mind had been once again stirred into revisiting thoughts best laid to rest. It was with great relief when finally I caught glimpses of Plymouth on the horizon and the vastness of the sea reflecting the sinking sun.

* * *

As I entered The Minerva Inn, all of my senses were assaulted. The stench of ale mingling with tobacco smoke tainted the earlier taste of food in my mouth. The jangle and bray of voices, each trying to be heard above the other, was deafening to my ears. The crush of so many bodies in a confined space, forcing me to touch and squeeze my way through all shapes and sizes of men. The frantic searching of my eyes, failing to see the two faces I needed amongst the many sailors, drinking away the last of their coinage. The atmosphere, though exceptionally jolly, was overwhelming.

At a loss of what to do next, I retreated back into the relative calm of the outside, asking each sailor that entered and exited the tavern, if they knew of the whereabouts of sailors known by the name of Flynn and Leary. Some shook their heads – foreigners unable to understand what I was asking. Others sought to know which ship we were sailing on and the time of its leaving? This I didn't know – a stupid oversight on my part. One brave fellow who was entering, dragged me in his wake, stood atop a table and boomed out the two names until the chatter abated and Leary, the taller of the two, could be seen in the far corner, frantically waving his arms. I thanked the sailor by pressing a coin into his hand and pushed my body in the direction of the far corner holding tight to my much diminished purse.

A beaker, half filled with a strong-smelling liquor, was pressed into my fist as Flynn asked what had kept me?

I dismissed his sarcasm with two questions of my own. What was the time of our leaving and which port on the near continent where we headed? My sailing companions looked at each other, laughter bursting from their drunken faces. They indicated in turn that I should drink and leave all such matters to them, ignoring my persistence to know exactly when and where we were headed. Leary, in a maddening fashion that I'd witnessed several times when wanting to avoid answering a question, began singing at the top of his voice. Within moments the loud bellowing of a sea-shanty was vibrating through the enclosed space of the Inn. Mine was the only silent voice.

I was soon to learn there had been a change of plan. That all places for crewing the schooner to France had been taken. And as a consequence, all three of us were hired on a ship leaving for the Americas on the very next day. Flynn and Leary had been hired as part of the main crew whilst I would be working my passage as assistant to the cook, a most important role, according to Leary as he burst out with laughter again. I knew full well about staffing levels on board merchant ships, and cooks' assistants were way down the list of importance, and renumeration in monetary terms was usually non-existent.

I protested strongly. My father had tried, and failed, to steer me in this direction and I was having none of it. Sailing across such vast distances required at least a year at sea. As a merchant, I was entitled to my choosing, of where I go. I was not a lad on his maiden voyage working his passage. I turned to go, needing to feel the cool evening air on my skin.

Suddenly, I felt a heavy blow to my head, my knees giving way under me. Hands supporting my body was the last thing my mind registered before total blackness engulfed me.

Chapter 13

On Board The Pindar

My life had become a living nightmare!

Twice before being in full control of my faculties, I'd partially surfaced to consciousness. Once whilst being half-dragged, half carried through narrow secret tunnels that ran between the timber walls of The Minerva Inn. In spite of my throbbing head, I'd fought wildly against my fate, for I now realized I'd been press-ganged into service. Another blow to my head followed rendering me once again unconscious.

The second time I'd surfaced, I was aboard ship. A ship, I was later to learn named Pindar. A ship that had not yet raised anchor, raising my hopes that freedom might still be possible. I'd rolled from beneath the bunk where I'd been abandoned, fortunately with my purse still attached to my belt and my memento mori on my finger. I'd tried to stand, my head pounding with the effort. Gradually, half stumbling, I'd reached the door to the cabin. It was locked from the outside, two fists beating on its surface producing no response. Eventually, I'd crawled to the nearest corner, collapsed in a heap and cried like a babe until the veil of unconsciousness fell and gathered me once again.

When I next came to, it was the toe of a boot that had bidden my entry into the conscious world. The boot belonged to a giant of a man who towered over me. I, an abandoned heap of rubbish occupying a corner of the deck. He'd bellowed out his name, Josiah, and proclaimed I was answerable only to him. The vessel rocked from side to side telling me that any chance of escape was now gone but also warning me that once I stood and caught sight of the horizon, dipping in and out of sight, my worst enemy, the dreaded seasickness, would be the one to gain mastery over my body. I attempted to rise from my demeaning position but the booted toe was again employed to stay me, followed by an order to drink the contents of a bowl the giant was offering. As I brought the vessel to my lips I smelt the strong aroma of ginger which floated in small flakes on the surface of the grog; supposedly a good remedy for seasickness, though I'd never cared to try it and, rarely allowed myself the circumstance where I'd need to.

As though reading my mind, he'd nodded encouragement to drink the full contents, saying it would stay the onset of the sickness, and provide him the help that was desperately needed in the galley.

***

More than a week had passed before I clapped eyes on Flynn; for rarely did I have time, or opportunity, to wander the upper decks and my sleeping quarters – a hammock in the cramped space of Josiah's cabin – was in the bowels of the Pindar. The ginger and grog remedy appeared to be working, although it could be argued that the amount of grog I was consuming could very soon lead to a dependence that was far worse than a bout of seasickness.

Flynn had ventured into the galley whilst I was just finishing scrubbing its deck. My first instinct had been to douse him with the bucket of filthy water but I knew this would earn me dire retribution from both Captain Blake and his cook. I continued my scrubbing whilst Flynn squirmed his apologies. Josiah was a fair master, a reasonably proficient cook and a lover of the oceans. I soon learned that my enforced labour could have been much worse. Provided I carried out what was expected of me, I was left in peace. However, I wasn't about to confer this to Flynn. As a friend, he had let me down in the worst possible way and I told him so. He made all manner of excuses claiming that without this ship, and the share of profit it would bring, we would all three be destitute and on our way to the debtors gaol.

Before leaving me, for I'd made it plain that I had much work to do, Flynn had pointed to my finger, where the only sign a ring had rested there was a paler band of flesh, and asked what had become of it, swearing to Mary the mother of God, that it was still on my finger when I'd been locked in the cabin. The ring was safe, but at the time, I wasn't prepared to share this knowledge with him. I was content to see his discomfort. Content for him to think that I thought my two companions thieves as well as Shanghai merchants.

It was Josiah who had warned me against wearing the ring. Apart from the incentive for any thief aboard to chance his luck and again render me unfit for duty, the daily scrubbings of decks, tables and utensils would soon, he'd declared, 'spoil its loveliness'. This declaration was given in a higher pitch of voice and a flurry of hand movements that mimicked one of an effeminate nature. I ignored his playful insinuation.

It had taken a good deal of effort and plenty of soap to remove the ring, leaving me to wonder if its very tightness had been the reason it was still in place. I'd pondered on my change of circumstance. On how my daily intake of food had much diminished. At the time, I had a strong, well-nourished body but I was under no illusion that now my diet had been reduced to rations of salt beef, salt pork or fish, supplemented with ships biscuits, my body weight would lessen. And the ring would become loose. I could move it to another finger but as Josiah pointed out, that would not save its loveliness from being spoiled. He'd suggested I attach it, using needle and thread, to the inside of my undershirt. The look on my face must have conveyed my thoughts. This was womanly work so how could I have been expected to know how to do it?

I have three sisters, needle and thread were in regular use as I was growing up. I had in fact, at the age of nine, taken part in the stitching of a cushion for our mother when she fell sick. Lydia, with much patience and encouragement, had shown me how to overstitch edges of cloth to prevent fraying, how to attach loops for buttoning up the cover and even how to apply the first letter of my name in a fancy loop stitch of bright-green silk. It was all done in secret. On the day it was presented, much flattery was directed at me; my mother especially pleased, stating that my vocation in life was evident within the lovely work. After she died, my father forbade me from any more joint activities with my sisters. The memory of that sad period was dashed from my mind by Josiah's scornful response. He'd raised his clenched fist declaring that to be wholly a man, you needed to be truly independent, capable of doing everything for yourself, including washing and mending your attire and cooking your own food. I could tell from this outburst, he had little regard for the upper classes.

At the end of that day, while the sea was relatively tame, I had, what Josiah thought, my first lesson in using a needle and thread. The ring was securely bound to the inside of my undershirt in the region of my mid-chest, for here the natural dip in my body assured its secret hiding place. As I'd bound the gold band over and over with the strong twine, completely covering and protecting its surface, my thoughts had been steeped in the few short months I'd shared with Agnes. I found each piercing of the cloth, akin to a stab in the heart. Mother would have loved Agnes and counted her as another daughter.

Josiah had asked no questions, as I'd sat by the lamp engrossed in my stitching, sensing that answers to questions would not be forthcoming. I was not yet ready to confess anything. Not yet strong enough to face the guilt that was gnawing at the deepest recesses of my mind. Perhaps my father was right. I was the only son of his four children but in certain aspects of my character, I was more like a woman than any of them. I was overly-sensitive to many things and what especially irked him, was my incapacities at sea. Many times as a boy I'd overheard him accusing Mother of bolstering my weaknesses by indulging them. At the time, I'd thought his pride in me fired these arguments, but the passage of years made me realize, my father held very little pride where I was concerned.

With the ring secure and out of sight, I was now determined to focus on one course of action. There was no point in ranting against what couldn't be changed. I would carry out my position on board the Pindar to the best of my ability. Experience what fate held in store and hopefully return to the shores of my country a much changed person. At that time I was ignorant of the cargo we carried for trading and what exotic goods we'd be importing back to Plymouth, but one thing I had been assured of, a share of the profit would be mine. From this profit, I would repay my father every penny of the ring's cost before using the balance to start afresh. I would have money enough to secure my own lodgings and be completely free of his influence. Cloth from the south western regions of England was in great demand the world over. My intention was to use my knowledge, my experience and my contacts by returning to the region of Newton Abbot. For here there *was space and opportunity for a man to succeed without the overbearing control of the Guild system and my father breathing down my neck.*

Chapter 14

In Sight of West Africa

The confines of the galley and the small cabin shared with Josiah became my whole world for weeks on end. Unlike my companion, I refused to keep tally of the passing days. In his position as ship's cook, it was very necessary, as was the strong lock to the door were provisions were held, restriction of food was not easily accepted by all.

On the tenth day after sailing out of Plymouth, on opening a new barrel of salted pork, Josiah had been incensed to find it stinking and rotten. I watched spellbound as he leapt from barrel to barrel then from crate to crate, opening up and checking the state of everything within them. He'd found one other barrel – its contents inedible – and a crate of ships biscuits infested with maggots. Wild with anger, he'd summoned the captain and together they'd rooted out the crew member who'd been given the task of checking the supplies before loading; for there were always dishonest suppliers looking for a willing blackguard who'd turn a blind eye for a shilling.

I was deeply saddened to hear that Leary had been found guilty of the crime, I'd never known him to be devious in that way. His punishment, a good flogging and his food rations cut by half, the rest of us having our daily measure fall by twenty percent due his selfishness.

He was lucky, men had been known to be clapped in irons and left to starve for putting their fellow crew members at such risk, but all hands were needed if we were to reach the West Coast of Africa alive.

My duties on board ship had been widened and I feel sure Josiah had a hand in the matter, although he strongly denied it, for I soon became known as the ships 'stitcher'. Impressed with my handling of needle and thread in hiding the death ring, Josiah had prompted me to widen my scope and try my hand at mending. I protested, stating that a simple needle and a length of thread, could not produce miracles. Without saying a word, he'd opened up his wooden chest – kept locked at the foot of his bunk – his broad, gnarled fingers searching reverently through layers of personal belongings. On finding what he sought, he secured the chest and slipped the key back in the leather pouch around his neck. His back was before me, leaving no chance of reading his expression but his body remained motionless for quite some time before turning and holding forth a bundle.

The bundle, when revealed from its outer wrapping of muslin, was a beautifully stitched, hide bag – soft but supple – the smell and feel of it reminding me of John and the handsome gloves he made. On looking inside, I found all manner of things connected to stitching: a boxwood case containing needles of various sizes, dozens of different threads from the finest silk to the strongest of linen, and squares of cotton and wool serge dyed in an array of shades. There was also a square of hide, rich brown in colour, strong but very pliable. It was a treasure trove of delight for any maiden. As I neatly slid the contents back inside the bag, my fingers touched on something small and hard pocketed in the wall of the bag. In this separate compartment, neatly folded, was a half-finished sampler and a silver thimble engraved with the initial 'B', far too small to perch on my middle finger.

Josiah had watched in silence until the thimble was revealed. He'd plucked it from my hand, stating that I wouldn't be needing it but I was free to use whatever else I required. I replaced the sampler, leaving it folded and unread, wary of igniting unnecessary sorrow. There were many questions I wanted to ask of him but now was not the time. He too had his secrets and like me, thought they were better kept hidden. I nodded to show my appreciation and felt a glimmer of hope rising from somewhere deep inside.

As time passed the scrubbing and preparing of food, was interspersed with stitching: the securing of a frayed shirt, the repairing of a split leather boot and the patching of a pair of worn out breeches.

On one occasion I was summoned on deck by Captain Blake to stitch the slashed arm of the sailmaker who had been caught by a violent swipe from a damaged sail – its brass eyelets split and sharp – resulting in a nasty gash down the length of his arm. I was placed in a quandary of which to mend first, the flapping sail or the bleeding arm. The captain bid me tend to the sail first and be quick about it!

I found myself searching out and holding onto all manner of bits and pieces. Scraps of linen, wool, leather, hemp of different thicknesses. Anything I could lay my hands on would be squirrelled away, knowing I may one day find good use for it, trying my best to use as little as possible from the fabrics held in the hide bag.

Although I was still affected in the head and stomach when the sea became violent with storm, the grog and ginger remedy always reached for, I felt my body to be strengthening due to the daily vigour of work coupled with a routine of walking the upper deck at dawn when a placid sea allowed. On one such morning, as I breathed deeply of the brine-laden air, I thought I saw a glimmer of land – a grey-green hazy line on the distant horizon. Thinking it possible that my imagination was playing tricks and not wanting to appear a fool, I headed for the galley to secure a second opinion; but before I had chance to share my excitement, a voice from aloft rang out, 'Land ahoy!'

By the end of that day, we were safely anchored close to the area where the new colonizers of the West Coast of Africa were always happy to see the arrival of a merchant ship flying the Union Jack.

* * *

It took several days unloading the cargo and I was not privy as to why it should take so long. It was clear the colonizers were in great need of the goods we'd brought. There were sacks of seeds, allowing them to cultivate a variety of food, cloth, copper, iron bars, – more precious than gold in these parts – and medicines to help combat the many tropical diseases. There was also a goodly consignment of weapons, alcohol, and boxes of trinkets, aimed – according to Josiah – for the local chieftain. On thinking about it, Captain Blake's strategy seemed obvious. The cargo was being ferried over in the order of least needed first. The bartering would be done on each batch, the captain threatening to sail on to another colony if a fair price wasn't met.

It seemed somewhat strange, standing once again on firm ground but the balancing of my body was quickly righted. The crew had been warned strongly not to venture inland from the coast, in fact it was stressed that even to move from the boundaries of the colony could prove dangerous. Not wanting to lose any men to the marauding natives or risk a bite from one of the many venomous snakes, the captain issued orders that all crew members return to the ship before darkness fell on each day. The initial excitement, of visiting this tropical land, soon waned and boredom followed. My first few days on land were spent exploring the relatively small area of the colony, managing to lighten my purse by three pennies on the purchase of two strings of tiny carved *beads — one of ivory, the other of bone. After this I was content to remain aboard ship, sitting on deck in the warm sunshine mending anything that was dropped into my lap, whilst other crew members rolled the dice, gambled with cards and drank their fill.*

The bartering, though slow, was successful. Within two weeks the hold was near-empty and the food and water stocks replenished. I was now anxious to move on to the middle passage of the Triangle Trade. But what did we have to trade? Ballast of some form was needed to stabilize the ship and it soon became obvious in what form the ballast would take. A cargo of slaves, would be accompanying us on the next leg of our journey.

* * *

Two hundred and ninety-seven souls, mainly strong, young males but also a handful of females, were dragged aboard and shackled together in the hold of the ship. There was much profit in this sickening trade and my father had been keen for many a year to secure a portion of this wealth for himself. How ironic, to find myself in such a circumstance. After all his encouragements, and all my refusals, here I was, drawn into a trading that did not sit well with my conscience.

Punishment for his earlier crime was still fresh in Captain Blake's mind, for Leary had been given the task of overseer to the slaves — a job most hated on slave ships. It was his responsibility to keep order and noise levels down, and administer the very occasional and meagre amounts of water and dried bread. The Africans were to remain chained and shackled for the whole journey without exercise. There were no sanitation facilities, so the less they consumed, the less stinking filth they had to lay in. Even so, the stench and constant moans from below, rose up in waves and polluted all our lives.

From time to time, contention broke forth. Loud, angry voices shouting words unknown to us, but their meaning clearly understood. Leary sorted these outbursts with the cat o'nine tails he carried. The flogged having now become the flogger. Due to his added responsibilities and his necessity to frequent the galley for water, I saw more of him as we headed across the Atlantic toward the Americas.

After about a month or so into the crossing, for still I refused to keep proper tally of the passing weeks, I awoke earlier than usual and headed for the top deck for exercise and the taking of some sweet, fresh air. The sun had not yet risen but the sky was lightened in readiness. All was calm, the sort of calm that precedes a raging storm. I caste my eyes across the eerily still water, my mind captured in wonder at how the ocean can show such placidity, and within a very short space of time be riled then roaring in anger. We'd been fortunate on the first leg of the triangle, the trade winds and currents our ally, keeping the sails taut and speed steady; but it crossed my mind that our luck was now about to change.

The pitter-patter of bare feet running on boards and a movement in the corner of my eye freed me from my idle wonderings. A woman, brandishing a blade, stood not more than four paces to my right. We stared at each other in silence. Neither sure what to do. Her limbs were bare, the only apparent garment, a tattered cotton shawl wrapped about her most private parts. Her jet-black hair was bound into dozens of narrow plaits each finished with the anchoring of a tiny ivory bead. Her molasses-coloured skin was flawless, the whites of her eyes almost luminous around the dark pupils. This woman was no peasant, her countenance betrayed that fact. She was indeed a beauty and was a great prize for any man who could meet the price on her head.

I slowly lifted my hands to show I meant her no harm and took a step toward her. She stepped back three paces and found nothing more behind but the sea. In panic I leaped for her. Catching hold of the coarse shawl. With perfect calm she spun half a turn allowing the cloth to unravel, dropped the blade to the deck and dived into the water – a black-skinned mermaid, naked of her tail – disappearing into the depths. I waited in shame. Unlike some men, I'd never overcome the fear and conquered the ability for swimming in deep water. Longer I waited, knowing full well a body couldn't survive that amount of time without taking breath. I clutched onto her relinquished shawl, wishing with all my heart that she were still here within it.

Suddenly, the first wash of dawn, spreading its bright rays across the deck and highlighting the discarded blade, it's edge razor sharp and wet with blood. On picking it up, I found the tang of the blade was bound onto two carved slats of hard wood. It was a handsome piece, better crafted than the ones I'd seen for barter back at the colony. Familiar voices filled the air, Leary and Flynn, arguing angrily. Without thinking, I wiped the blood from the blade using the shawl and concealed it beneath my shirt, dropping the shawl into the ocean. On seeing me, they halted, their argument put on hold. An awkward silence followed before Flynn broke it by asking if I'd seen a black whore, running wild and naked on the deck?

My shame masked the truth. I told him I'd seen nothing, just the sound of light steps and the splash of water. We all three peered into the depths, a ragged shawl floating on the surface, giving sign that the woman lay somewhere beneath. Flynn spat upon the shawl and before turning to leave, told me my newly found craft of stitching would be required again.

Before the sun had been an hour in the sky, Leary lay before me with an open wound, measuring the length of nine inches across his chest. Fortunately, the slash was not deep, but the slightest movement would again bring on the bleeding. It was my task to remedy this, enabling Leary to continue his duties as soon as possible. As regards to the stricken *woman, I was told a blade was concealed in her clothing and she used it to advantage at the first opportunity. It was later, much later before I was to learn the truth of what took place on that eerily calm early morn.*

Chapter 15

Heading Toward Jamaica

Storm upon storm battered the Pindar as we pushed toward the Caribbean. Such was the violence from the sea, that two crew members, washed overboard by huge waves whilst trying to secure rigging, were swallowed up and never seen again. Twice I'd been called to re-stitch Leary's chest, enabling him to take his turn upon the pounded decks but his reserves of strength were diminishing fast and this was reflected in the wounds failure to heal. In his place, I was ordered (on pain of death if I refused) to oversee the slaves and pay particular attention to them remaining secure.

The remainder of the passage to the Americas is not clearly defined in my memory. The violent storms we endured played havoc with body, mind, and most devastatingly, strength of will. My dependance on the grog was out of control. I lied to myself that it was necessary to calm my queasy guts, when in truth, it was to chase away the fear lurking and ready to snap and snarl at the heels of my self respect. Waiting to ridicule and remind me of all the shortcomings that were part and parcel of the man named Edmund Rowe. No sooner had a bout of intoxication wore off, I was again reaching for more, not caring whether flakes of ginger were floating within. I became one with the crew, underpinned by the transient fiery liquid. Captain Blake and Josiah seemed to be the only ones in full possession of their command. Perhaps accepting that the use of grog was the only way when the threat of death was so close.

We were three crew down for Leary was now too weak to be of use anywhere on board. He was despised by all and had it not been for me, he would have been thrown overboard before his due time. I allowed him my corner of the cabin and fed him like a babe on a watery gravy. His wound was festering and rotten, no amount of stitching could alter the fact that he was close to death. In spite of his crime, before this nightmare of a trip I'd counted Leary a friend, a little simple-minded and easily led, but friend nevertheless, and I felt duty bound to do what I could to ease his passing.

On one such a occasion while attempting to feed him, he'd grabbed at my shirt, not caring that the upturned bowl spilled its contents over us both, and began to utter all kinds of accusations regarding Flynn, my father and the paymaster behind this trip. I thought him at the mercy of the fever. His rantings were preposterous, interspersed with pleadings of meeting his maker stitched up in proper fashion for a sea-burial. On this score I couldn't make any promises – there wasn't the cloth available and I doubted I'd be given the time to carry it out. But he wouldn't leave it be. He truly feared entering the deep without the protection of the stitched cloth and without baring his soul of all its sins. He also gave brief mention of the beautiful slave girl, accusing cook of ordering Leary to unshackle her and bring her to him. But once freed, she'd lashed out at him with a concealed blade and run like the devil she was.

On the day I last saw Leary, he seemed calmer and more accepting of his fate. He made much of my kindness before stuttering and stumbling through half-spoken, half broken sentences foretelling much danger to me from one who wielded great power. 'Keep the death ring safe', he'd warned, 'for without it you'll surely lose your son!' Confused, and desperate to learn more, I bid him explain but a sound from behind me stilled his tongue. I turned and found Josiah, face as black as thunder glaring down upon us. He barked at me to attend the Captain's order to 'check the cargo' which, for the life of me, I hadn't heard. When I returned a short time later, Leary was gone. No service of respect was given, in fact no mention of his name was uttered again. I reached for the grog to douse the horror that circulated round and round in my head.

Time passed and so did more lives. The slave count was diminished by eight. Three had been hauled from their chains in the dead of night, their bodily strength needed for the pulling and staying of rigging. Flogging and threats of the gun barrel meant nothing, for at the first opportunity, each had willingly thrown themselves overboard and were swallowed by the raging swell. Four others had died shackled in their own stinking filth. One a woman, her wrist deliberately rubbed long and hard against the metal that bound her, finally opening her vein and allowing her life to drain away. Flynn had helped me move the bodies and flush clean the areas, for we'd been warned that any further losses would not be tolerated.

***

Eventually, we arrived at the British-held Port of Jamaica. Three more slaves had lost their lives and I was close to losing my mind. There may well be good profit in such a trade, but to be party to it required having no scruples, required being willing to sacrifice everything for a purse of coins. It was hard looking upon the withered-spirited Africans as they were herded off board to the jeers and cheers of my fellow crew. Two proud souls remained upright and defiant, their eyes piercing into the eyes of each of their captors as they were harried along with stick and whip. When all was clear, I stepped upon the sweet greenery of solid ground, inwardly vowing that once I was back on my own territory, I would never set sail again.

It took several days of scrubbing and cleaning to make ready for the final passage home, carrying a cargo of molasses, rum and tobacco. The crew appeared giddy with excitement and relief, spending their days on land and on their return, dancing and making merry late into the night. My daytimes held much mending to keep me occupied. Due to the sailmakers arm turning gangrenous, I was told the mending of sails was now my priority. Tough and arduous work on the hands, even with the use of a sailors palm and needle, but it pleased me to do it. I was kept from the grog and my hours of introspection passed without notice. As I stitched, I became lost in a reverie of plans on my return to Devon. I would team up once again with John and Lydia, putting my newly found skills to good use. I had a fancy for crafting hide bags, beginning with simple holders such as coin purses, sheaths for short blades. First of all, a small pouch to hold the memento mori about my neck where it would be safe from damage and out of sight to those who seemed drawn to know of its secrets.

However, during the hours of darkness a cloak of negativity and doubt descended upon me, mocking my future plans and tempting me into becoming one with the drunken crew. But while safely anchored my mind remained fixed, I would not allow grog to pass my lips!

Josiah became more talkative, trying his best, he said, to ease the pain of losing my wife by confiding his own losses. His wife and daughter had succumbed to a virulent fever from the tropics shortly *after his return from a sailing two years previous. Without show of remorse, he'd concluded that he'd been the carrier of the disease and they, having no resistance to it, had sealed their fate. I asked why such a tragedy hadn't put paid to his sailing? His answer was a bark of laughter and four words, 'sailing is my life'. Then, on the tail end of those four words, he asked the strangest of questions. 'Who is caring for your son whilst you're sailing?' We were yards apart, the candle playing light on my hands as the awl pierced holes in the hide. My face in shadow, hiding the shock of his sudden enquiry. I mimicked him by keeping silent until I'd thought through my response. Was it an innocent mistake? Or were my personal circumstances known by all? I steadied my breathing and answered him in nonchalant manner, explaining that my wife died giving birth to a still-born child. He added nothing more but I sensed from his impatient sigh that he disbelieved me and this was not the end of the matter.*

***

The ocean was much kinder as we sailed toward home; maybe because of our benign cargo, we were less targeted by the Gods of tempest. I didn't hold much store with such superstition but it has to be said, there seemed more lightheartedness of atmosphere and much fairer attitude of the men, as the Pindar glided elegantly across the third arm of the triangular trade passage. Food stocks were plentiful and although crew numbers were three down, the workload was manageable, giving me time enough to work on stitchings of my own design. I had retrieved the square of hide from the maiden's bag and marked out a two and half inch circle which, after being punched around its circumference, was laced with cord and drawn into a pouch giving space enough to hold safe my ring. My undershirt was in dire need of a good scrubbing with soap and water and would be put to dry on the upper deck, needing a secure place for the ring elsewhere. With care, I found the remaining hide was just about sufficient for the making of a sheath for the African short blade, for this too needed to be secured somewhere about my body, without risk of its sharp edge cutting into flesh. Unlike my father, I'd never carried weapons about my person. However, this blade had been made with such care. It was pleasing to the eye, comfortable to hold and it held a memory I wasn't yet ready to relinquish. And, remembering Leary's ramblings and the shock of Josiah's prying questions, maybe it held a little insurance against attack from a yet unknown blackguard. I decided this too would be suspended on a cord and worn crossways over one shoulder, out of sight but easily available beneath my coat.

I was almost finished completing the sheath when Josiah came upon me, enquiring of its purpose as he lifted it from my hand. I'd asked his permission to use the hide which he'd given readily, but now it seemed, I was to pay back my due with information. With a shrug of my shoulders I made light of his compliment and as to its purpose, that was plainly clear, but I made no mention that the blade it would hold was mine. The blade itself was well-hidden, had been since the day I came upon it, for even then I had a mind to keep it for myself – part of me sensing unknown forces meant me harm. Josiah, impatient with my continued avoidance of his questions, shocked me into response.

'I hear-tell your wife bore twin boys and one survived,' he announced as though giving me Captain Blake's summary of the weather. He continued in the same vein and in the same calm manner, 'I also hear-tell that the child wasn't sired by you and as the mother is dead, the true father means to claim him.'

My composure was shattered, I blustered through accusation after accusation, demanding to know the perpetrator of such slanderous gossip but I was fooling no one, least of all myself. Eventually I felt silent, my head cradled in my hands, at a loss of what to do. How could it be that someone aboard this ship knew my deepest secrets? Suddenly, a hefty swipe across my head sent me crashing to the floor; followed by Josiah's angry bellow. 'Don't sit in my presence like a wimpish child, your father was right, may his guts rot in hell, at least be man enough to face the truth.'

The mention of my father reared such anger in me, completely altering my mood. I, was now the one demanding information, engendering a look of satisfaction on Josiah's ugly face. He poured a good measure of rum and waited until I'd thrown it down my throat before sidling up beside me. We sat, huddled together like bosom friends, exchanging information whilst the ship rocked in accompaniment to the song and dance that raged above our heads. I wasn't sure I could trust him. I wasn't convinced I could trust anyone with the truth. I wasn't even sure what the truth was anymore. But I was desperately in need of baring my soul, and he was the only one around sober enough to listen.

It was clear there was now more at stake than my own miserable existence. What of the child? Whoever had seeded him, Agnes had given her life bringing him into the world. There was also Lydia to consider. A sister who had always given freely when help was needed. She'd promised Agnes the boy would be kept safe, loved and well taken care of. I knew she would defend that promise to the death, unlike her brother who had fled at the earliest opportunity.

I poured forth all my concerns, unable to curb the flow once the imaginary gates to my personal hell had been opened. Another measure of rum was tipped down my throat, oiling my vocals and giving Josiah his turn to speak. He informed me that my father was well known among the Plymouth merchants and so too was the wealthy politician, Sir Charles Mannering, who between them, were financing this passage.

Little else entered my brain after the mention of the name, Sir Charles Mannering. Mannering was at the root of everything that had blighted my life since meeting Agnes. The stocky, swarthy-faced, dark-haired, black-eyed man was the monster who had raped my betrothed – stole her innocence and in its place left his own vile seed. And now he meant to take possession of the very child that had caused her death.

Missing pieces of a nightmarish puzzle began to slot disturbingly into place. I'd heard rumours about a certain ambitious politician who had married into the landed gentry of a Cheshire manor. According to rumour, the wife was barren and well into her middle years. However, the goodly size of the house and the fertility of the land surrounding it, was compensation enough. Years passed and his wealth, power and position grew in leaps and bounds. However, we all have to die and without a sired child there'd be no heir to succeed him and the manor would pass to his wife's much hated cousin. With his wife's blessing, they decided he should take a healthy, young mistress to take on the role as surrogate mother. It seemed obvious to me, the character in the rumours I'd heard and Sir Charles Mannering, were one and the same person.

A loud clatter broke the spell of my meandering thoughts as two crew members stumbled into the cabin, crying out for more rum. Josiah grabbed a hefty chunk of wood and chased after them, leaving me slumped on the ground in a dazed stupor.

When I awoke it was fully light and my head felt as though I too had been clouted with the wood. Josiah was nowhere in sight, but I could hear a raging wind and much activity on the upper deck. Not *wanting to attract the wrath of Captain Blake, I hurried forth to join the remainder of the crew. The strong westerlies, bloating the sails and pushing the ship along at a great speed of knots, meant that we were expecting to reach the shores of England later that very day. All faces showed pleasure at this news, but none more happy nor more relieved than mine.*

Chapter 16

Plymouth-July 1707

It was late afternoon before the Pindar arrived at Plymouth, with still much to discuss and argue regarding pay to each member of the crew. All my previous sailings had been to the near continent and were easily executed. My father would arrange and see to the financial side, whilst I did the legwork and secured the traders for both buying and selling the goods. It was a simple family affair without the need for partners or crew. My father, no doubt made a handsome profit, for in return I was given a generous yearly salary and allowed free lodgings in the upper rooms of our family home.

What a difference two years can make, I reflected, as my eyes glanced over the ill-fitting, threadbare clothing I'd been forced to hire from the 'slop chest' – a battered wooden box that held equally battered clothing, plundered in the main from slaves and dead seaman. I soon came to realize that Flynn's insistence on securing a passage by boat from Topsham had made sound, economical sense. He and Leary had arrived at Plymouth in suitable seamen's clothing, baggy shirts tied at the waist, tunics, breeches and wool stockings, topped off with Monmouth caps. I, on the other hand, having spent a goodly sum on a carriage and gentleman's lunch, had sealed my fate to being fleeced by arriving in attire more suited to a toff. I wished to God I'd listened more carefully to Flynn's argument, eschewing the overpriced hiring of these rags and a hefty payment to Josiah for securing my merchants apparel under lock and key. No matter, I'd worked tirelessly for more than ten months and felt confident that I'd soon be dressed once more in clothes befitting my station with my purse filled to brimming – providing there were no more trumped-up charges against my name.

Trumped up charges, turned out to be the least of my concerns. During the lively period when payments were being issued to crew members, I was ordered to the galley. As cook's assistant I was sent down to scrub every surface until spotless. I couldn't help but wonder, especially after witnessing whisperings between Captain Blake and Josiah and harsh words between Josiah and Flynn, that there was much scheming and conniving afoot regarding what I should be paid in relation to the rest of the crew. By the time I'd finished and the galley inspected, the sun had set and the ship was abandoned apart from myself and Josiah. I curtly demanded my wages and my own clothing for I was was eager to be off this ship and never to set sail on the likes again.

Josiah held forth a double measure of rum, encouraging me to toast our new friendship. I refused, we were safely harboured and I needed a clear head to organize my transport home. I just wanted my money and to be gone. With jolly talk and many smiles he informed me that my father had arranged a seat on the morning carriage to Exeter the next day and he'd promised to make sure I was on it. Dumbfounded, I allowed him to continue. He went on to say he'd made promise that he wouldn't allow me to mingle with the peasant sailors in the inns and whorehouses. 'After all,' he'd continued, 'Look at the trouble it landed you in the last time. And with your purse full of coinage and gold about your neck, who knows what may befall you?'

I still hadn't spoken a single word but my mind chattered furiously trying to read within, behind and beneath his words. I mastered the urge to confront him, allowing him again freedom to speak. Behind the main thrust of his joviality was a stark warning. I was to remain on board until the morrow. Josiah's cabin was at my disposal. My wages, minus any monies owed, would be paid on Captain Blake's return at dawn. An idea rose from somewhere deep within – someone had to compensate for the slaves who had died, and I had the strongest feeling it would be me. Still I remained silent for I knew for sure, there was more at stake here than money.

Josiah made ready to leave by donning red-silk breeches, fresh linen shirt and buckled shoes over clean wool stockings. He was anxious to taste food more exotic than that of his own making and to share company of a fairer kind. For women would be plentiful on this night and he was dressed for attracting the best. I asked that I might join him, a strong urge to feel again my own clothing about me overriding the distaste of his company, but with a smile that possessed a hint of maliciousness, he shook his head. 'Sorry Edmund. Captain's orders. There has to be at least one person on board overnight. It's usually me. However, you're my assistant and as you need to be around until the morning for your carriage and your pay, I've decided you can wait on board. There's ship's biscuits to keep you from hunger.'

Braying laughter followed in his wake.

* * *

Noises of frivolity carried on the breeze from the inns and taverns of Plymouth. Darkness had fallen and it was time to carry out my plan. My plan had begun to hatch after carefully thinking through all that had been revealed to me, partly through Josiah but also through the ramblings of Leary. When a man is close to death, there's no incentive to lie. 'Keep the death ring safe', he'd warned, 'for without it you'll surely lose your son!'

I now realised how important it had been for Lydia to have the Memento Mori. It gave credibility and proof that the child was passed to her with the mother's blessing. In law, when it came to adoption, the mother's wishes came first. If Mannering took possession of the ring, he too could use this same credibility to bolster his scheming plan to claim the child as his own. Whilst there was still breath in my body, I would not allow that to happen.

The ship was firmly anchored but unlike the rest of the crew, I had no means of getting to shore, other than swimming. My more refined clothing, as earlier stated, were under lock and key, and even so, were unsuited for plunging into salt water. Again I found myself delving into the 'slop chest'. Having time enough to spare, I raked through every piece of clothing to find suitable attire. Eventually, a small pile of rags lay before me; peasant clothing, coarse, hardwearing cloth of dull colour and stinking of dead man's flesh. The salt water would freshen the cloth and the look of it would help me become less visible once I'd left the ship. I had no plan to swim in boots, so they were swapped for a pair of pumps, so worn that the very fabric could be crunched into a fist-sized ball. Before taking to the water with the aid of rope, I slipped the Memento Mori into my purse of diminished coinage and concealed it with the pumps under my cap. Around the cap, I tied a black bandana as holder for the scabbarded blade, for keeping it clear of the salt water was paramount. My clothes would dry. If wetted, the blade would rust and lose its edge.

I was no great swimmer and the necessity for keeping my head high of the water was irksome, but the distance was short, the water temperature tepid and the determination to put right a wrong, powered my muscles. In short time, I was dragging my dripping bulk onto the foreshore and staring back at the dark shape that had been my home for nearly a year. Should I have left a lantern burning? My sense of concern for safety to the ship answered no. However, I feared my decision was flawed. Would it not appear strange that an occupied ship should have no light?

I adjusted my clothing allowing the breeze to blow through it as I headed away from the vibrating, drunken melee and into the dark streets of Plymouth.

* * *

My clothes had all but dried by the time I came upon the place I sought – a farmstead, close to where the carriage from Exeter had terminated when I'd arrived in Plymouth ten months ago. Well, more precisely, what had actually caught my eye on that day, was the battered sign hanging from its door which read in bold letters HORSES FOR HIRE, I had a mind to use this service if distance to the port was too far to walk but as it turned out, it was not.

Before approaching the door, I held back in the shadow of a neighbouring barn. I'd had a strong sense of being watched since arriving on shore but nothing more to justify this fear. Nevertheless, I waited.

The quiet of the evening was suddenly interrupted. In the distance a sound of horses. Horses coming closer. Pressing my body tight against the barn I watched as two riders dismounted at the very door where I'd been heading. What did it mean? And what now the chance of hiring a horse? I calmed my nerves, trying to instil confidence that I'd taken every precaution against being seen. But still I waited. Then, edging stealthily toward the door I heard laughter and voices filling the space behind it. My heart was pounding like a drum but the need to know the nature of their visit compelled me forward.

'But how will I know?' one voice asked. In answer, another voice, *softer and less clearly defined, answered, 'He wears a death ring. Get your hands on it and you'll be well rewarded!'*

Using the laughter that followed as cover, I gently took hold of the reigns of one of the horses, stroking its neck and whispering close to its ear as I remembered Agnes doing. The beast was a gentle mare and in minutes we were lost from view of the door. In a few minutes more I'd mounted and was galloping along the soft turf that ran alongside the track leading inland. I could hardly believe the boldness of what I'd done. But what choice did I have? Mannering, it seemed, would stop at nothing to get his hands on the ring.

When well-clear of the farm, I pulled to a halt, the jingling of the purse under my hat unnerving. I retrieved the ring from the purse and slipped it back onto my little finger – the tightness of it giving me a sense of peace and security that had been sorely missed. The bandana was used to secure the sheathed blade around the waistline of my shirt, out of sight beneath my tunic but easily accessible. For who knows what lay ahead this night?

* * *

I rode like the wind gathering up the miles that led toward Newton Abbot. Reaching Lydia and handing over the ring, I knew, was the only way to prevent the child from being claimed by Mannering. How the swine had come to learn of the surviving child, I had no idea, for I was certain, Lydia would have kept the secret close to her heart.

All of a sudden it hit me like a bolt from the sky. The farmhand's wife. She knew everything. And may God forgive me for these uncharitable thoughts, but I perceived her to be more than a little sly when it came to dealing with others. The day Agnes gave birth and died, I experienced at first hand how callous a woman she was. Yes, I would stake my life on it, this woman was the root cause behind the treachery. Lydia had been dependent on her until the child was weaned, maybe the void that followed left her bitter of heart and empty in pocket.

Little Percival, for now I remember this was the name that was favoured by Lydia – the given name of Agnes' father – would now be almost a year old. Maybe he was walking, maybe even talking a little. I found myself wanting to hold him. Wanting to see how much of his mother was evident in his small body. The mare was panting heavily. On hearing the sweet sound of chuckling water I halted to allow us both the quenching of our thirst. Then I heard it, faint but unmistakeable. Horses in the distance. Good God in heaven would they never give up? And here was I, leading them to the very door where Lydia, John and little Percival lay unsuspecting of the heartbreak that may befall them. In panic, and unable to give rest to my mare or myself, I veered in a north easterly direction toward Torquay, for here I would surely find respite from the riding this night and continue my journey back to Wolborough on the morrow.

Tired from the unbroken riding, angry because of my own stupidity and lost in the purpose of protecting the ring at all cost, I rode like a madman, the mare taking the brunt of my wrath. Eventually I came in sight of the very place where Agnes lay cold and decaying. Fixing my eyes on the square bulk of the chapel's tower, black as coal in the moon-lit sky, I pressed toward it – knees digging into ribs and reins flaying the neck of my carrier.

The mare's legs suddenly gave way beneath her. In panic, I was dragged to the ground, misjudging the way I should roll I lay vulnerable to the hefty weight of her kicking, dying throes.

It was no time for sentiment. I knew my pursuers were close. Half-dragging, half-crawling, I managed to put distance from the panting, *dying beast, thankful that adrenaline was still pumping through me. Tracks would be easy to follow in daylight, but for now I had to be content with hiding, resting and waiting.*

Chapter 17

Cockington 1707

The sound of thrashing sticks interspersed with voices brought Edmund to full consciousness. Instinctively he edged deeper into the bank, ignoring the flash of agony down his badly injured arm. The henchmen were close. Too close. Daylight had come hours ago, a dead mare easily spotted for miles and the tracks of a dragging, crawling man easy to follow. He wondered why it had taken them so long. The answer came readily. They'd stopped at the inn to rest their horses and refresh their bodies.

It was only a matter of time before the thrashing and probing of their sticks would reveal Edmund's hiding place and all would be lost. The ring would be taken. His body left to rot, or worse, carted off to Exeter and dumped at the feet of his father. No! He would not allow it to happen!

With his good hand, he lifted the other to his face – his fingers red, swollen and throbbing, making it impossible to release the ring – the skull on it seeming to mock his feeble attempt. He reached for his blade and in panic swiped towards the ringed finger. He missed the mark, cutting deep into his wrist. Blood spilled profusely from the deadened hand. He grabbed it with the other, cursing silently as he pushed it above his head, anchoring it into the hedge. The flow of blood began to slow, allowing more time to carry out the task properly. More slowly, more carefully, he cut into his little finger, hacking deep around the middle joint. Blood gushed forth, the wetness of it allowing Edmund to free the ring. What now? It must be hidden. No time for probing the dry earth to bury it. The thrashing sticks were almost upon him! With trembling fingers he lay the ring upon his chest and plucked a dog-rose bloom. Using it as wrapping, the glue of his blood binding the petals, he made a neat parcel. Then, with mouth opened wide, he dropped the bundle in as though it were some delicate bon bon. And swallowed. And swallowed again. But his mouth was dry and the ring became lodged. Stuck in the area where breath needs free flow.

The sound of choking coughs brought his pursuers to his side. The loss of blood and lack of oxygen brought light-headed confusion upon Edmund. He saw two relieved faces. Flynn and John Glover, as they gently held up his head to ease the choking. A gurgling sound rang in Edmund's ears, clouding and distorting the words they pressed upon him. Flynn brought his water flask to Edmunds lips, trickling moisture down his mouth. More coughing, spontaneous gulping then one last swallow and the precious package slid down to the intended place of rest – hidden within the stomach of the doomed man.

As Edmund's heart fluttered and stalled, he heard Flynn cursing the name of Mannering, suspecting that his henchmen had caused this outcome. Believing the rogue now held the ring in his possession.

In response, John's words were sad and gentle; growing faint and difficult to hear. Somewhere within the space, or time, of life and death, Edmund felt sure he heard a promise that he'd be laid to rest alongside his beloved Agnes.

PART TWO

Found and Lost

Chapter 1

Cockington – August 1884 – Wednesday Morning

I'd been pulled from my bed at the break of dawn, breeches and boots flung at my feet minutes before being dragged the distance from Old Mill Road to the excavation site at Cockington Court. The one doing the dragging was Ma. It was embarrassing, I was a well-built man of eighteen years, my height bordering on six feet and Ma, beginning to wither under the strain of life, barely reaching five feet. As if her domination of me wasn't shameful enough, her physical abuse was accompanied by cursing. Cursing in loud voice. Turning heads which lowered in pity of me.

On reaching the village alehouse, the cursing ceased, Ma giving one last push to my back before disappearing into it's dark interior, leaving me at the mercy of the pitying locals and the searing heat. I continued up the steep incline which led to the place I was doomed to spend another day, sweat pouring from my brow before I'd even laid hand on pick or shovel.

This was my third day in employ of the squire. I was extra labour, hired for the removal of weighty stones, tree roots and many other things held fast in the sun-parched earth. According to Baldwin, the man in charge of the diggers, some things coming to light were

99

not to be spoken of to anyone but him. He had given severe warning against idle gossip concerning any of the goings on here at the Court. I disliked the work, not because it was hard – I was used to hard labour – what I disliked was the air of suspicion, the lack of trust from Baldwin and the man's total disregard for the dead and buried.

It was common knowledge to all the villagers, the area being dug and reshaped to make way for the laying of tennis courts was part of the old church graveyard, and the depths required for such, meant some of the graves were being disturbed. Common knowledge is one thing, speaking out against it, especially when it involved the gentry, was another matter. Even so, what happened during the early eve of yesterday was beyond all reasoning, and anger flares within me each time I bring it to mind.

There'd been no show of rain in over a month leaving earth hard as rock and difficult to penetrate, even with the sharpest of tools. The squire had become much impatient with the slow pace of the work, ordering his head-groundsman to secure extra labour. Young strong men who could start on the digging as soon as possible.

Ma was employed at the village alehouse, scrubbing tables and cleaning floors (although her thirst for the cider and the goodly amount she consumed, left her all but nought to show for her efforts) and four days earlier the court's head-groundsman entered the alehouse, making it known he was seeking extra labour in the form of young, strong muscle. He named the daily sum to be paid to any fortunate applicant deemed suitable for the task. As this daily sum was higher than that earned preparing ground and digging trenches for villas in the early stages of construction, Ma, there and then sealed my fate.

My first day had been simple enough. A great mound of stones and tree roots needed removing from the site to allow the earth beneath to be lowered for matching with the rest of the excavation. It was hard toil and by the evening of that day my back ached with a vengeance, but the pay was fair and half of it would be laid aside in my secret place for saving, the rest handed over to Ma.

On the second day, having cleared the way, I was given pick and shovel and ordered to dig and remove the earth to a goodly depth of five feet. It soon became obvious that this area was going to be especially difficult to work. Roots from an ancient yew wrapping and tangling around stones of hefty size, were much in evidence.

After hours of swinging the pick, cutting the roots with shovel and heaving out the stone, it came to light that a family grave was in the throes of being desecrated. Feeling uncomfortable with this abuse, I put aside the pick and began with care to scrape around the stones with a finer tool, thus revealing the edge of a blackened oak box. Having continued in this slow deliberate manner, loosening soil which I then shovelled to one side, I came upon the upper part of a skeleton that as yet had not been disturbed. The arm bones, smaller than that of a man's, were crossed over the ribs, holding in place the tiny bones of a babe.

My heart raced, not in fear, though I knew many who would panic at such a sight, but in wonder of who this woman was? I'd continued with care, picking and scraping at the nearby broken stone, for although I had no learning to boast of, my memory for shapes and letters was sharp and having once studied them, felt sure I could later transfer that memory to slate. When the bones were transferred for reburial, it was important to have names and dates.

Suddenly, a sharp dig from behind had sent me off balance and crashing into the nearby mound of soil. This was followed by loud, angry bellowing.

'Grimshaw, you are not here to ponder what the soil holds, take hold of that pick and clear this area and be sharp about it!'

I'd righted myself and turned to find Baldwin, overseer to the digging, standing with hands on hips, his face wearing an expression as dark as thunder. He turned to go, satisfied he'd made his point, but before leaving, his eyes fixed on the exposed part of the female skeleton, her arm bones still locked around the tiny remains of her babe. He shoved me aside, reached for the female's finger bones and tore them one by one from their loving embrace.

'This was a wedded woman,' he'd said with a leer that exposed crooked, yellowing teeth, 'See here her brat, which no doubt caused her demise.'

The symmetry of the tiny bones were cast asunder as his calloused, impatient hands fumbled and searched the earth around them. Then turning to me he'd spat words loaded with accusation. 'Where's the ring from this mother's finger? For this be no pauper's grave?

In defence of my honour, I made plain that the fingers were undisturbed until *he* had rent them apart. Raging at my forthright remark, he'd grabbed at my shirt, almost tearing the sleeve as he grappled for purchase. We struggled on the unevenness of the ground, drawing attention from the squire who was discussing matters with another groundsman a few yards away. In less than a minute he was upon us, silently absorbing the scene before him. He turned to Baldwin and in a commanding voice that gained the attention of all in earshot, had asked outright, what had become of the dead mother's ring?

With head bowed, Baldwin stated there was no ring to be found. The squire then asked further, why the finger bones be scattered and broken when he'd given strict instruction that any bones found should be treated with respect before being re-interred? Baldwin had nodded in my direction while his voice remained mute. As though seeing me for the first time, the squire turned to me and asked my name. Before I'd had chance to answer, Baldwin had found his voice.

'This be Digory Grimshaw of Chelston, the eighteen-year-old son of Digory Grimshaw Senior, transported to New South Wales, Australia, in the year 1867 to serve seven years hard labour for thievery.' Having found his voice, it seemed Baldwin could no longer hold rein on it. He went on to describe Bridget Grimshaw, Digory's Ma, as an unfortunate wretch whose days were spent in the alehouse, whilst her four brats fended for themselves.

My shoulders had slumped in shame at Baldwin's words, for what they described was part-truth and part malice. Nevertheless, the squire had me searched in full view of all and when nothing came to light, in the same low, commanding voice, spoke harshly to me in regard to keeping respect for the dead of this manor of Cockington.

I was paid nought that second day, and I felt sure it would be the same no matter how many days I toiled. On my return home with empty hand, Ma had been enraged, refusing to listen to my side of the sorry tale. There and then I'd vowed not to set foot on that site again. But, by break of dawn on the following morn, I was dragged from my bed and shepherded the distance from Apple Cottage in Chelston to Cockington Village.

* * *

A sly smirk rested on the face of Baldwin as I took pick and shovel and lowered myself into the area dug the day before. There was no sign of the previously discovered bones, and I kept to myself the curiosity as to where they'd been taken. Before my eyes, the older man had scratched a line using the point of the pick, indicating the area to be fully dug out before the ending of that day; warning me that any further bones exposed should be immediately reported to him. Before leaving me to my digging, he spat these emphasized words in slow deliberate manner, thinking me a half-wit and wanting to make sure I clearly understood their meaning. 'Do not loose thyself in role of this new fangled archeology and do not remove anything found, even if it be just a farthing piece, for rest assured, you *will* be searched at the end of each day.'

Hours passed, and somewhere in the distance I heard the strike of two. Lifting my face to a clear blue sky and a sun that showed no mercy in the heat it caste forth, I was glad to lay down my shovel. The area previously excavated, had gone some way to providing shade, allowing me to make decent headway towards Baldwin's marking, for I knew I'd be held there until I reached it. Having cleared to the depth of three feet in over half of the area during the cooler temperatures of the morning, I was now faced with working in full sun, until once again the fiery ball dipped to an angle. Unbidden, a deep sigh escaped my weary body and the thought, *even slave labourers were entitled to a break.* Straightening my back, I climbed from the earthy pit, dragging my body to a stand of trees where, on a row of wooden crates, refreshments were placed at the middle of the day for the groundsmen on the site.

Only one other stood within the shade. A much older man wearing coat and cap in spite of the high temperature – his back supported by the trunk of an oak whilst his lips pulled greedily on a clay pipe. He acknowledged my arrival with a nod and the words, 'Not much left, lad. Cider's all gone and the left-overs from yesterday's dinner disappeared down their gullets in a flash. Refreshments arrived an hour ago. What kept you?'

Confused and disappointed I responded. 'Yesterday's refreshments were placed at the strike of two, I…I thought each day to be the same,' I mumbled, as I reached for the battered pewter jug that contained a short measure of water of dubious colour.

'Yesterday was different, lad. Yesterday, cook had a half day off and her assistant likes to make plain she has only one pair of hands. Didn't Baldwin make clear the change of time for refreshments on Wednesdays?'

I didn't know this man. He appeared friendly enough but I wasn't about to land myself in further trouble with Baldwin. I said nothing as I lifted the jug to my lips, eyeing the two insects that floated belly up in the water. The other man's hand and his kindly voice stilled the jug before liquid touched my lips.

'Wait awhile lad, I've had my share, but they won't refuse me more, I'll bring cider and food to keep thy strength pumping. It was callous of Baldwin not to let it be known the workings of the court's kitchen.'

'Thank you Sir, but I prefer water to cider.' Having seen what cider had done to Ma, I made sure to keep well clear of the stuff.

'You'll have what I brings you, lad, and it won't be water. My name is Albert, I'm not of the gentry so no need for fancy title.' Albert chuckled as he walked the twenty yards to the kitchen door – held open by a hefty piece of broken, carved stone – an angelic face torn from its rightful place.

On his return, I'd already removed the dead insects from the small measure of water, my thirst so fierce that I'd been sorely tempted to swallow the warmed polluted water, but I'd held fast, Albert may well turn out to be my only ally at this place.

'Here we are lad, a cool jug of cider. In my opinion the only trusted refreshment at this time of year when insects are prolific, pissing and using their poisonous, devilish bodies for all kinds of activity in the well water. The cider may leave you a little light-headed, but it won't give you gripes in the gut and frequent runnings to the hedgerow.'

Albert took hold of the battered, pewter jug, tipped the remains of its foul contents to the ground, poured in a tiny measure of cider, swilled it around and tipped it in the same place. I watched as it disappeared into the parched ground. When I looked up, the jug had been half filled from the other and was being handed to me. With the remaining half-filled jug, Albert touched it lightly to mine saying, 'Here's to your good health, lad.' Then a goodly portion of it was down his neck in one, long gulp.

I followed his lead and would have emptied the jug before the taste of it had chance to make itself known, but again, my arm was stayed by Albert.

'What's the hurry, lad? The liquid will serve better if drunk slower. Don't follow my habit, nor that of your mother, sip it slow.'

His sharp eyes caught my change of expression at the mention of Ma. He said nothing, just the hint of a smile as his hand delved into the gaping pocket of his coat. He brought forth a slab of pie, chunks of rabbit trapped in jelly clearly visible where the knife had cut.

'Don't expect the likes of this every day,' boasted Albert. 'If you're lucky, it'll be stale bread and moulding cheese. I'm happy to share this delicacy with you lad, so long as it's clearly understood: don't assume all men are as Baldwin. Also, you don't mention of me bringing you this lavish treat. I knew your mother, and your father, long before you was born and that gives me right to speak of them when I choose, even if you be in earshot.'

My eyes fell on the slab of pie, the smell given off causing my mouth to water in anticipation of its taste. I nodded my acceptance of his terms, not caring at this moment who Albert did and didn't know. I was starving and desperate that I and the rabbit pie become one as quickly as possible that I may return to my work. I reached to take it from his boney hands but he seemed to think better of it and pulled back a little.

'Not so fast, lad. As with the cider, this be for sharing.' From the same pocket that had held the pie, Albert removed a folding knife, flicking it open at the touch of a button. The slab of pie was placed on the crate for cutting, but before the blade reached its mark, I could see, crumbs of pastry stuck with jelly clinging to the knife's sharpened edge. This was the same knife that had cut into the whole pie. What power did this man hold at Cockington Court? Or, was he just a common thief? Taking advantage of the kitchen's routine and its staffing. Right now, I was only mindful of wrapping my moistened lips around my half of the prize. All other questions could wait for another time.

No sooner had the delicious treat reached my stomach, helped there by my remaining half of the cider, I heard the distinctive roar of Baldwin's voice coming towards me.

'Grimshaw? You'll be digging till midnight at this rate, get your idle body into the earth and remove everything to the mark I made!'

I nodded to Albert, hoping this alone showed my gratitude, before walking slowly, head held high, back to my digging. The cider had indeed refreshed me. It had also given me something else I couldn't quite put into words. I just hoped that Baldwin didn't come too close, provoking with his viscous words, for I was in no mood for his bullying ways. Albert had cut across Baldwin's path and on looking back, the two of them could be seen, heads pushed forward, arms in motion adding power to their words, reminding me of deer sparring for territory. After deciding, if no pay was forthcoming this day, I would take my fist to Baldwin and weather the consequences, I took hold of the pick and worked as a man possessed!

* * *

By late afternoon my muscles were feeling the strain from the constant heaving of roots that lay at a near depth of five feet. I knew in my heart there were more bones to follow. It was just as yesterday, at this level, roots of the yew tree, large stones and bones of the dead. Probably another member from the same family grave. I needed to find Baldwin, ask what was required of me if such came to light.

After searching the site, Baldwin was nowhere to be found and it was Albert, once more, who came to my aid. Again, he stood in the cool of the trees pulling on his pipe in a relaxed stance, as though overseeing this project was his sole responsibility. Maybe it was.

Glad to be upright, I strolled over to where he stood and asked if he knew the whereabouts of Baldwin and followed my asking with the reason for needing to see him. Without comment, Albert took hold of one of the wooden crates and handed it to me.

'Put a few shovels of soil in here, lad. If you do come upon bones again, lay them gently in there ready for re-burying. If you see markings of a name on stone, make copy of it on the crate with this.' He slipped his hand into his coat pocket and brought forth a piece of dusty, white stone, causing me to wonder at the variety of oddments that lay secreted within his coat.

'And Baldwin?' I asked, hearing concern, nay, hearing fear in my voice, for the effect of the cider had grown dim and my resolve had weakened.

'Leave Baldwin to me, lad, but bear this in mind, if his marking on the earth is not reached by your pick and shovel, he has right to deny pay.'

Relief and elation that pay was possible after all, powered my body as I returned to my digging, helped by the whispers of cloud that now covered the sun, cooling the late afternoon temperature.

All was going well, the roots were mostly dead and snapped easily from their hold and there were no hefty stones held in this part of the parched earth. I was making good progress to the mark, good progress for coinage in my pocket. Until the next strike of the pick, and the show of black in red-brown soil. A plank of oak, rotten and crumbling as the shovel loosened it, stilled my breath for what was to follow. The bones of a man's arm and hand were to follow. A man who must have died in battle, for the bones were fractured in several places and the smallest finger-bone on the hand was missing – non of it my doing, for I had been most careful in this removal. Yet who would believe the word of a Grimshaw? Son of a thief and a drunken wretch!

As instructed by Albert, I lay down the damaged bones on a blanket of soil in the crate and continued with my probing of the earth. The bones of the chest seemed intact as did the skull. The larger tools were laid aside and my careful hands wrestled them from the earth.

A dark shadow falling across my back gave me cause to turn. Again, Baldwin showing himself at a time when it appeared I was slowing my pace of working and he looking non too pleased at the sight of more bones. Foul cursing followed at my slowness in removing the bones. Lowering himself into the gaping mouth of the earth beside me, he grabbed the pick and began tearing at the soil like a lunatic. Ribs cracked and broke away. The skull, freed of its earthy hold, shifted and rolled toward his booted foot. Halting there, a hideous grin upon its fleshless face, blind eye-sockets seeming to stare with malice. He stepped back in shock of it – or was it fear that his brutality might well have haunting repercussions – before scrambling from the violated pit.

'I want every bone from this carcass placed in the crate before that cart leaves for the reburial site at the stroke of six.' His shaking finger pointed in the direction where a hand cart was piled with stones, sacks and God knows what other unmentionables. 'Any bones found after the stroke of six, are to be re-buried below the five foot level. Is that clearly understood, Grimshaw?'

'If I'm to re-bury any further bones found, I may not reach your mark this day.'

'And if that be the case, there will be no pay! And Albert will have no say in the matter.'

I'd heard the half-hour strike but a few minutes earlier, drifting from the open door of the court's kitchen, and knew I'd be hard pressed for time. For all my sins, I could not allow a dead man's bones to be buried in two separate places. I put aside the thought of pay and allowed my energy to focus on retrieving the whole of this unfortunate corpse.

As the strike of six began, I was dragging the crate toward the cart, one eye fixed on it, willing that it should wait a minute longer. Eventually it was reached and panting from the effort, my own body almost collapsed upon it. The words, 'Sorry young Grimshaw, there be no room left on the cart, leave the crate there for the morning run,' almost brought forth a flood of tears, adding womanly weakness to my sorry reputation. A man with a pock-marked face known by the name of Jon the Carter, was the owner of the voice and the cart. He smiled broadly, showing two rotten teeth in his upper mouth and one only in the lower – that too being in rotting state. There was no malice in his words, for it was clear the cart was well-stacked with all manner of things. If more was loaded atop, it would surely send all asunder. In desperation, I offered Jon my company to the re-burial site, promising to carry the crated bones myself. By way of answer, Jon shook his head with vigour, lifted the bars of his cart and pushed it onto a well worn dirt path that led toward Ladypark Crater.

Accepting there was no more to be done, I dragged the crate back to my digging place and reasoned what was best to do. Dig deeper and rebury the bones below the needed level or swing the pick like a madman until Baldwins marking was reached? Two hours of light was all I had, time enough for one or the other. I looked toward the trees, probably hoping to see Albert, offering forth a jug of refreshment, then realized that thoughts of fancy would not help in the matter. I descended into the shadow of the pit and began shovelling deep into the earth.

Time passed and the sun sunk low, I kept on digging, aware only of what must be done. Curiously, the deeper ground seemed less dry, less difficult to shift, less tiring on my body. With a sky still bright from the west, warm streaks reflecting the setting sun, the lower grave became ready to receive the nameless man.

With care, the bones were placed as best they could. Baldwin's violent interruption had made no easy task of putting them in proper order. On taking up the back bone and querying the way it should lay, I noticed something strange, a glint of light reflecting off a lump of stone or metal held fast in the rib area of the spine. The light was fading fast but as I plucked the strange lump from its anchored place, rubbed it against my sweat-laden shirt, I found myself staring at a handsomely ornamented ring of gold!

Chapter 2

Apple Cottage – Chelston – Wednesday Evening

Bridget Grimshaw stared at the cold hearth, the stewpot covered and pushed to one side, its contents thickened with time. Time, she thought, time was such a curse. There was a time when Bridget Grimshaw, known to most folks of this manor as Ma Grimshaw, was happy and carefree. There was such a time when she possessed everything a woman could want: beauty, a loving man, a comfortable homestead with orchards of apples and a store stacked high with salted fish. All providing a goodly living for those that belonged to the Grimshaw family. Time had robbed her of everything. She cursed and spat at the cracked floor, dabbing her eyes to her skirt as she continued her pacing back and forth, back and forth.

Eventually, she sat at the table, head cradled in hands, trying to stem the concern that gnawed in her gut. Where in God's name was he? No one with sense would take pick and shovel to the earth once the sun had left the sky, especially probing into soil that held bones of the long dead. Everyone knew there'd be hell to pay for allowing it to happen. And she, Bridget Grimshaw, mother to Digory, had been the one to push her son into it.

Casting thoughts of spirits and demons from her mind and focussing on the more down to earth, she wondered, was he drinking his pay away? No, not Digory, he had more sense. Had he been jumped and robbed of his wages on the dark, lonely path home? Most unlikely, the size and strength of her boy, who would dare? Or, was it as the day before, Baldwin, the mean-spirited villain, holding back his pay, leaving him shamed into facing his own family? We'll see soon enough, she thought, grabbing her shawl with a mind to go find him.

Eme and Constance, Bridget's thirteen-year-old nieces, were bickering in the main bedchamber they shared with her. Drew was asleep in the smaller room opposite – a bed barely big enough for Digory to stretch his legs, let alone share it with his four-year-old half-brother – a brother that spoke little but wailed much.

The twins' bickering grew louder, followed by the bedchamber door being slammed shut. Following that, Drew's wailing cries!

'Oh God have mercy! cried Bridget, 'I need a jug of cider to calm my nerves! Where is my son?'

'Probably found someone to marry and escape *this* miserable place!' screamed Eme, slammer of the bedchamber door, oldest of the twins by half an hour and the more aggressive of the pair. She scraped a chair from beneath the kitchen table and plonked herself down on it, arms folded, face as sour as an unripe apple.

'Go tend to your cousin,' Bridget ordered. You was the one woke him from sleep and mark my words girl, if I hear any slapping, I'll take a stick to you!'

With arms still folded, Eme flounced back toward the stairs, her mop of chestnut curls flowing loose behind her, muttering low that Drew would get more than a slapping if he didn't cease his wailing. Drew's wailing stopped abruptly. So too did Bridget's worrying, for she heard the distinct footfalls of her son walking up the cottage path.

The latch lifted and there he stood, her beautiful boy, her pride and joy.

'Where in God's name have you been, Digory? My stomach's all churned and twisted with concern for you. Have you been drinking? What woman has tempted you to her bed?'

'Ma, must we go on this way every time I'm out of sight for more than a few hours? You know well where I've been, hard-labouring till the fall of darkness. I'm tired and I need my sleep.'

'I can see you're tired son, but don't think me stupid. I smell cider on you and I knows you don't care to drink it. No lies now, Digory, no one labours in the dark, unless they be up to no good.' Bridget sidled closer, 'Give me the name of the woman who takes advantage of you and I'll scratch the eyes from her head!'

I turned away, moved towards the stairs but Ma cut ahead of me hand held open.

'Have you money for me? The remains in the stew pot is all that's between life and starvation until the girls get their pay from the stables.'

'Then you'll have to use your earnings from the alehouse,' I said, my voice sharp with impatience. 'Baldwin's holding back my due until the labouring's finished. My mind's fixed, Ma, only one more day will I labour for that man. But I swear to you, I'll have every farthing that's owing to me and it will be yours, all of it. My mind is set, I intend to move away, far away. Seek my fortune in a place where my name is not linked to thievery and drunkenness.'

I didn't wait for her ranting. We had had many exchanges such as this. I climbed the narrow stairs, feeling the precious ring concealed in my boot, pressing against my ankle. I'd been aware of it since slipping it there a minute after it's discovery, and every single minute since. An awareness that gave me hope for my future plans. During the walk home, the rubbing had become a hurting, a hurting that was bitter-sweet and welcome, reminding me that the little money I had hidden would take me as far as London. Once in the mass of that great town, all possibilities would then be open to a young, strong unattached man, whose name was unknown. A man in possession of a hefty gold ring. A ring easily transferred back to a lump of valuable metal, providing coinage enough to travel the full distance of my greatest desire.

I wrapped my arms around little Drew, taking care not to wake him. I thought upon all that had happened that day. My mind lingering on the knowledge imparted from Albert as I'd supped in his company after the setting of the sun. He was content to talking and I was content for listening. As his words settled softly into my memory, the ring rubbing reassuringly at my ankle, I knew for sure the direction I would be heading after my last day labouring for the villainous Baldwin.

* * *

Bridget Grimshaw pulled the shawl tight about her shoulders as she left the cottage and headed towards the alehouse. The evening was warm, the pulling of her shawl was to help keep her temper in check and still her tongue from ranting to the heavens above. It was certain then. He meant to leave her. Just as his father before him.

Digory was heavy in Bridget's belly when she'd last seen her husband. Although more than eighteen years had past, it still seemed as yesterday. In spite of her ungainly condition, she'd insisted on travelling with him to Torre Station, both happy and excited as he boarded the train heading for the throbbing mass of London Town. The hide bag, filled with curios they'd cleared from the adjoining cottage, was almost left behind as the pair became locked in an embrace that lasted a long time – such was their affection for each other.

To this day, Bridget will never understand how and why her man had been caught up in thievery. He was the most trustworthy person she'd ever met. Remembering him as a boy, he was honest and straight-talking and as Old Ma Grimshaw often stated, "My boy's no scrump, even for a single apple, he'd always ask first." Besides, money was plentiful. The main reason for the journey, being to purchase a fashionable perambulator for the babe's arrival and the taking of the unwanted curios to sell at the market, would go some way in paying for it.

When Old Ma Grimshaw heard of his fate, it broke her heart and her spirit. Within the year she was upon her death-bed. Bridget dabbed the shawl to her moistened eyes in memory of it, then spat at the ground, cursed at the moon and hurried her step, refusing to continue revisiting times long past.

Before long she heard sounds of merriment drifting her way. She could smell and almost taste the pressed, intoxicating juice of the apple. A juice she'd drank daily since she was younger than Drew. A juice that was more commonplace than water for quenching a thirst. A juice that cheered the heart and dulled the pain. What right had anyone to deny her such a juice?

She spat once more before pushing open the heavy oak door, her eyes seeking out the landlord, for without his patience for payment, there'd be no supping here this night.

* * *

Once satisfied that my half-brother and cousins were asleep, I moved with stealth from the small bedchamber and descended the stairs. Secure in the knowledge that Ma had gained the landlord's sympathy and wouldn't be back for some time, I lit the lamp and brought forth the gold ring to its light. This was the first opportunity to see clearly the precious find and with racing heartbeat, I marvelled at its craftsmanship and artistry. Skulls and bones had always filled me with wonder and to see them here, carved perfectly on so tiny a scale, enlarged that wonder. I felt no shame at having kept the ring for myself, it's rightful owner was long gone, and if I'd offered it up, it would have been the likes of Baldwin who would profit by it. There were words and numbers scribed on the inside surface of the ring, and thinking now of the bones that had given up the ring and the man who once fleshed out those bones, I felt a strong urge to copy down what was written, even though the bones had now been re-buried.

Carrying the lamp through to the scullery, my eyes swept the area, searching for a suitable surface to copy down the scribing. In one corner, half-forgotten, dusty lengths of timber stood concealing a back door that had been bolted and unused for years. The lengths of skirting cut and shaped in more positive times when Ma and Uncle Richard had a mind to refurbish the scullery – new wood to provide a new start after selling off the cottage next door. Back then there was money enough to build on an extra room, a room offering more privacy for me. Back then Uncle Richard was alive and Ma was happy carrying his child. Back then Ma was ignorant of the fact that Uncle Richard, along with five other fishermen would soon perish in a storm that cost the whole community a terrible toll. The positive dreams of a new start fading to nothing, as did the money from the sale of the cottage next door.

After much shifting of the timber, I found what was needed. A short length, angled at both ends for fitting into a corner. The wood had darkened with age and was smooth to the touch. I struck a line on it using the chalk stone from Albert's pocket and a clear white line showed back. My intention was to transfer the scribing using the chalk stone first, before rendering it more permanent. I would then follow the lines with the use of a small chisel. The unknown man was now buried away from his family, the least I could do, was to match up the markings at the new burial site and indicate, even though not entirely true, that here too rested another family member. It might be some time before I could carry this out but at least the inscribed timber would be safe here.

So engrossed was I, checking the ring and copying the letters, checking the ring and copying the numbers, that a sudden sound from behind startled me, causing the wood to slip from my hand and clatter to the floor. I turned to find Drew, face flushed with shame, as a puddle of piss spattered to the ground. He was about to start wailing. My fault. I'd not taken care in being quiet and the lad was stunned with fright.

I reached toward him. 'Hush now, Drew, Ma's not gone far and she'll be back soon. I'll clean up the mess, you go on back to bed and nothing more will be said.'

'You won't tell Eme?', asked the four-year-old with a shiver.

'No, I won't tell Eme, now…'

And you won't tell Connie? interrupted the boy without moving a single step.

No, I promise I won't tell anybody in the whole world that you pissed on the floor, if you go back…'

Drew started to whimper, and I knew it would soon develop into wailing if I didn't act quickly. Without thinking I lay down the ring by the lamp, took hold of Drew by the shoulders and squeezed them reassuringly.

'I'm sorry, Drew, I didn't mean to frighten and upset you. I have a job to do here and as soon as I'm finished I'll be back up to bed. If you're still awake I'll sing you a lullaby.' I took hold of a cleaning rag and swiped the floor with it. 'There it's all gone, no one will ever know it happened, now off you go, I'll be back up there very soon.'

'What's that?' Drew's eyes were locked on the ring, his finger pointing directly at it.

I snatched it from sight, slipping it behind the length of wood. It's…it's just my work, Drew, I'm cleaning it for someone.

'Can I hold it?'

'No! Like I said, it's my work and it's been cleaned so…'

'My hands are clean, look. Drew stroked both his hands down the front of his night shirt and held them forth for inspection.

'One quick hold and then back to bed, right?'

He nodded and held forth again an open hand. Before placing the ring there, I asked him who he loved most in the whole world. He hesitated, thinking it to be a grown up trick.

'It's Ma, right?' I said, relief flooding across his small face. He smiled and nodded. 'Well if I let you hold this ring, you have to promise not to tell anyone about it, anyone at all, not Ma, not Eme or Connie, no one. If you do tell, then the person you love most will die!'

May God forgive me! I watched passionless as Drew stiffened again with fear. 'It's a magic ring, Drew, and that's why I don't want you to hold it, because you're only a little boy and I know it's hard to keep promises from people you know and love. Now off you go to bed and forget all about what you saw. It was nothing more than a dream.'

'Please let me hold it, Digory, I promise never, ever to tell.'

As the ring was placed in the centre of the child's small palm,

Drew's fingers closed around it like an activated mantrap. Then just as quickly, the trap sprang open and his young, bright eyes gazed on the band of black and gold and all its intricate artistry. Before offering it back to me, I watched as he bent forward and kissed its surface, just as I had done shortly after finding it – cool metal against warm lips.

Drew smiled and said, 'I promise, I won't tell anyone about it. I don't want Ma to die!'

Chapter 3

Apple Cottage – After Midnight

Distant voices, angry and argumentative, carried on the breeze, spoiling the peace of the night. I'd finished my task. Found a new, more secure hiding place for my coin purse and ring before returning to bed, relieved to find Drew sleeping. Relieved that I too, may now find rest after the turmoil of the day.

The voices continued their loudness, having no regard for the late hour, having no care that others were being kept awake. Carefully, I slid from my bed, snatching boots and over-shirt before descending stairs two at a time. Once outside the voices became clearer. It was Ma and Baldwin, angry words flying, pointing fingers stabbing the air, at each other like cat and dog. In minutes I was upon them, dragging Ma to one side and expecting to use my fists on Baldwin but relieved when he stepped back with arms raised in a gesture that halted any further action.

'See you on the morrow, young Digory,' he said, hiccuping before and after his few words. No mention of what he was doing close to my home. No explanation or apology for the disturbance. He gave a curt bow to Ma, turned, and in an ungainly manner, headed toward the village, hiccuping as he went.

'What was going on, Ma? You were making enough noise to wake the dead. If Baldwin didn't owe me, I'd have shown him my fist. Drew's been restless for hours and I need my sleep.'

'Oh stop your complaining, boy. Baldwin was the only one to stand me credit this night, alls we were arguing on, was how much I be in his debt. He's a sly one, but I knows exactly the amount that passed these lips and I'll remember right enough to tell thee in the morning. If he docks a farthing more from your pay, you has my permission to floor him. But, remember this, my handsome boy, Baldwin and me was the best of friends for years and there was a time when he was as handsome as thee.'

* * *

Sleep evaded me for a long time because of my concern for Ma and how she would manage after my leaving. Eme and Constance earned what they could, mucking out the stables of the coachhouses, handing over three quarters of their pay. They too were sick and tired of seeing their hard-earned money go to waste, Eme threatening to run off with the first man who gave her the eye. She would do it too, not caring that Ma had raised the pair since their mother, Grace, died of the fever during the winter of their second year.

As a seven-year-old, I well remember Uncle Richard. Owner of his own boat and usually absent at sea, I remember on his return, smelling strongly of fish, all of us happy to welcome him home – the only man of Apple Cottages. Ma seemed brighter when he was around, made more of her appearance.

Then came the excited talk of selling off one of the cottages, along with the orchard. How we'd be rich beyond our wildest dreams. The talking included the recently extended rail line to Livermead, and how its improvement would draw the prosperous folks to set up second homes in this beautiful corner of England. Soon we were all squeezed into the one cottage. Ma and Uncle Richard in the one bedchamber, me and the twins in the other. A temporary arrangement, according to Ma, as they talked some more about adding extra sleeping space with the extra money to carry it out.

Ma got fat, and talk soon turned to welcoming another child in our midst. Then one hot summer's day, I walked with Uncle Richard to where his boat was moored, hand in hand exchanging hopes and promises. *His* hopes were for welcoming another son into the family, so both of us when older, could join the family trade, three fishermen, harvesting the fruits of the sea. *My* promise was to take good care of Ma in his absence and do without question or argument, all I was bid. It was the last time I saw Uncle Richard. Later that day the hot summer's day turned humid and dark. By nightfall, violent storms raged across the whole of the South West. For the next few weeks, the only talk was of the biggest storm in decades to hit these parts. Robbing families of menfolk and their livelihoods. The whole community was in mourning for weeks. In Ma's case it lasted years. The cider, she claimed many times, the only thing that eased her broken heart.

Long since I'd grown weary of keeping my promise to Uncle Richard. Talking, hoping and planning is of naught, unless action is to follow. Time was now ripe for action and that action would be according to my own plans.

* * *

In the deathly quiet of the early morn. Bridget sat at her kitchen table, her mind picking through all that she'd heard whilst supping with Baldwin – the villainous Baldwin, as he's often named. The fact being, he was the only one to show mercy and guarantee her credit, and had kept company with her throughout the evening. She wasn't fooled, it being his opportunity for gathering information on what was happening in Chelston. She knew him well. The slyness and callousness he carried was a front, a hard shell protecting a simple-minded soul ruled by fear. He knew where she'd be, her habits were known to all around. His habits were to sup closer to home in Cockington village, but truth to tell, I dare say he was being constantly heckled by villagers unhappy with what was taking place up at the court.

As the evening progressed, she soon realised he was here to find reason behind Albert Wilson's befriending of her son, and what they discussed whilst supping together after dark at Cockington. Bridget it seemed, gained more information than he, for her son had said naught about where or who he had spent that time.

Most folks in these parts classed Bridget as a drunkard, a person of few scruples and no regard for those in her care. Forgotten was the high standing she held in the community of years ago. Forgotten was the young beauty, who, at the age of sixteen had three young men vying to wed and bed her. Forgotten was the goodly sum of coinage paid to her grandfather in exchange for her hand in marriage to the youngest male of the well-respected Grimshaw family.

Bridget had a sharp mind for numbers and a keen memory for everything that passed before her eyes, honed since childhood when she helped in the orchards. Old Ma Grimshaw, amazed at how, after gathering and filling the apple barrels, Bridget, at the tender age of five, could count and then recall, without marking it down, the exact number and weight of each barrel. And even if some be removed for reason of badness or for making an apple pudding, Bridget could say without delay the number of apples left and the gauging of the barrels weight. Old Ma Grimshaw appreciated Bridget's gift for numbers and recall, she encouraged the development of it, often saying, "No amount of schooling could improve on what's already there. Pure intelligence is what you have, child, and when you grows into a woman, you'll be a real asset to any man."

As Bridget grew, so did her popularity, especially with the menfolk. Digory, Albert and Baldwin were all acquainted due to their fathers being fishermen. By the time she was fifteen, there was many a falling out and often a bloody nose from fists raised in jealousy.

On the day before her sixteenth birthday, Bridget's grandfather, her only guardian and good friend to Old Ma Grimshaw, asked her straight out which of the three lads she'd prefer as husband? And before deciding, he'd warned, give plenty of thought to your prospects for the future. As far as Bridget was concerned, very little thought was needed. Back then, all three were handsome in their own way, including Baldwin, but the Grimshaw's owned land, property and a thriving business. She was soon promised to Digory and they were wed the following year, moving into the larger of the cottages with Ma Grimshaw and Digory's younger sister, Grace. Being a newly-wed, she then saw much less of Albert and Baldwin.

'Ma? Is it morning?

The small voice from behind was barely a whisper but it pulled Bridget back to the sorry state of her life. Without turning she said, 'It's still dark, child, go back to your bed.'

'I'm thirsty, Ma.'

With a heavy sigh, she rose from the chair, wood creaking at the shifting of her weight, and shuffled to the scullery where a pewter jug, half filled with water stood covered by a square of muslin on an old wooden barrel. As she reached for the jug, a startled mouse shot out from behind it, scurried down to the floor and cut across her path to a hole in the far corner of the wall.

Drew clapped his hands in excitement, 'Vernin! Vernin!'

'Shush, child, you'll wake everyone!' She tipped a splash of water into a cup and shoved it into his hands. Drink it down then go back to your bed.'

'Ma, is Digory leaving us?' Drew's wide, beseeching eyes locked on hers.

'Don't talk nonsense child, sup up and back to your bed!'

* * *

Drew gently placed the empty cup by the jug. Ma had forgotten to cover it. He placed the muslin carefully over the top, making sure no gaps were showing. Vernin was out on the hunt for food, he wouldn't want to find his friend belly-up in the water. When Drew was alone, he would put tiny scraps of food by the mouse hole. He would call softly to Vernin, bringing him out to play. Waiting behind the jug was Vernin's favourite hiding place.

'I said, back to your bed!'

Drew jumped in fright. A yank on his arm and a push toward the door followed Ma's sharp words.

Once out of the scullery, he pressed his body close to the kitchen wall and peered through the gap in the door, watching, looking to see if Ma was poking a stick into Vernin's hole like Eme had done. She was standing on the stool, reaching for something on the highest shelf. Drew's eyes widened as he saw Digory's private box in her hands. The box that once held smelly sticks called cigars which came from a far off land. Every time Digory opened the box, the smell escaped into the room, just like now as Ma opened it, tapped it, shook it and tipped it upside down. It was empty and she looked disappointed then angry. She cursed out loud and spat on the floor.

Drew moved quickly to his bed.

* * *

I was roused from a restless sleep by Drew scrambling into bed, wrapping his cold arms about my waist, his heart pounding against my back. I remained quiet, in no mood for listening to his child-like escapades. If I allowed that, we'd both be wide awake.

Drew's venturings in the dead of night, seeking out a mouse, beetle, spider, anything that moved, was commonplace. I'd witnessed with my own eyes how he'd corner them with crumbs, scraps and plenty of soft talking. It was just his way, he seemed happier unloading his feelings to creatures that couldn't talk back. There were days when Drew barely spoke at all, a nod or shake of the head sufficient for most questions asked of him. The twins had little time nor care for his company. Seeing him as being backward and in line for being named the next village idiot. They were wrong. He had no one of his own age to parley with, so he found friends where he could, his latest being Vernin (introduced as Vermin by Ma, as she chased the mouse through the kitchen, hoping to crush it beneath the high held broom). Drew holding his breath and clapping when the mouse survived the run. Without thinking, I laughed briefly and Drew seized the opportunity.

'Ma found your box of treasure, Digory, but it was empty. Just the smell was left.'

'Thank you for the warning, Drew. Now you rest easy, we both need our sleep.'

'I think your new hiding place is much harder for anyone to find. And I promise on Ma's life not to tell anyone, not even Vernin because he's a really good digger!'

I thought as much, Drew must have hung around, watching me through the gap in the door, but I trusted his word not to tell. Now there was more at stake than just money. As a precaution against Ma finding the ring. I lifted one of the flag-stones in the scullery floor and buried my money and ring in an old tin-box beneath it. Only someone with strength to match my own would be able to find it. I would have told her of the find, but without a shadow of doubt, she'd have insisted on me returning it. Not because of purity of heart but because she feared the spirits of the dead. And all the talk of desecration and reburials banded about the village had only added to that fear.

Folding my arms about me, I pulled Drew closer. Our breathing slowed in perfect rhythm as we each entered our own night-time domains.

Chapter 4

Apple Cottage – Thursday – Early Dawn

The repeated cries of a cockerel pierced the tranquility of pre-dawn, alerting Chelston that a fox was possibly on the prowl. Moans and groans rang out from the larger bedchamber. It was an early start for Eme and Constance and before long their moans and groans developed into bickering and then arguing. Ma's voice, louder and arresting, demanding they be more considerate of those still sleeping. Now we were all awake, including Drew.

I kept out of Ma's way as she busied about the kitchen, cutting lumps of bread, smeared over with a lick of pork dripping. When on occasion her eyes found mine, I sensed anger mingled with fear and accusation. Words were unnecessary. We both knew the outcome at the end of this day.

Drew remained silent, head bowed in concentration, both hands holding bread as he nibbled off tiny bites like a rodent, much of it spilling onto the table. He was lost in his own world as the hustle and bustle developed around him. At one stage, Eme confronted him, demanding to know what had become of the small mirror? But his own world held strong.

'Drew! Are you deaf as well as daft?' she shouted, giving his head an aggressive tap. 'Where's the small mirror? It was there yesterday.' Her finger pointing to the shelf above the hearth, then both hands returning to her hips as she awaited his response. Silence. Except for the chatter of small teeth nibbling hard bread.

Eme's hand drew back in preparation to swipe. I caught it before contact was made. 'Leave him be. What would Drew want with a small mirror used by women to powder their faces? It was cracked anyway and in danger of breaking up completely. If you must keep looking at yourself, use Ma's large mirror in the bedchamber.'

Unable to resist, Eme gave Drew a sly dig before heading for the stairs, feet pounding noisily as she went. Another pounding returned her to the cottage door, which opened then slammed shut. Constance, with bread in hand, rose from the table and without saying a word, left to follow her sister.

I tried to focus on a time when our lives were different to this. Before Drew was born, before Uncle Richard had died. Yes, there was a time when life was better, but it seemed such a long time ago.

I waited till Ma left us alone, as I knew she would, not wanting to be available for a peck on the cheek from her eldest son – a son who was soon to desert her. Once the bedchamber door had closed and the tell-tale creaking of Ma returning to bed died away, I turned on Drew. 'Where is the small mirror?'

Without any hint of shame for the ruckus he'd caused, his answer was simple. 'It's in my secret place.'

'I know Eme is not the kindest of people but to take something to spite her, will only make matters worse.'

The nibbling stopped. Drew lifted his eyes to mine. 'It's just an old mirror. I didn't take it to spite anyone.'

'I know it's just an old mirror but why did you take it? It's been on the hearth shelf for years. I want you to promise you'll put it back and nothing more will be said.'

His eyes lowered and his lips curved downward, what remained of the bread pushed to one side. *Here we go,* I thought, preparing for the inevitable wailing. I was about to leave for work, leave the wailing for Ma to deal with for my patience was wearing thin. Then I realized I was mistaken. The lowered eyes and the curved down lips, were Drew's adopted look of concentration, his look of determination.

'I need the mirror', he said, staring me straight in the eye. 'That's why I took it. When I've finished needing it, I promise to put it back.'

My curiosity burned, but now was not the time to ask. A long day of hard work awaited me, and I had no intention of giving Baldwin any excuse for him not paying me in full, minus the sixpence owed for Ma's two jugs of cider.

* * *

The cottage door closed behind Digory, silence falling and opening up a world of infinite possibilities. Drew loved this time of day, early morning when Digory, Eme and Connie were at their work, Ma was in her bed and he could do as he liked. First of all, he would tend to the needs of his best friend. Carefully gathering all the crumbs from the table into the palm of his hand, he tip-toed to Vernin's hole at the back of the scullery. He shook the crumbs onto the ground, making a trail from the hole to where he would sit waiting for Vernin to appear.

Taking the mirror was part of a good idea, for when Vernin came face to face with himself, he'd be able to see what he looked like and how different he was from the boy who was his friend. Drew's secret hiding place was in the kitchen. Beneath the table top where struts of wood gave space enough to hide the box – the box no longer needed by Digory. Pushed under the table top at the corner where he sat, was easy to reach but out of sight to everyone. Yes, it was a good place to hide things. No one would ever think of looking there.

He reached for it now. Carrying it to the end of the crumb trail, he sat, crossed his legs and carefully opened the box. The escaping smell was really strong, making him sneeze three times. Taking hold of the mirror, he reached forward and angled it into the hole. There was nothing interesting to see, just dust and bits of spider web. He returned to his crosslegged position, confident that Vernin would appear before too long.

With the box open on his lap, Drew began sifting through his treasures. His favourite, given to him a few days ago, was a large finger ring with the body of a snake wound around it, its tail disappearing down its own mouth. Two tiny eyes shone red in the light from the window, giving it the look of the devil. It wasn't made from gold like the one Digory showed him the night before. Digory gave him this ring because he wouldn't be here for his fifth birthday in seven weeks time. He said it was made of brass and copper and it used to belong to my father who died when I was a baby in Ma's belly. Digory said it was only right that I should have it for when I grow up and my fingers grow big and fat like his. Drew had remembered seeing it in Ma's chest upstairs and he felt sure she didn't know that he'd been given it, so he would have to keep it a secret.

So engrossed was Drew with the contents of his box, and his own thoughts, he didn't notice the tiny creature appear and begin gobbling up the crumb trail, until it was nearly upon him. He reached for the mirror and held it firm at the end of the trail. It didn't take long for the crumbs to be eaten and Vernin to be left sniffing at the image of himself. Drew was delighted. Suddenly a sound from upstairs told him the fun was over. The lid was on the box, the box was hidden from view and the mouse was back in the hole.

Chapter 5

Cockington Court – Thursday Morning

No one was around when I arrived at the site, the morning cool due to a breeze drifting in from the west, showing good promise that I might reach Baldwin's marking of yesterday before he arrived. My mind was set firm, I would earn my full pay of yesterday and full pay today, making sure at the end of the day, I held every penny of it in my hand before leaving Cockington Court. Even if it meant using my fist. I'd promised that much to Ma, and she deserved my kept word. God only knows how she will manage after I leave on the morrow.

As I swung the pick and shovelled the earth, thoughts of my father pressed for attention, details supplied by Albert of the kind of man he was and the man he'd apparently become – a thief feathering his own nest – resulting in him being shipped out to Australia for seven years hard labour. Ironically, transported on the Hougoumont, the last convict ship to be sent from England. From his flippant choosing of words, Albert gave the impression that my father had not been ready for marriage. That he hadn't adjusted well to the thought of becoming a father. That he was a free-spirited fisherman and would never cope with being harnessed on land. He almost made it sound as though being shipped off to foreign parts was preferable to his life at home.

Ma's version, heard many times when the cider loosened her tongue, never varied. Their love knew no bounds and he was proudly awaiting the arrival of their first child. He travelled alone by train to London Town, taking curios to sell at one of the many markets in exchange for buying a perambulator, a carrier on wheels not yet available in these parts, for the expected child – myself. His absence was expected to be no more than three days, for the child was due soon. When after a week, he hadn't returned, Ma and Old Ma Grimshaw, frantic with worry and convinced he'd been robbed by a cut-throat, began to make plan to send a paid investigator to London; to follow his trail and attempt to discover what had become of him.

The day before the paid investigator was due to leave, a letter arrived at the door of Apple Cottage, marked for the attention of Mrs Bridget Grimshaw. A letter, printed on handsome paper with the name of an official printed in gilded letters at the top of the page. A letter, giving facts that Digory Grimshaw had been arrested and found guilty of selling stolen goods. Goods robbed and proved to be from Cockington Court.

Ma was near to giving birth and Old Ma Grimshaw was in too bad a state of health to travel the distance to London, contesting what was being said. In their stead, Albert joined forces with the paid investigator, offering to put forward to the powers that be, a written testimonial signed by many, to show that Digory Grimshaw was of good, sound character. But it was all to no avail.

I'd reached the marking line before Baldwin arrived and uncertain of the direction to proceed, for no overall plan was ever shown to me, I paused for rest and water to refresh my body. As I stood, drinking my fill from the newly placed jug, I caught sight of Albert walking toward me.

'I see you're in no mind to heed my words, young Digory. Lucky for you that water has just been placed and has come from a clean source.'

I was in no mood for idle talk. 'Have you seen sign of Baldwin? I'm anxious for his marking of todays line, time is drifting by.'

'I understand he's been summoned by the squire to the re-burial site. There's been complaints. Villagers angry about the disturbance of their ancestors and little respect shown to their reinterment. Daresay he'll be a while yet. He took out his pipe and began pressing tobacco into it from a battered tin box. Albert's easy-going way was starting to irritate.

'And I'm to stand here like a fool, earning no pay?'

'Easy lad, the day is young, but if you be that anxious for your digging, I'll mark a line for you. I'm sure Baldwin will be back afore you reach it.'

I watched as Albert sucked rapidly on the pipe and when sure the tobacco had taken hold, closing his eyes he sucked deep and long, an expression of sheer joy on his face. On opening his eyes, he smiled. The sort of smile, I feel sure, won him many favours.

'Now lad, what's it to be, shall we continue our conversation of last night whilst awaiting Baldwin? Or shall you use your own initiative, your own sense of independence, and continue earning your pay?'

Chapter 6

Apple Cottage – Thursday Morning

After splashing her face, dragging a brush through her hair and tying a clean pinafore about her, Bridget called out to Drew to make himself ready for leaving. There was extra work on offer at the alehouse and as much as it pained her to admit it, if she was to continue enjoying a jug of cider, she'd have to earn more money. As well as scrubbing the tables and making fresh the floor, John, the keeper of Cockington Village's alehouse, had been trying for months to get her to work more hours. But why would she be interested? Her pay was given in one hand, and mostly taken back in the other. Especially during the hot summer months, when more cider was drunk for quenching a thirst brought on by vigorous scrubbing and cleaning.

She knew well that help was needed in his kitchen. Alice, his cook, was unhappy. She was forever complaining that the extra trade from groundsmen and builders was putting strain on her already poor health. Yes, the time was ripe for Bridget to awaken the businesswoman she once was, and if John didn't like what she proposed, she'd take her proposal *and* her supping elsewhere.

Chelston had alehouses too, didn't she spend many an evening in one of them. The evening before, whilst one ear was on Baldwin's leaking of information in regard to Albert, the other was tuned to the tittle-tattle of Chelston's community – from the perspective of its menfolk. She'd heard that at least two establishments were looking for female labour. For when it came to kitchen-work, cleaning and scrubbing, women were far more suited to the task.

Construction work in the area was booming, leading to an imbalance in the demand and supply of refreshment at the hostelries and alehouses, and the staff they required to keep them running. 'Yes, now is the time', whispered Bridget as she stood before the large mirror in her bedchamber, her voice, though low, holding a strength of determination she hadn't felt in years. 'Let the boy go. Let him find for himself that the dream that pulls him, is naught but a dream.'

'Ma, can I stay here? I'll look after the cottage. Clear out all the beetles, spiders and…'

'No! I'll be away for a longer time than usual and I have a better plan for you.'

Drew knew what was coming and he hated it. He put his hands over his ears and shut his eyes tight, willing the words to fly over his head. He knew it wouldn't happen, it never did. Before he counted to five, Ma would have hold of his arm pulling him to the place she wanted to go. The place he hated. And wailing in protest would only earn him a slapping across his legs.

* * *

It wasn't far to the coachhouse where Eme and Constance spent three mornings a week mucking out the stables, but with an unwilling child in tow, it seemed to be taking forever. Now that

Bridget had set her mind on change, she was eager to put thoughts into action. For a start, she needed to have words with the owner of the Coachhouse, Arthur Gilbey, who owned three handsome carriages and at least a dozen beasts for pulling them.

A winding drive led to his fine residence, which lay to one side and forward of the stables, Eme's voice, loud and aggressive, could be heard chivvying her sister to work faster. Drew stopped in his tracks pulling back in protest.

'Please Ma, I hate it here. The smell from the dung makes me sick and Eme…'

'Hush now, or you'll feel my hand!'

As they neared the entrance, the heavy, oak door swung open, it's owner seeming to be aware of the unexpected visit. He walked slowly toward the pair, smiling only when he was but a few feet away.

'Ma Grimshaw? To what do I owe this pleasure? You considering sending your youngest out to work?' he asked, ruffling Drew's hair. 'I'm afraid you'll have to wait a few years for him to be of any use to me.'

Drew pulled back, half hiding behind his mother's skirt. Bridget pulled him back beside her with one hand, gripping it tightly. With the other she pointed at Gilbey's belly, an indication of its portly size, 'I'm glad to see you looking so well, Arthur. However, I'm not here for pleasantries. I'm here on the serious matter of giving notice that from the end of next week Eme and Constance will be removed from your employ.'

The transformation on his face from proud confidence to wary confusion was plain to see. Then confidence returned along with the smile that belied his true feelings toward this woman. 'Don't you think that's a matter for the twins? They are happy working here. Eme has taken a shine to Francis, my head stableman. The matter might be out of both our hands before long.'

'That's as may be, Arthur, but I be their legal guardian and what I says, goes. Besides, Francis Bolt, I hear tell, already has a woman, a woman heavy with his second child and I'll be having words with him later. I'm here to discuss a far more serious matter. In the year and a half since the twins took on labouring for you, you've cheated them out of half their pay. Two workers for the price of one – two hard workers. The one wage for both of them was meant for a trial period only, as a way of making sure that kin as close as twins can work together without dispute. That trial period, agreed on by all, being one month. And you've seen fit not to honour that agreement.'

Gilbey's smile broadened, 'As you no doubt heard for yourself, Bridget, the girls have many an argument, which *does* interfere with their workload, but I know things are difficult for them at home, and I do like to be charitable where I can.'

A bark of laughter erupted from Bridget, a short, sharp burst of noise cutting through the air – the sound akin to a fox defending its territory. She took two steps closer. Gilbey held his ground.

With her face but inches from his and in a voice laced with determination, she said, 'Any arguments the girls do have, are about money and the unfairness of their pay. Constance has broached the subject with you several times, but you lead her to believe they're not worthy of any more. If truth be known, Francis Bolt is part of a plan to keep Eme sweet and cause friction between sisters and that is your undoing, Arthur Gilbey. For there's work aplenty in these parts for hard-working lasses.'

As though to underscore what was being discussed, hollering rang out from the stables. Constance, announcing to all in earshot that she couldn't work any faster. Eme, verbally hitting back that in ten minutes she'd be needed in the other stable. A clatter followed, as though a pitch fork was thrown to the ground.

'The girls don't sound happy to me, Arthur. I think they'll be happier elsewhere, with better pay.'

Gilbey cleared his throat. 'It's true there's been an oversight regarding their pay, but I can put that to rights straightaway, Bridget, if you withdraw your notice. You're right, hard-working girls are not easy to find.'

Bridget looked about her, appearing to give the matter serious thought. Gilbey had come far. His business growing well and his pockets growing fat at the expense of the poor. But change is a constant happening and before you know it, trains and other forms of transportation will one day rob him of it all.

She looked down at Drew, his sharp eyes and ears taking in all that was being said. Before raising her eyes to Gilbey, Bridget produced a flicker of a smile and a left-eyed-wink in the boy's direction, giving indication that all was well. 'Well, after serious thought, Arthur, I'll consider withdrawing my notice on one condition. You've short-paid my nieces for eighteen months. If the rightful pay be backdated for a period of nine months – for I feel that to be a fair estimate of meeting you half way,' Bridget held up a hand to still his intended interruption. 'Also, if either one of my nieces prefer my employ to yours, there'll be no binding them here. Are we agreed?'

Gilbey made a huffing sound which corresponded well to the displeased look on his face. Eventually, he gave a curt nod, and turned to go.

'And if it be all the same to you, Arthur, I'll take the back-dated pay now. If you need the exact figure,' Bridget tapped the side of her head with one finger, I have it here.'

Without a word nor invitation to follow him, Arthur Gilbey returned through his heavy oak door before closing it behind him.

Bridget bent close to Drew's ear, explaining the need for him being here and the importance of carrying out her wishes. He nodded seriously. Too seriously for a child of his years. She planted a kiss on the top of his head then watched as his small legs carried him in the direction of the stables.

A goodly time passed before the oak door opened and Gilbey emerged carrying box and ledger. Her reputation for figures was well known. The amount he'd entered in his ledger, matched the amount in her head. Not a farthing more nor a farthing less. She offered forth her hand and said, 'I've instructed Drew to stay close to his cousins, reporting back to me anything untoward in regard to Francis Bolt.'

Gilbey counted out the coinage into Bridget's gaping palm. Then slammed-shut the money box, closed the ledger with more force than necessary and without smiling said, 'I must admit, Bridget, your morality is somewhat warped. The baby guards the twins, while you sup away the twin's rightful pay.'

Bridget spat on the ground, causing Gilbey to flinch as sputum the size of a penny-piece, landed inches from his fancy, square-toed shaped boots. She turned and with head held high, marched away.

Chapter 7

Cockington Court – Late Thursday Morning

Without interference from anyone, I was making good progress. I'd marked my own line, since Albert swore to give honest account that Baldwin's marking of the day before had been reached. He also swore that the direction of the next area to be dug, corresponded with the master plan. I sensed that he thought me mistrustful. Maybe I am, but this being my last day, I'd leave nothing to chance.

The site was deserted except for me. No sign of Baldwin, no sign of any other activity at all on the site. Further knowledge from Albert stated that the regular groundsmen were still occupied at the new burial site. A small group of villagers, unhappy at their ancestors graves being disturbed, had then heard they were being reinterred at an ancient site used for victims of the plague. In these parts, as I suppose in many others up and down the land, any mention of 'the black death' evoked panic and superstition. Because of this, the small group of villagers had now developed into a troublesome, angry mob, elaborating their grievances by saying that their families' remains were being flung into pits of hell without proper regard or piety.

Albert also informed me, his charming, laid-back smile still in place, that the groundsmen were well-armed with sticks and picks, and as further measure against trouble developing, the squire had called upon the vicar to help reign in his unruly flock. It was clear who Albert sided with and I came to wonder, not for the first time, his place in the ranking at Cockington Court; for he showed no sympathy at all for the grievances of the villagers of this manor.

The earth I was now clearing, although equally parched from weeks of dry weather, was far less burdensome. No trees had set root, no large stones had been placed or erected and no bodies had been laid to rest here – apart from the bones of the unknown benefactor I'd reinterred the evening before. Try as I may, I found it difficult to keep my thoughts from wandering back and forth in regard to the skeleton buried just a short distance from where I stood. I was curious as to how he met his death? Why he found it necessary to conceal his ring in such a dramatic way? Clearly, swallowing the ring had thwarted its theft by his attacker.

I recalled the heartache I'd felt at not being able to transport the bones along with others on the cart, but after hearing Albert's account of what had transpired at that place, I was content that my decision was the right one. On the other hand, should I not have been more honest and anchored the ring back in the location where discovered?

Growing weary of my mental tussle with right and wrong, I settled on the cold, hard facts. The cold, hard facts being: this unknown warrior had been long-dead-and-buried, no one knew, apart from me, of the ring's existence, I am alive and whilst there is blood pumping through my veins, I need to search out the truth about my father. Finding this ring will help me to do that. Even though the ring be on course for the melting pot. Providence has seen fit to grant me the means for reaching my goal. Not just for myself, Ma also deserved to know the truth and I am the only one strong enough, and committed enough, to uncover that truth.

* * *

The Coachhouse Stables

Eme glared at Drew as he sat cross-legged on clean straw in the corner of the stable block, refusing to go out of their sight. For company he had one of Arthur Gilbey's fox terriers tucked close by, in rapture of the boy's constant stroking.

'Drew, go on out of here, take a walk, that's what you usually do. Me and Connie has work to do.'

Drew, remained silent and continued his stroking. The terrier huddled closer as though knowing trouble was brewing.

Eme marched into the next stall where Connie had just begun forking out the soiling 'You talk to him, Connie, he'll take notice of you.' She lowered her voice to a hissing whisper, 'Francis'll be here soon and he won't be wanting the next village idiot gawping at us, will he?'

'What's the difference? You don't mind me gawping at you. Or listening to your giggling when Francis has a mind to start mauling your body. Have you no shame, Eme? Francis already has a woman, and because she's carrying, he's using you.'

Eme gave her sister a shove and the hissing continued. 'How many times do I have to tell you, Francis intends to leave her. You're jealous that's all. Now do something about that brat before I pitchfork him out the door.'

Connie, stayed her ground. 'And if he leaves her for you, where will you live? I know it as a fact, Francis and his woman live in the same house as her father. I can't see him allowing you to move in, can you? Can't see Aunt Bridget allowing the pair of you to move in with us neither.'

'Why not? Digory'll be gone after tomorrow, the brat can move into my space and me and Francis can have Digory's room.'

That wouldn't be fair on Drew and Aunt Bridget would never allow it.'

'Drew! Drew!' Eme, screeched in a high-pitched whine. 'I'm tired of hearing that name on everyone's lips. Everything was fine before *he* was born.' You know that as well as I do, Connie. I know you feel the same as me. *He* was the one who should have died, not Pa!'

Chapter 8

Apple Cottage – Thursday Afternoon

Bridget returned to the cottage, her arms filled with provisions bought at one of the local farmsteads. Added to this, a cart would soon be arriving with delivery of flour from the mill, a keg of cider direct from the press and a crate of eggs that was destined for Brixham market until she offered to take the lot at a discounted price. Dan, the sixteen-year-old son living at the nearest farmstead, was owner of the cart and willing to transport the lot to her door for a small sum.

She had a gift for figures and it was time she put it to good use once again. She also had another skill, long since been let go. The skill of pie making. Any woman who wasn't half-witted could put together a plain fruit pie or fruit pudding. Bridget's skill went beyond that. She had top notch pie making skills, game pies being her main speciality. Rabbit, pigeon, venison, pheasant, she'd used them all to fill the fancy decorated pastry casings. Secret recipes passed on from generation to generation. Coupled with the orchard seasonal work, that's how she earned a living for herself and her grandfather for many a year. Her grandfather, one time gamekeeper to the landed gentry, had contacts aplenty for a whole variety of game.

Once she was wed, it was the ledger and the keeping of figures that kept here nose to the grindstone. Old Ma Grimshaw was no fool and ensured that Bridget's skill for figures had been well harnessed, while Old Ma maintained her place as queen of the kitchen for she wasn't about to relinquish that title to anyone; especially not to her wet-behind-the-ears daughter-in-law. Mind you, in spite of the age difference, the pair rubbed along together well. On days when Bridget was allowed to help in the kitchen, the two women would exchange pie making tips with each other.

Back then, they were living in the bigger cottage next door. Old Ma had seen fit to have a large cast-iron range installed, which consisted of a coal burning grate flanked by an oven and boiler. The range was enclosed on top by a hot plate which forced the hot draught to circulate around the oven and boiler before being lost to the chimney. These closed ranges were held to be cleaner and more efficient but in reality they burned huge quantities of coal and were time-consuming to maintain. Neither of which bothered Old Ma. Money was plentiful and scallywag labour was cheap.

It had been a long time since Bridget had seen money to spare and she liked it. Really liked it. Some would argue that the money belonged to her nieces, but hadn't she taken care of them for many a year? Wasn't she still? If they had a mind to listen and focus on the opportunity that she envisaged, between them they could share a handsome living. Yes! With help, Bridget felt she could make it happen. She felt alive with the possibility of having her own business. Her very own family-run pie shop. Even though a drop of cider hadn't passed her lips this day, she felt closer to the state of happiness, than she had done in years.

Other facts also had to be faced. The man of the house was leaving, the twins would no doubt follow before too long and where would that leave Drew? Wanting! No one could see it but her, and maybe Digory, the boy had intelligence and with a little money spent on education, he could well be able to support himself in the future.

'There you are my beauties!' cried Bridget in a flurry of excitement as she rummaged in the cupboards of the old pine dresser. A dresser which had stood half-forgotten in the corner of the kitchen since Richard drowned. Before selling the cottage next door, they'd carted, dragged, lifted and near broke their backs on bringing as much of the furniture and fitments as this smaller place would hold, each excited at the promise of a fresh start together. And to her shame, it had barely been used, let alone appreciated. She'd wasted a chunk of her life mourning the loss of her men. Allowing opportunities to pass by. The time was now ripe to put that to rights.

Holding her discovered prize aloft, she counted no less than four pie moulds. Three of various size in metal, slotted comfortably inside the largest and the grandest pie mould she'd ever seen. It was pottery-made and decorated in raised, colourful scenes showing hares frolicking in grass. On its lid, a reclining hare formed the handle. They'd all been bought by Old Ma. She, being proud of the fact that we could live well and afford the things that once was unavailable to ordinary, hard-working folks.

Poor old Ma, thought Bridget, *losing her son in such a shameful way, ripped the heart and soul from her, leading to her death within the year!*

Seeing these beautiful things that were used and cherished by her mother-in-law made Bridget realise how wasteful her own life had become. She couldn't change what her son had decided to do, but she could change the way she dealt with his leaving. She had to, if only for Drew's sake.

After her profitable visit to Arthur Gilbey's fine residence, Bridget had gone to see John, keeper of the tavern where she scrubbed tables and kept floors clean. He'd smiled as she entered, a smile easy to read for it didn't happen often. He thought she was here to help in the kitchen and be paid in cider. The smile soon disappeared by the time Bridget had informed him of the reason behind her unexpected visit. He'd scowled, huffed and puffed, kicked the dog as it lapped spilt ale on the floor, then demanded to know...

'So where..? I mean how..? Who will..?'

Bridget had filled in the gaps, saying, 'You'd like to know why I won't be scrubbing and cleaning for you anymore and where I'll be taking my refreshment in future? Is that what you're asking, John?'

'Well yes, you know you're my best customer, Bridget, I should hate to lose you. Besides all that, who'll scrub the tables and freshen the floors?' John had lowered his head, caught sight of his dog lapping at the floor again and toed it in the ribs before continuing. 'I was hoping you was here to tell me you'd be working extra hours, like I said yesterday, cook needs help in the kitchen. With young Digory gone... I mean, pardon my assuming for all of us knows your situation, Bridget. Well, I just thought...'

With a smile, Bridget remembered every word of her response and it pleased her to repeat the response out loud. 'No one really knows my situation, John. They sees and hears what I let them see and hear. And as news travels faster than a fart in these parts, you can let it be known that Bridget Grimshaw will soon be setting up shop selling the best game pies for miles around. As you are the first to be given this news, maybe you'll be wanting to place your order before the other establishments beat you to it. Buying in your pies should relieve a large portion of cook's burden.'

She hadn't expected a smile at her humorous choice of words and half expected a verbal tussle but John had stood dumbfounded, allowing the gravity of her news to sink in. His hound, taking full advantage of his master's inactivity, found more spills to lap up.

On realizing his state of shock may well take time to pass, Bridget had turned to leave, nodding toward the dog as she did so, again remembering well her parting words. 'Looks to me as though you have your answer for keeping the floor clear of spills, John.'

* * *

Three loud raps on the cottage door and the sound of Drew's voice, halted Bridget's effort in organising the scullery.

'Ma? Dan let me ride on the cart. He says he has flour, eggs and a keg of cider for delivering. Is that the truth, Ma?"

'Hush your hollering, lad. Where's Connie and Eme, didn't I tell you to stay close by them.'

Drew waited until Dan had the sack of flour on his back and was heading into the scullery. Keeping his voice low, he said, 'They're not far behind. I was the only one wanting to ride the cart. He asked Connie first, but she just giggled. When Dan said he was delivering to Apple Cottage, I asked him if I could ride instead. Francis didn't come to see Eme today, Ma, and she's in a really bad mood. She clipped my ear three times for nothing.' Drew held three fingers in the air. 'What's happening in the scullery?'

'Questions, questions, give me some peace boy, I'll tells you what's happening when I'm good and ready.'

Dan finished his unloading and smiled when Bridget pressed a threepence into his hand. 'Thank you, Mrs Grimshaw. Pardon me mentioning it, but you'll need to be rid of the mice if this be the place for storing your flour and such.'

'I knows that, Dan. I have someone in mind who can do that for me.' Bridget looked pointedly at Drew and Drew looked pointedly at the mouse hole. 'In the meantime', she continued, 'I'd much appreciate it, if you keep this little problem to yourself.'

Dan, feeling the coin in his tightened fist responded, 'Don't you worry Mrs Grimshaw, I'll not say a word to no one.'

'You still here then, Dan?' It was Connie, smiling brightly and breathless as she'd walked faster and ahead of her sister.

Dan, turning pink in the face, snatching his cap from his head and wringing it as though filled with water, shyly smiled back. 'I'm…I've finished now. Yes, I'm just finished.'

'Would you like a drink? You must be thirsty after all that lifting.'

Both Connie and Dan looked to Bridget. And Bridget sighed heavily before declaring, 'One cup each and let Dan open the keg.' She was beginning to wonder what had become of Eme.

Moving toward the scullery, Connie asked, 'Shall I fill cups for you and Eme.' She wasn't that far behind me.'

'No! No, you two go ahead and enjoy the refreshment, I still have much to do in the kitchen and Eme will no doubt arrive when she's good and ready.'

Bridget had no doubt that Eme had seized the opportunity to return to the stables and find Francis. *Well so be it,* she thought, *I can only do my best, if the girls too smitten or too stupid not to see the making of the man, she'll just have to learn the hard way.*

Bridget recalled the brief conversation she'd had with Francis Bolt earlier – the man had no shame and probably little intention of altering his behaviour. She did however leave him in no doubt, there was no room at Apple Cottage for the likes of him.

Chapter 9

Cockington Court – Early Thursday Evening

I had done all I was prepared to do in regard to seeking out Baldwin. It seemed no one knew of his whereabouts or when he'd be back on site. Albert was witness to my hard work. Witness to markings reached and new ones scribed in the earth. Markings that he'd entered on a simple copy of the master plan showing my name as the one who was digger. On showing me this plan, he'd gone on to explain, slowly and deliberately as if talking to a child.

'Here's the area you've cleared, lad,' he'd said, tapping the plan with the stem of his pipe. 'And here is your name, showing as you was the one that dug it.'

'I can read my own name, Albert, I can see clearly where I've spent hours digging and shifting the earth – my back knows full well I've done the work. However, what I don't know and what I can't see, is the man's whereabouts with the coinage to pay me my due.'

'All's I'm about to say lad, if you can't get your pay this day, I'll make sure your Ma will have it before too long. I knows your intention is to leave on the morrow for London. I just want to assure you, Baldwin'll not get away with not paying your due.'

I was taken aback. Who was the one keeping tally of the comings and goings of Apple Cottage? Who was the one privy to my private dreams? My tongue was never loose and as for Ma, she had more sense than to engage in tittle-tattle. Albert folded the plan and tucked it into the pocket where all manner of objects lurked. He seemed content to have had the last word but I wasn't done yet.

'I'm going nowhere until I'm paid in full and I can place every farthing of it into Ma's palm.'

He frowned, tapping his pipe stem against teeth yellowed with tobacco stain, before asking, 'How will you pay your way to London, lad, if all you've earned is given over to your ma?'

Although his words were spoken gently, laced in friendly tone, the challenge and prying contained within the words, caused anger to rise in me. 'That be my business not yours and who, may I ask, is feeding you my personal intentions?'

Albert slipped his arm around my shoulder. 'Calm yourself, lad, I'm not your enemy. You are the son of my old friend. A very dear old friend. I understand how you need to find the truth behind the conflicting accounts of why your father left. Bridget was a beautiful lass, heavily pregnant with you, the envy of many a man. Although it has to be said, some men can't be tethered, not in the way Bridget was demanding. She'd declared that after you was born, your father was to put an end to the skippering of the fishing boat. To leave that to those who had no choice in the matter. Money was growing more plentiful and why should he risk his life unnecessarily. But your father was never ruled by money, nor by women. The sea was in his blood, lad. Besides, ask yourself this, if, as your Ma says, they was besotted with each other, why didn't he return after the seven years hard labour was done? I know it might grieve you to hear it, lad, and it pains me to say it, but I reckon your father to be dead. Or, he had no plan on returning at all.'

All this and more was given in hint at the end of yesterday when we supped together in the cool of the starlit sky. Albert doing the talking and I doing the listening. Hearing it a second time, only helped to confirm my earlier notion. Truth passed from person to person becomes hearsay. Real truth is experiencing it for yourself, and that was my intention. However, before leaving Albert's company, I needed two things from him, so on reigning in my anger, I nodded my agreement to his repeated opinions.

'Albert, the copy of the plan you have marked with what I'm owed, can I have lend of it? I promise its return before I leave for London.'

Again that frown and the teeth-tapping. Then a smile as his hand delved into the cavernous pocket and pulled forth the folded document. 'Keep it lad, as I say it be only a copy. Baldwin knows right enough what coinage is due to you, and I have access to the master plan if I care for its use again.'

I gripped the document tightly in my hand, not yet knowing how important a piece of evidence this would turn out to be. Albert turned to go, then thought better of it, reached for my hand and squeezed it hard. My last request rolled easily off my tongue. 'Who was the one told of my travelling to London? I know it wasn't Ma, for even now she doesn't believe I'll leave her, and to speak of it, even to an old friend as you, would mean it gaining power to become real.'

'Your cousin Eme, delightful as she is to look at, is selfish in nature, greedy for prospects and loose in morals. And there are many who would take advantage of that. Don't take too harshly to her lad, we are all a mixture of blessings and curses. Young Eme's are just easy to read.'

* * *

I was at least two-hundred yards from the cottage when the delicious aroma of baking filled my nostrils and quickened my step. Ma had long since lost the urge for making pies – a gift she was once well-skilled in – but as a boy, I well remember the delightful taste of them. The untimely death of uncle Richard had robbed them all of many things.

On entering the cottage door, held back with Ma's flat iron, seldom used for its intended purpose, I was engulfed by a rush of warm air loaded with mouthwatering odours and the babbling chatter of Connie and Drew. They were clapping and shouting praise as two pies were being lifted from the gaping oven – the oven I hadn't seen used in ages. As I stood unnoticed, lost in the scene, I wondered if this was Ma's final attempt to hold me here, trying to recreate happier times to fill the void that had grown between us.

Suddenly, Drew turned and caught my wonderment. Squeals of delight followed. 'Digory! Digory! Ma's setting up a pie shop! Connie will be assistant to her and I'm to be in charge of keeping the kitchen and scullery clear of all creatures and...'

Ma placed the pies carefully on a board before interrupting him, 'Calm yourself, Drew, give Digory chance to get through the door.'

As her eyes found mine, I could see something had changed. They were bright and alive, not with the drunkenness that had plagued her life of late, but with something than ran much deeper – determination. I lowered my gaze, wondering again if whether my act of leaving on the morrow would cause that light to dull.

My wondering was cut short. 'Once Eme shows her face, we'll feast on these beauties,' Ma declared, moving the beauties to the open window where a cooling breeze would soon make them ready for the eating.

'Would you like me to go fetch her, Aunt Bridget?' asked Connie, brushing flour from her hands and pinafore. 'I know where she goes when she's pining for Francis.'

'That's kind of you, Constance. Take Drew with you. Don't press her too much mind, it's not easy learning the truth about the one you've given your heart to.'

Connie grabbed Drew by the hand as they skipped down the cottage path, leaving behind them an uneasy silence in the cottage.

'So, how was your final day, son, did you get your full due from Baldwin?'

'He's been absent from the site the whole day, but don't worry none, I'll make sure you have your money before I leave.'

'My concern is for you, son. You'll be needing all you've worked for to attain what you're after and we both knows what that be. I'll not hold you back from what you need to do. Needing to find out the truth about your father is natural. Just remember that life is fleeting and don't go wasting your time, youth and money on my account. My pain is mine alone to deal with.'

Wanting to leave the subject of my father – a man I'd never set eyes on, although according to everyone who'd known him, *I* was his very image so every still pool held his face – I asked, 'Are you aware, Ma, Eme is making known all that takes place under this roof?'

'She's young, confused, lost her way that's all. She'll do anything to escape it but you can't run away from yourself. Besides her tittle-tattle could prove to be useful, very useful for bringing in orders for my pies. Use your head, Digory, only voice the things you don't mind the whole village knowing.'

'So you're serious about this pie-making-business then?'

'I've been given another chance, son, and for Drew's sake I shall make the best of that chance. One thing I ask of you before you leave. The lengths of timber stacked in the scullery, would you fix them for me around the bottom of the walls? Drew's encouragement of vermin has taken hold there but I have him on side to be rid of them. The skirting will block their holes and the careful placing of Strychnine will keep them at bay. I would appreciate the fixing of the boards before the ending of the day. As you know, the timber is already cut to size and your skill with hammer and nails is all that's called for.'

If I didn't find Baldwin this evening and demand from him my due, for all Albert's crowing, I knew my pay would be gone forever. 'I'm sorry, Ma, I need to go out this evening. I'll do as you ask when the sun rises on the morrow, I promise you, I'll not leave till the task is done.'

Ma looked at me long and hard, her expression difficult to read. 'So be it. Sit at the table, son, I'll cut us each a chunk of pie, washed down with a cool jug of cider. The first that'll have passed my lips this day.'

Chapter 10

Cockington Village – Thursday Evening

The continuos sound of loud voices, scraping of tables on the uneven flagged floor and the pitiful whining of the landlord's hound, halted my steps at the threshold of the only village tavern. Baldwin had to be in here, I'd already checked the Chelston alehouse and no one had laid eyes on him. If I was to succeed in getting my due, I would have to enter the lion's den.

After the jug of cider I'd shared with Ma, my mind was set firm, not a drop more of intoxicating drink would pass my lips this night. There was much to do and even more to think about and a man needed his head clear to master both. Besides, I had no desire to parley with John the taverner, let alone hand over my hard-earned money – his only aim being to fleece the villagers dry.

When Ma had put forth to me her plan for the pie shop, what had impressed me most, was how she'd stood firm against the likes of Arthur Gilbey and John the taverner, gaining funds from the former and a promise of orders from the latter. Turning the tide of their scant regard for her and the twins. She'd shown her true mettle and it lessoned my guilt to know she wouldn't be taken advantage of when I wasn't around.

Allowing the thought of that mettle to rub off on me, I pushed my way through the crush of bodies, my eyes sweeping from left to right as I moved slowly into the bowels of the den. I began to fear that yet again I'd been outfoxed, for I saw no sign of the man I sought. Then a light tap on my shoulder, followed by Baldwin asking, 'I hear tell you be looking for me, young Digory?'

My fists clenched instinctively as I turned to face my quarry.

Baldwin's hands raised in submission. 'Don't worry none, I have what you're owed. You've done a fine job, boy, and the squire'll be sorry to lose you. He was especially pleased with how you reinterred the last skeleton to come to light. There's no further risk of bones being uncovered and the loutish behaviour of some of the villagers has all but gone away.'

I was dumbfounded! Not only was the man being civil, he was actually smiling, something I'd not witnessed until now. Also, a fleeting thought that he was quite handsome when he allowed his face to show pleasure instead of ill will. In fact, he seemed pleased that I was here. The taverner's hound suddenly released a long, loud howl when its hind quarter came in contact with someones boot, making it difficult for us to continue our talking without filling the ears of all around. On draping his arm about my shoulders, Baldwin guided me back to the door and as one, we stepped into the sweet air of the starlit sky.

Straightaway, I began apologizing for seeking him out during his free time, his due time of relaxation, but he banished my deference with a wave of his hand. The same hand that began counting coinage from a purse tied to his belt.

'I think you'll find that tallies with what you have written on your copy of the map, young Digory.'

'How did you know..?'

'Albert let it be known, you required your pay as a matter of urgency. Saying that you was leaving these parts on the morrow in search of what became of your father when his seven-years-hard-labour was done. I salute you for that, young Digory. Your father and me was good friends and it'll be good to hear that he hasn't yet met his end in some God-forsaken foreign land. We was all good friends at one time, me, Albert, Digory, and Bridget, as kids we was never seen apart. After your Ma and Pa was wed and the Grimshaw's fortune increased, jealousy reared its ugly head. I'm not giving names here but there was loose talk that the child in Bridget's belly was not Digory's. Well, I ask you, any fool can see you to be Digory's son.'

Baldwin paused for breath as he took a gulp from the jug of ale he'd carried from inside – a goodly portion of it spilt on the way.

In that pause, I asked a question that had irked me for some time. 'If you and Albert were such good friends, why are you not so now? And why does *he* see fit for me to turn my back on searching for my father, while *you* applaud it?'

'Hopefully, you'll have your answer in due course. In the meantime, I give you my word, boy, your Ma, my friend Bridget, will be looked out for.'

I nodded, offered my hand as a gesture of my appreciation. Then asked one final question of him. 'What role does Albert play in regard to Cockington Court?'

A bark of laughter and a final long gulp of the ale – dropping the empty jug on the grass where he stood. 'He'd have you believe that high-born blood runs through his veins, when in truth, both his parents were in service to the court and his brother and sister-in-law still are.'

Chapter 11

Apple Cottage – Late Thursday Evening

My steps were hurried as I headed back to the cottage. There was much to do and my mind flitted from what could be achieved before tiredness forced me to my bed and the mulling over of Baldwin's revelations. I was still somewhat surprised in how different the man seemed. Then, I recalled Ma's words on the night the pair were arguing about how much she was in his debt; she'd made a point of telling me that *she* and Baldwin had been the best of friends for many years. Did that friendship develop into something more? Was the rearing of jealousy he spoke of, in regard to money or the loss of love? And who was the one corrupted by the green-eyed-monster? All manner of thoughts raced through my head, betrayal at their core.

On reaching the cottage, lanterns burned brightly and the homely smells of baking still hung in the air, even though the oven had cooled. The kitchen had been scrubbed clean and no doubt every crumb of one of the pies had been eaten. On cooling, the second pie had been placed in the meat safe, along with a verbal threat from Ma that her stick would mark any hand that touched its lock. There was no sign that this threat had been carried out for the faces of all family members seemed content. Even Eme, who rarely smiled these days, at least not for us, seemed more relaxed – the welcome outcome of having more of her own money and more importantly, more choices on how to earn it.

I walked through to the scullery, wanting to make sure my hiding place of the ring hadn't been discovered by Ma. Yes, it was important for the money it could generate and I knew she wouldn't steal it from me. However, if it had been discovered, leaving me no alternative to tell how and from where I had come by it, there'd be hell to pay. With the current unrest of the villagers in regard to desecrated graves, reburials alongside victims of the plague, and being highly superstitious of both, Ma would march me to the very place it originated and stand, arms folded whilst I dug the hole to rebury it – caring not for the consequences that followed. With a sigh of relief, I could see the large stone was undisturbed although the floor had been swept clean around it. She had also been busy with the lengths of timber, laying them in order of how they should be nailed in place, covering at least two holes where vermin could hide. I heard her close on my heels.

'There'll be time enough for you to do this fixing of the skirting in the morning, son? All is calm between us on this evening and there is much to discuss with the rest of the family.'

I drew forth the money that Baldwin had handed over and pressed it into her hand. She tried to give it back, as I knew she would. 'Ma, I insist you take it. I have money enough for my needs and I am capable of earning more wherever I find myself. The coinage I have saved lies beneath the stone your standing on and I need to retrieve it before any further work is done in here.'

She looked down to the floor and a wry smile crossed her lips. 'I'll close the door on my way out then, shall I?'

* * *

As Bridget closed the door on her eldest son, she found her youngest son cross-legged on the floor directly outside. 'Drew,' she said in a whisper that carried anger. 'I've told you before, it's wrong to listen in on private conversations.'

'Well how am I to know what's happening? No one tells me anything.'

Bridget held back from slapping him, for hadn't she encouraged the very same in regard to finding out about Eme and what went on at the stables. She hadn't asked him to actually eavesdrop on conversations. Just to be aware of what was going on and to remember what was being said – like herself, he had a sharp memory. Most folks thought this child dull-witted, including the twins. If keeping quiet and holding what you know to yourself be dull-witted, so be it. Knowing it to be different could come in very handy. His babyish wailing for attention had all but disappeared since he'd become aware that Digory was leaving. Once Digory left for London, Drew would be the only male in the cottage. He would have a bed to himself and be responsible for banishing all vermin from the cottage. It seemed that her youngest son was now on the threshold of growing up.

* * *

In spite of Ma's anger, Drew remained where he was, his back to the wall with his left ear in line with the gap of the scullery door. He'd heard every word between Ma and Digory and could hear now the grunting breath as Digory lifted the large, flat piece of stone that covered his tin box of treasures. With eyes closed, he could see in his head the stone being carefully rested against the wall, Digory's hands probing the earth beneath, the tin box being lifted out, the earth smoothed level by his boot and the stone lowered carefully back in place. He'd witnessed Digory doing the same thing the night before. The images still clear in his memory. But where would he hide his treasures on this last night? Once he'd heard the 'thump' sound of the stone dropped in place, Drew, in one swift, silent motion, turned his face to the crack of the door and pressed his eye close to it. His greatest fear was for Digory to place the box high on the shelf, a place that couldn't be reached by a small boy – even standing on a stool.

A knowing smile crossed his lips as he shifted quickly from the door. Digory emerged and headed for the small bedchamber they shared. No one could see, but the small boy knew, the tin box was concealed inside Digory's coat.

* * *

Ma and the twins had been busy. Not only below, where the ground floor of the cottage had been spruced throughout in readiness for the pie-making enterprise, the bedchamber had also been spruced and fresh linen covered the beds. My shirts and undergarments, what few I had, had been laundered – sun and breeze rendering them soft and fresh-smelling – folded neatly and ready for me to slip into the leather satchel that once belonged to uncle Richard.

Melancholy tinged the earlier excitement of travelling to London, and possibly from there to a strange land thousands of miles away. Should I leave the past be? Would I not miss my family too much and regret the effort of the daunting task awaiting me? There were many ups, downs and many difficult decisions to be made, but there was one thing for certain; Ma would have continued in her destructive ways had I not taken this firm stand. God-willing, on my return, I'd be welcomed back by a family to be proud of.

'Supper's ready, Digory, I should come now or all will be gone.' It was Connie's voice that carried up to me. She sounded happy and confident. Hopefully, the same will rub off on Eme and help to carry her through this tricky affair with Francis Bolt. When I'd first become aware of it, I was set on confronting the man – a man thirteen years Eme's senior. Ma had stopped me, saying it would do no good, that the ending of it had to come from Eme herself. She then gave a sly wink and added that once each of them realized they'd have no roof over them if the nonsense continued, common sense would follow.

I opened the tin box and removed the ring from its bundling – a torn piece of muslin found in the scullery drawer. My gaze once again lingered on the beauty of it, my mind taken back to the unknown man who had felt obliged to force it down his throat. For who else but himself would want to hide such a treasure? What was this man's story and who was *his* family?

A slight creak on the third stair told me it was time to hide it away again. Without panic, for I could tell it was Drew creeping up the stairs, I kissed it, again in gratitude for it coming my way. For without it, I couldn't have foreseen a way to finding the truth. I reached for the clean neckerchief folded atop of my laundered garments, parcelled the ring within and slipped it, along with my purse of coinage to the bottom of the satchel. The neat pile of garments following, fattening out the soft leather but still allowing plenty of ease for strap and buckle to fasten.

The bedchamber door opened. 'Ma said to come and get you,

Digory. There's bread, cheese and apple pie. We can't begin the feast till you join us.'

Drew's face was bright with excitement and expectation, he chatted on about the bed, the one we shared. It would be moved into Ma's bedchamber for him to sleep in alone. The bed that the twin's shared would be moved to this smaller room. It was clear, he was happy with this change.

A rebuke, loud with impatience brought us both to attention. 'Be it on your own head, Digory Grimshaw, if the table be empty when you honour us with your presence.' It was hard to say if Ma was annoyed, or just being sarcastic. I grabbed Drew's hand and we pounded down the stairs.

* * *

Bridget had worked non-stop all day and tiredness was beginning to fall about her like a dark shrouding mist, threatening to oust what little patience she had left. She wanted this last evening with her son to be perfect. She may never lay eyes on him again and it was important that he left with good memories and the knowledge that he was loved. He needed to know that his return was important to all of them.

Hadn't these very same notions plagued her mind all those years ago when she was heavy with him in her belly. The day before her husband was due to take the train from Torre to London, the day they'd had a scolding row about whether or not he should put an end to fishing off-shore, how he could afford to let others take the risk of the ever-present danger of the sea.

She recalled now, harsh words during that row, words spat forth without pre-thinking, words that would come back to haunt her when her husband didn't return. Words that had somehow become hidden in the deep recesses of her mind, showing themselves now at this inopportune time. She'd insisted on sharing the carriage. Travelling with him to Torre station. Pouring out her apologies for words said but not really meant. Blaming her ranting on fear, fear of losing him, fear of being left with a fatherless child. As the train had slowed to a stop, and all about rushed to board, eager and excited to be visiting this place where blue-blooded royals resided, she'd held him firm to her breast, anxious not to let go until she was sure of his forgiveness. The smile on her husband's lips looked sincere and his kisses felt warm, but his eyes, eyes that were tired from the tossing and turning we'd both endured the previous night, had a look of sadness, a look of deep loss. The whistle blew and he'd peeled away from her. Ran for the train and boarded as it shunted away. Not once looking back.

Pulled back from the dark memory by the pounding of Digory and Drew descending the stairs. Bridget quickly moved to the scullery. Filled a half cup of cider from the keg and poured it down her neck.

'Sorry I kept you all waiting, and thank you for tending to my clothes, it is truly appreciated.' Digory sat on the vacant chair, the best one in the cottage, and reached for the knife to cut off a chunk of bread.

Bridget felt that her life was in a spiral of repetition. It was all happening again. Her heart ached and her eyes filled with the burden of it. All she could hope for, was this time the traveller would want to return.

Chapter 12

Apple Cottage – in the Dead of Night

Drew moved carefully from the warm closeness of Digory's back, halting for a while until he was sure his brother's breathing remained deep and slow. The bedchamber was dark, the window, only a lighter shade of dark. Outside, an owl let free a hooting cry. A bad omen for the small creatures foraging but not likely to disturb anyone in the cottage. In stealth and silence, small hands reached for the leather satchel sitting atop the only piece of furniture – a small oak chest positioned below the window. Carefully resting it on crossed legs, the buckle was undone. One small hand entered it's leathery embrace, feeling its way between folded cloth, around a purse of coins and finally, in the furthermost corner, touching upon a cloth bundle the size of a plum. Small fingers squeezing the cloth plum and feeling its hard core.

Within less than a minute, the satchel and its contents, all but one of the contents, were back in place on top of the chest and Drew was heading down to the kitchen.

* * *

Bridget stirred in her bed and grumbled in low voice, 'The hooting of owls, the creaking of stairs, how was a body expected to sleep with this manner of disturbance abroad?' She flung the blanket from her, preparing for confrontation with her youngest son. He, like the creatures he admired, would on occasion spend part of the night wandering downstairs.

He'd done well that day. Trapping three mice in the tightly woven bread basket that was then carried to the bottom of the lane to empty. Connie accompanying him to bear witness to this, for Drew refused point blank to have them dealt with in permanent manner. Assuming he'd gone downstairs to check that none of the vermin had returned, Bridget relaxed back on her pillow to await his creaking return.

* * *

Needing to see more clearly, Drew tiptoed through to the scullery and with the aid of the stool, and the memory of the many times he'd seen it done, lit the oil lamp, knowing there'd be trouble if Ma found out. The scullery was now much altered. Cupboards, emptied of useless oddments, were scrubbed clean with new papers covering the shelves. On top of the cupboards, lengths of shaped skirting filled every inch of surface, waiting Digory's fixing of them in the light of the early morn. The only surface available to him was the stool. Lowering himself before it – small knees pressing onto stone-flagged floor – he placed the plum-sized bundle at its centre, with eyes fixed in concentration on the knot holding the bundle together. On opening the knot, he counted each twist and turn of the cloth, committing it to memory, before the hard core was laid bare. Finally coming to the last flap of cloth, pinched between two small fingers, Drew folded it back and there it was. The magic ring of black and gold, resting in the middle of Digory's neckerchief. How could that be? This was the very ring that he was told belonged to someone else. The very ring that Digory insisted he was cleaning for its owner, returning it to him the following day. So why was it bundled up and concealed at the bottom of his satchel? The satchel Digory will be taking with him to London Town.

Drew felt sad and confused. Why couldn't his brother trust him with the truth. He felt disappointed that the childish talk of magic and Ma dying if the ring was spoken of was just a way of frightening him. Drew's only fear was the magistrate sending Digory to gaol for thievery, for how else could Digory have come by it? If he'd found it fair and square, why keep it a secret when all would have rejoiced in his good fortune. The ring must be stolen and the inside scribing will point to its rightful owner. And If Digory is sent to gaol like his father was, Ma would surly die of a broken heart!

* * *

Tired of waiting for the return of the creaking but not relaxed enough to slip into sleep, Bridget cast aside her blanket and with a heavy sigh and outstretched arms felt her way towards the bedchamber door. She slowly descended the stairs, avoiding the one that creaked for she had no intention of pre-warning the child. Common sense told her he was probably making sure the vermin he'd spent half the day moving, weren't back in their holes. For the twopence promised, wasn't payable until her kitchen and scullery had been vermin-free for a whole week.

Her eyes, having become accustomed to the dark, could see he wasn't in the kitchen – no sign of his small body crouched in possible places that creatures could hide – four-legged creatures that had ruined many a baker's profit. However, a lighted lamp in the scullery, with its tell-tale line of flickering brightness around the closed door, filled her with uncertainty. *Had I left the lamp burning?* thought Bridget, knowing in her heart she would never do such a foolish thing.

Holding back the urge to lift the latch and throw open the door, she pressed her ear close to the gap. No soft words of encouragement to the creatures of the night. In fact no sounds at all. Her curiosity growing, she closed one eye and peered through the gap, a habit Drew was fond of, in spite of the slapping if caught. Though the line of vision was narrow, she saw clearly. Drew was in there. With his back to the door and in light of the lamp, kneeling before the stool, his head bowed as though in prayer. Her eye moved to the lamp and she knew for sure. After all her warnings, after all her forbiddings, Drew was the one who had lit the lamp.

She grabbed for the latch, then mindful that the sound of its metallic rattle might wake Digory and the twins, she calmed her touch and eased the latch more slowly. The door wouldn't move. Something was holding it shut. In frustration, the latch was attacked again, accompanied by her angry voice. 'Drew, open this door or you'll feel my hands across your legs!' After hearing shiftings, and liftings and the pulling of the wedge from the scullery side of the door, Bridget lifted the latch and the door swung easily open. Drew stood before the stool, his face giving nothing away. 'Who lit the lamp?' asked Bridget, knowing the answer but needing it to be confirmed.

'I did, Ma. It was dark. I couldn't see.'

'And it didn't enter that head of yours, there was chance of the cottage burning while we slept in our beds?'

A shrug of tiny shoulders followed by. 'I was careful. I don't want anyone burned.'

Exasperated, Bridget asked, 'What are you doing in here, Drew? The vermin has gone. And it won't be back or you'll not see your twopence. What was you doing kneeling in front of the stool?'

Again, the shrug of shoulders. No explanation followed.

'I asked what you was doing kneeling in front of the stool?'

A thoughtful pause, before the answer, 'I was thinking of Digory. Hoping he'll come back to us soon.'

'You was saying a prayer then?'

Drew didn't want to lie, and Ma knew this. She also knew that Drew's way of getting around telling an untruth, was to say nothing and shrug his shoulders. 'There's nothing wrong in praying, Drew. So long as your praying is for good things to happen. Now back to your bed and be sure not to wake Digory, he has much to do before boarding that train.'

Chapter 13

Apple Cottage – Friday – Break of Dawn

In spite of mixed emotions churning my insides during the evening, I'd slept well and without dreaming. No disturbing scenes containing omens or messages to test my resolve. I felt content and certain that the journey I was about to take was in my own, and my families, best interest.

In the stillness of the early morn when thoughts come clear, unfettered by the chaos of surrounding dramas, I again felt sure my father was still alive. Whether it be in England or in the Australian Colonies across the globe. If he'd died, surely with our remarkable telegram system which was developed many a year passed, word would have reached Ma.

My own thoughts on the matter, and I hereby confess, the matter has plagued my mind for years, is that my father, having served his time of hard labour – his mind and body prematurely aged because of it – felt too shamed and embarrassed to return. For all he knew, Ma might bear a grudge so severe, that forgiveness wasn't possible and if my father can be found, I'd like to be the one to reassure him in that regard.

Drew was still sleeping, lying in his usual position behind me, one small arm half reaching around my waist. I gently lifted it from me and slipped from the bed, my eyes taking in the leather satchel where I'd left it atop the small oak chest. I smiled with glad anticipation that Ma would help fill out what space was left in it, with a chunk from the remaining pie, for the journey to London was indeed a long one.

Pulling on my well-worn breeches and boots, I left the bedchamber as quietly as I could. All was silent in the cottage. Outside however – led first by the local cockerel, a riot of birdsong was erupting, welcoming the new day and lifting my spirits to immeasurable heights. Fanciful thoughts began drifting through my mind like featherweight clouds and I imagined myself in my father's company. My very own father whom I'd never clapped eyes on, returning to apple cottage. The cottage where he and I were born. My imaginings grew more whimsical as I saw in my mind's-eye, the look of surprise on Ma's face. Then surprise turning to delight when their arms enfolded.

Eme's loud complaint for the birds to cease their noise, at once put an end to my time wasting and set my concentration back to the task in hand.

There was much to prepare before hammering the wire-cut nails through the walls. So there was no fear of waking anyone else for some time yet, although Eme's hollering may well have done that. As previously mentioned, the planks were already cut and shaped but I wanted to pre-drill all the holes to accommodate the nails. This would make sure that none of the timber split whilst being hammered to the wall, for there was no timber to spare and no time available to remedy that.

Ma had helped, saving time by laying in order the sequence the skirting should lie. The simple number-markings, scratched on in charcoal by uncle Richard, were faint but still visible. A sudden thought crossed my mind. Did Ma, like me, offer up a heart-felt thank you to the man whose only real trade was harvesting the sea. And yet, numbering the timber in this way, meant that after years of abandoning the improvements, the materials were ready and waiting to be easily put into place.

With the hand-drilling almost done, I caught sight of Drew standing in the doorway. I nodded and bid him, 'Good Morning!' He smiled shyly but remained silent, his hands gripping the cracked mirror that had caused upset with Eme 'I thought you might return the mirror to it's old place, now you have no further use for it.' I said conversationally.

'I need to use it one more time.'

I continued my drilling and Drew continued to stand in the doorway, eyes fixed on the mouse hole now supposedly abandoned. Then I realized, 'You want to use the mirror to check the mouse hole? You want to make sure the creature hasn't returned before I board over its door?'

A slight shrug and an even slighter nod of the head.

'Well that's thoughtful, Drew. I suggest you also check the holes in the kitchen, Ma wants them boarded too. There is no pre-cut skirting for the kitchen but if you can find two small sections of timber about this size – I made squares with my fingers measuring about six inches by four inches – I'll drill then hammer them in place. A temporary fix until I return.' The child seemed full of concern and I wanted him assured of my intentions.

When I had almost finished the drilling on the final timber, I looked up to find Drew still standing in the doorway. Hearing impatience in my voice I said, 'If you want to check that hole, Drew, I should do it now. The first timber to be hammered in place will be the one that covers the hole. There's no time to spare, I'll be back in five minutes with the nails and your chance will be gone.'

* * *

Drew stood aside, allowing Digory to leave the scullery. He knew where he was heading. The washhouse, back to back with the privy, had shelving for tools and all manner of fixings. He also knew, he had no more than two or three minutes before Digory's return.

One of those precious minutes was spent positioning the mirror, angling it just right for seeing into the hole, first looking left then right then straight ahead. Satisfied that nothing, absolutely nothing, could be seen, he moved swiftly to the kitchen. With stealth and speed, as though copying the creatures he so admired, he was soon below the kitchen table, two small hands reaching for the box, the box that smelled of tobacco when opened. As the second minute passed, Drew was already halfway up the stairs, box tucked under his arm. As Digory's footsteps, laden with the weight he carried, were heard entering the kitchen, Drew was quietly closing the bedchamber door and placing the wedge beneath it. Shutting out all possibilities of being disturbed.

As the hammering of nails entering the scullery walls rang out, moans, groans and shifting could be heard from Ma and the twins in the bedchamber adjoining. Drew put this from his mind and focused on what needed to be done.

When what needed to be done was accomplished, Drew was left with a near-empty, cigar-smelling box. A box measuring almost the size of the wood that Digory needed to cover the holes in the kitchen wall.

* *.*

Thanks to the pre-drilling of the timber, fixing the skirting to the walls was an easy task and done in less time than I'd predicted. I moved into the kitchen leaving Ma and the twins to clear the shavings, sweep the floor and make ready the cupboards for another delivery of provisions.

I gathered, from snatches of conversations overheard, the twins would continue their work at the stables until Ma had sufficient custom for needing their full-time help. All three seemed happy and excited about the pie-making venture. And all three seemed amused at the prospect of leaving Arthur Gilbey to the mercy of finding two new grafters and even more amused at the thought of him having to do the grafting himself.

A creak on the stairs told me that Drew was not where I supposed him to be. I *was* hoping he was outdoors scouring the area where two newly-built villa's would have off-cuts of timber in abundance, for I made promise to Ma the two holes would be covered before I left.

With the shy mood of earlier gone, Drew approached with a smile on his face, offering up the wooden cigar box I'd once used to conceal my savings in. My impatience with him returned. 'It's kind of you to return the box, Drew, but what I really need right now, are two pieces of timber for covering these holes. I feel sure you'll find what is wanted up at the villa site.'

Drew looked from the box to Digory, realizing that what he had discovered about the box, hadn't yet been seen by his brother. 'This box will do well for our needs, Digory,' he said in earnest. 'If you remove the hinge and pins that hold it together, the top and bottom can easily be used to cover the holes if you drill first in the corners, as you've done with the skirting.'

He was right! He was absolutely right! It was good strong wood that was flimsily put together and easily taken apart. It's size of seven inches by five inches was ideal and there'd be no work in smoothing edges and whitewashing to match the wall. The colourful letters and image of a strange, long-necked-bird printed on its surface, adding intrigue and a constant reminder of this special day.

I looked at Drew, a small boy of four-years old and tried to imagine the man he would become. His scope of intelligence seemed boundless considering his few years of experience on this earth. On my return, I would make sure he had the schooling to broaden and develop that intelligence.

Drew, his face searching mine, expectantly awaiting a response, said nothing more.

'That's a really good idea, Drew, but where will you keep your own treasures if we take apart this box?'

'I'll use the tin box that you no longer need.'

Everything seemed simple and straightforward to Drew. At that moment, I wished with all my heart that after I left, it would remain so.

* * *

Bridget finished her dusting down of the last cupboard top and stood back, hands on hips to admire her new workspace. Years ago, the original plan for the scullery was to turn it into an extra bedchamber, for who needs good wood-skirting in a scullery, but much had changed since then. However, having laid out the substantial cost for the timber and the shaping of it, plus the time dear Richard had spent carefully marking each section, it would have been a crying shame not to have used it. Another bonus was the second door, bolted and hidden behind the stack of timber for years, could now be unfettered and opened easily to good fresh air and the expected growing band of customers. For the thought of anyone, anyone who wasn't family, traipsing through her kitchen, filled her with displeasure.

'Well done girls, you have done a fine job. Time now for a hearty breakfast. Eme see if Digory's finished his work in the kitchen. I'd like to see us all around the table once more before he leaves us.'

Eme could be heard clapping her hands, her voice gay with the words, 'Yes, I do, I like it. What a good idea, Digory.'

Bridget, followed by Connie left what she were doing to see what Eme's joyful outburst was all about.

On seeing them, Eme burst forth again. 'Look, aunt Bridget, how Digory has dismantled that old cigar box to use in covering the mouse holes. Don't you think that's clever of him?'

Bridget caught Digory looking at Drew and Drew looking back at Digory with a slight shake of his head. 'And what say you, Drew? For I believe the box was given over to you for your treasures?'

Drew looked shyly upon all who awaited his response sighing heavily as though carrying the world on his tiny shoulders. 'The box smelled strongly of tobacco,' his nose wrinkling as he said it. 'I didn't like the smell of it and neither will the vermin, so we won't have to worry about them returning. Drew turned to his Ma and said, Digory has given me his tin box for my treasures. It's big enough now I don't need the mirror.'

Bridget watched as her eldest son climbed the stairs to change into his best clothes, clothes fit for a traveller. He'd told her to discard the worn, torn, breeches and shirt he'd worked in for many a year. On his return, *dear God allow his return*, she beseeched inwardly, he'll find them to be mended, laundered and folded around lavender and laid in the chest.

She sent the girls to pick flowers from the garden and roses from the hedgerow. Wild and free for the picking, cheering any table and hearth on this happy but sad occasion.

Chapter 14

Apple Cottage – Late Friday Morning

I was all but ready to leave. The expected provisions hadn't arrived as yet and it wasn't possible for all of us to walk the distance to Livermead Station. I knew Ma wouldn't want to be there, too many bad memories would be rising up to taunt her. So it was good she had this excuse. And it seemed, Drew also preferred to say his goodbye on familiar territory. Why? Only he could answer that and as was often the case, he chose to keep silent on the matter. So it was to be me and the twins only.

The breakfast Ma had set out was indeed hearty. The second pie from yesterday was cut into deep slices – two of them put aside and then carefully placed in the satchel for the long journey ahead – the rest devoured over good-natured banter about choosing a name for Ma's new business, settling on 'Grimshaw's Game Pies'. When finally we all knew it was time I left, I looked about for Drew, for he'd left the table first.

I found him in the scullery, gazing upon the change a few planks of wood, a second door thrown open and plenty of scrubbing, could achieve. Realizing this was the first time he'd seen it since Ma declared it finished, I well understood his fascination.

'Well, what do you think, Drew? Do you think Grimshaw's Game Pies will be a great success?' His response to my question was, well frankly no response at all. His focus seemed to be locked on the first piece of skirting I had fixed to the wall. He moved toward it running two small fingers over letters I'd begun marking on there from the ring. I'd done this before realizing, the wood may one day be used for its original purpose. Better to copy the markings on its inner side. A wise move indeed. I could wait no longer, otherwise my train would be gone. 'Drew, I have to leave now, but I promise you I will return as soon as I'm able. You do understand that don't you?'

He nodded and smiled. The sweetest of smiles, it almost broke my heart. Then he walked toward me with his outstretched hand and said. 'Don't worry Digory, you will be quite safe now.'

Bewildered by his words but having no time for explanations, I took his small hand in mine and shook it as though he were a grown man. Then an unbearable thought. *Maybe that is what he'd be when I next laid eyes upon him.* Unable to resist the urge, I took him in my arms, squeezed his small frame and tried my best to transfer the strong bond of love I felt toward him. On releasing him, I kissed his cheek briefly and ran from his presence before my moistening eyes had chance to strip away my dignity.

* * *

Drew walked back to the marked timber. Pressed two fingers on the few letters showing, his eyes closed in concentration, reliving his actions in the dead of night. The gold ring decorated with bones and scribed inside with words – damning words to show who the ring belonged to – was now resting deep within vernin's old hole.

Making sure Digory would remain safe from the locked doors of gaol.

* * *

It would take a whole day before Digory found that the hard core of his plum-sized bundle was not the gold Memento Mori ring. In its place was his uncle Richard's brass ring. A ring of very little value. A ring that would not pay passage across vast oceans. Two folded papers were also found inside the satchel, put there by his mother along with her muslin-wrapped slices of pie.

One paper was old and faded – a letter, from the learned solicitor who informed her of her husband's fate, before Digory was even born. A letter that may well prove useful when searching out information. The second paper was of recent newness, though marked with mud-stained prints. When unfolded it was recognised by Digory – it being the copy of the master plan of Cockington's digging site – Albert's neat script writing, scrawled here and there upon it. His mother having found it in the pocket of his worn breeches, thought it prudent to enclose it with the other.

* * *

It was time once more for the Memento Mori to rest unseen and untouched by human hand until another century passes. For providence had decreed, this ring was not yet destined for the melting pot. Nor was it destined to leave the fair shores of Devon.

PART THREE

Full Circle

Chapter 1

Thursday – 31st July 2014 – Burnley, Lancashire

It was midday, the sun beating down from a cloudless sky as the car pulled up outside Mum's house. You could see at a glance that Gemma was here. Viewed through the large front window, which was perfectly aligned with the large back window in Mum's 1960s semi, was a scene of colourful chaos and abandonment: a limp trampoline devoid of any trampers, a Wendy House, showing no sign of anyone at home through its half-open door, a pink, three-wheeled scooter on its side, only half visible as it poked above grass badly in need of cutting, and the most galling of all, the huge box of lego which had cost me an arm and a leg a few weeks ago for Gemma's third birthday, had been upended and was strewn everywhere, including the path to the front door.

Three footsteps on that path and a toot from Jenny's horn followed by a shout from the rolled down window of her car, 'Don't forget your suitcase, Kate. Oh and about weekend, I'll give you a bell, yea?' Another toot as she roared away. I turned, lifting my hand in a cursory wave to a car that had already turned left out of sight, leaving me with a suitcase and gaping bag of shopping on the pavement and my handbag precariously hanging from one shoulder. I was hoping that Mum might have been here on her own for once with the kettle on whilst we had a welcoming chat before my drive back to Halifax.

It was school holidays and I'd been on a four-day-trip to Blackpool with three other teachers – all badly in need of just letting rip, then chilling out before settling into August and all that came with that month. Andy was on another one of his courses and wouldn't be back till Sunday. Just like teaching, you were never fully-qualified when you were in the police force, there was always another course you were obliged to attend.

As I neared the front door, a small face appeared in the corner of the window wearing a smile more beaming than the sun. It was Gemma, abandoner of all the colourful plastic, relinquisher of the tiny house, forsaker of the arm and a leg building blocks, the child that held everyone of us in the palm of her hand.

Dropping my baggage and moving to the window, I pursed my lips and planted them directly onto Gemma's, our breath misting the double-glazing on both sides – cool hard glass separating warm soft lips. It was a childish game we'd played since Gemma was about six months old, a game played less frequently now and no doubt as the years gather, will be lost to us completely.

Mum's voice calling from the other side of the front door broke the magic of our cold kiss. 'Go round back, love, Gemma's got her farmyard setup in porch.'

'I'll put my luggage in the car first,' I called back, 'I can't stay long, I've got shopping that needs to be kept cool. Can you shove the garage key through the letterbox?' The face in the window had gone but the voice that belonged to it could be heard talking to the cats, my cats. They were being told, in comforting tone, that their mummy was back to take them home.

Mum's garage was in a block of eight, a hundred yards up the road. When finally the key began to emerge through the rectangular hole, I grabbed it, gripped its leather tag in my teeth and trudged back down the front path with suitcase in one hand and shopping in the other, Gemma's uproar at me leaving, filling the air.

Minutes later I was back, standing at the kitchen door as the kettle began to sputter into its screaming alarm call. 'Sod it!' I shouted, the naughty word well hidden within the crescendo of the kettle's whistling. I had forgotten the cats' baskets on the back seat of my car and there's no way I could carry the two of them without being scratched to ribbons. The ear splitting-din of the kettle suddenly died and Mum's voice filled the silence.

'Where's the cats' baskets? You're not off gallivanting again are you? Only I intend going to Manchester tomorrow and I'll need to get an early start.' Without pausing for breath, or my response, she continued in a lowered voice, 'Only I really wanted to go today, Thursdays are a lot quieter than Fridays or Saturdays and the buses don't get filled up as quick, but as you can see…'

'Sheba and Minx don't need constant attention, Mum,' I cut in, 'as long as they get fed, they'll come in and out as they please. If it's Liz you're annoyed with, why not just come out with it. She should be looking after Gemma in the holidays, after all it's her granddaughter and like me she's got the time off to do it.'

'Kate! Kate! Kate!' The sound of Gemma's voice rang through the air as she ran into the kitchen. I'd just dropped into the nearest kitchen chair and she scrambled onto my lap, her excited chatter overriding Mum's complaining.

'How many times 'ave I told you, Gemma. It's Auntie Kate, or more precisely Great Auntie Kate. Same as I'm your Great Grandmother.'

'No your not,' she giggled. You are Nanna and this is Kate.' Chubby little arms encircled my neck and the cool, hard lips of earlier were pressed once more to mine – warm, soft and tasting of chocolate. An unsatisfied longing reared up deep in the pit of my stomach. I swallowed, forcing it back to its resting place. 'So, have Sheba and Minx been good? Any scratches to show off, lets have a look.' I inspected arms, legs, neck and back, tickling as I moved around her squirming, squealing body. Yet another game that would soon be lost to *old father time*.

A car door slammed shut and Gemma scooted off my lap and ran to the front window giving me the chance to check on my own babies. Unlike Gemma, my cats weren't too pleased to see me. As usual when I left them, even when it was just for a few days, they became aloof and moody. Punishing me for daring to desert them in unfamiliar territory.

'Its Grandma', Gemma hollered, returning with me to the kitchen, both of us accepting the drinks offered by Mum.

Liz, my older sister – older by five years – was tall and elegant with sleek blond hair, and by far the most beautiful of Mum's two daughters. She sauntered into the kitchen, a waft of Chanel No 5 overriding the scent of PG Tips, her nail-polished hand reaching for the mug of tea on offer.

'Oh, hello Kate, how was the trip? I bet Blackpool was teeming with trippers. Wouldn't you have preferred somewhere more peaceful? You were always the one for getting away from the crowds.'

'There were four of us,' I said between sips of tea. 'I would have preferred the lakes or the dales but I was out-voted. The change of scenery was good, but I'm looking forward to getting back to Andy.'

'What was the letter about?'

I paused, confused by my sister's sudden nonchalant question, the confusion growing as I saw Mum, flustered as she put a hand to her mouth.

'Oh! I forgot all about that,' she said, jumping up from her chair and rushing from the room.

'What letter?' I asked to Mum's disappearing back, before turning my enquiring gaze to Liz.

Liz sipped slowly on her tea, miraculously managing it without wetting her coral-painted lips, enjoying the power of holding my attention. 'A couple of days ago a letter arrived here addressed to you, postmarked Torquay and it looks a bit official.'

Mum arrived back brandishing a cream envelope with my name and Mum's address in neat hand writing.

For the attention of: Mrs Kate Radcliffe

The flap of the envelope looked disturbed and lifted easily, I looked at Liz accusingly.

'It arrived two days ago, and we weren't sure how important it was, so I opened it. Old Aunt Winifred, remember her, she lived in that old ruin of a place just outside Torquay. Well she's popped her clogs. Her solicitor wants you to visit, says you may hear something to your advantage. God, the way these people talk, like they're living in a bygone era, a law unto themselves the lot of them.'

My eyes ran down the letter trying to take in the words while my mind was back in the old cottage, picturing Great Aunt Winifred who was stern but always kind. I stopped reading and looked up. 'The funeral was yesterday. Did anyone from the family go?'

'Don't be daft, Kate,' said Mum, plonking her self down at the table again to drink her tea. 'Even if we had known Old Aunt

Winifred had died, who's got time to go waltzing off to Devon at the drop of a hat?'

'Dad would've, if he'd been alive, and so would I. I liked her.'

'Well of course he would,' cut in Liz, 'she was his auntie. He'd insisted on visiting his auntie every year, and dragging the two of us with him for most of those years. I hated the place. It was too quiet and boring in the daytime, and after dark, what with the owls and the cockerels from the nearby farms, you were lucky to get a good nights sleep. Anyway, she's dead and buried and nothing can change that. I suggest you phone the solicitor here and now and find out what the letter's all about.'

'I'll phone when I get back home,' I said, feeling the pressure and hating it. 'She's probably left me the family photographs, I was always fascinated by them. I will probably need to be on the phone for quite some time arranging to have them sent by carrier rather than driving that distance. At this time of year the traffic will be manic.'

'Just do it now!' Two voices in unison and Mum pressing the hands-free landline phone into my hand.

Annoyed at being cornered by the pair of them, I pushed the phone to Liz. 'If you're so eager to find out, you ring the bloody solicitor!'

'Naughty word, Kate. No sweets for you today!'

Gemma's voice was no match for her grandmothers. I could hardly believe my sister's own admission that she had already phoned the solicitor on the day the letter arrived, explaining to her that I was on holiday and she'd pass on any information on my return. The solicitor – the female solicitor that sounded about seventeen years old, Liz made a point of saying, wouldn't budge on the rules of confidentiality regarding her deceased client and the clients beneficiaries.

I could picture the scene. Almost feel Liz's frustration as she cut the connection to this young madam who had the audacity not to do her bidding. 'I'll use my mobile, Mum, I don't want to run up your phone bill.' Without saying another word, I stuffed the letter in my bag, picked up the mug of tea and wandered out into the back garden, my eyes searching for somewhere privately to sit.

Beyond the abandoned chaos of colourful plastic stood a rustic arch, sagging from rot and the weight of an overgrown climber laden with yellow scented roses. I squeezed through its narrow passage, catching my top in two places and spilling some of the tea. Before me lay ghostly impressions of marked out squares where Dad once grew his vegetables, still visible amongst the takeover of weeds. A brick path, also overrun with unwanted growth, led to the shed. The place Dad had called his sanctuary. The key to it was still in the same place – dropped in the head of a hollow gnome. On opening the door, a rush of familiar scents and memories that clung to them. In the corner, an old leather armchair beckoned, as it had done many times when I'd come here to unload my tears for his loss. Dad had died three weeks into the new millennium from a ruptured-brain-aneurism. While everyone else was still celebrating the start of the twenty-first century, I was mourning the loss of the best friend I'd ever had.

I slowly drank the remainder of the tea, my eyes flitting around the walls of planked wood. Interspersed amongst shelving and once sharpened tools that now showed rust creeping over their surfaces, were posters from the Royal Horticultural Society, depicting ferns of all shapes and sizes. Dad loved ferns, but they didn't grow well here, in spite of his efforts. I lay down the empty mug and opened the letter, reading it slowly, a picture of the lady it referred to fixed in my mind. A lady who had boasted on many an occasion that she never took a holiday, had at the age of seventy-eight, travelled the distance from Torquay to Burnley, to attend her nephew's funeral.

The phone was picked up on the third ring. A moment of silence before a bright clear voice. 'Hi, Sam here!'

My first thought was that I'd dialled the wrong number, and in my flustered state came a clear thought – a girl named Sam is as bad as a boy named Sue. 'I… I'm sorry to have disturbed you, I think I've made a mistake.'

'Samantha Devreau of Devreau Wilkes Solicitors, my apologies for the informal answering of the phone, my secretary is on an errand and I thought it was her ringing. How can I help you?'

I went on to explain who I was and why I hadn't been able to respond earlier. I wanted to apologise for not being at the funeral, for not knowing that Great Aunt Winifred was at deaths door. *Christ, apart from the yearly scribbled Christmas card, I hadn't been in touch in over three years and guilt was tightening its grip.*

Her words halted my agonising. 'Thank you for ringing, Kate. Is it possible for us to meet before Monday? I'll be on leave for three weeks from Tuesday and it would be in your own best interest to get the paperwork signed off before I go.'

'Well…Why the rush? Are we not talking about a few photographs here, they can be just as easily sent in the mail?'

A long pause… 'Kate, you were your great aunt's only living relative. The cottage, everything inside the cottage and what money she had saved has been left to you. I wouldn't normally release the contents of a will over the phone, but Winifred led me to believe you already knew of her intentions. Furthermore, the cottage is unoccupied. I drive to and from work via Cockington, keeping a watchful eye on the place, but for three weeks…'

'So the cottage is mine? But what about my sister?'

'The cottage is yours, Kate, it's entirely your decision what you do with it!'

'I'll come down by train from Manchester. I...I'll leave tomorrow morning. I should be there by mid-afternoon.'

'Good. Text me the time of your arrival and I'll get my secretary to meet you and bring you straight to my office. Would you like me to book you in somewhere close, for bed & breakfast? At this time of year the more popular hotels won't have any vacancies.'

'Can't I stay at the cottage? Aunt Winifred always had the guest bedroom available for me.'

Another long pause before the solicitor's answer, her voice hesitant. 'Kate, the cottage is... The cottage hasn't been occupied in over three months now. Towards the end, Winifred lost her sight completely, and I'm sad to say, the authorities deemed it necessary to move her into a nursing home!'

Chapter 2

Friday – 1st August – Manchester

We'd barely spoken a word, as Liz drove Mum and me to Manchester, the morning rush easing by the time Piccadilly Station came into view. Mum was dropped off first, close to the bus stop she was familiar with. I'd offered to get out here too, save Liz getting caught up in a one-way system that required one-hundred-percent concentration, but she'd insisted, saying that she didn't want to be branded as selfish.

They'd both thought I'd gone mad, agreeing to shoot off to Torquay at the solicitor's command. Mum whined about me leaving the cats again, pointing out that if the Alsatian across the road savaged one of them, it would be my fault not hers. Liz argued that I ought to think more about my husband and less about myself. In short, they'd done their best to persuade me to phone the solicitor back and rearrange to meet after she was back from her holiday. For my part, it was the most opportune time for going. Andy wouldn't be back from his course until Monday, and I had nothing planned for the next three days – except a half-hearted arrangement for a drink on Saturday night with my three colleagues.

Staying overnight in the house I'd grown up in and getting a lift to the station was all I asked. I'd told Mum straight, if she wasn't prepared to have the cats for two more days, I'd book them into a cattery. And if Liz couldn't be asked to run me to the station, I'd just book a taxi.

I hadn't slept well, the single bed in Mum's spare room was narrow, old and lumpy. The thin polyester quilt lying under the bottom sheet did little to hide the evidence of a knackered mattress. In addition, there'd been an avalanche of unanswered questions swamping my mind, such as *why was I the sole inheritor and what was meant by the solicitor's remark of me being the only living relative?* Had Aunt Winifred actually gone senile, forgetting my older sister, her three children and grandchild? It was possible, as I had been her only, albeit infrequent, visitor since Dad had died.

After speaking with the solicitor and hearing the news of my inheritance, I'd sat for a while in Dad's old leather chair, allowing the enormity of it to sink in. And, allowing sadness to accumulate like storm clouds on the horizon of a clear blue sky. Sadness at the news that Aunt Winifred, the most independent person I'd ever known, had been forced to spend her last few weeks on earth in a nursing home. My God she would have hated that!

It was Gemma's voice interrupting my dark mood after being sent out to find me under the guise of hide and seek. Out loud, I'd heard her count to seven then jump to fifty before shouting, 'Ready or not I'm coming to find you, Auntie Kate!' For some reason I couldn't quite fathom, I hadn't wanted her to discover me in Dad's old sanctuary. In fact I hadn't wanted her in here at all. Creeping from its peaceful confines, I'd locked the door and dropped the key back in its hiding place. Her hearing was sharp and she was beside me in seconds, squealing with delight. 'Found you! My turn to hide,' she'd hollered, leaving no room for my refusal.

'OK. OK. I'll count to ten but you must hide somewhere in the kitchen,' I'd said, seeing the disappointment cross her face and the complaining 'Oh' on her lips. 'Be quick then. One, two, three.' She'd shot off to the kitchen, my con working a treat.

I'd entered the back door and for several minutes all attention was focused on Gemma, hidden under the table between two pairs of legs, but once Liz had enticed her into the front room with a new toy she'd bought that morning, attention was turned to me and the knowledge I'd gained from the solicitor.

Before long, a heated argument had developed, partly due to me wanting to rush off to Torquay the very next day, but mainly because of my announcement that I was sole beneficiary. When I had repeated the solicitor's words on this point, both Mum and Liz had exchanged strange, but knowing, glances that I sensed was for my exclusion.

'What?' I'd said.

Mum said nothing, just collected the empty mugs from the table and began scrubbing them under the running tap, her face turned away, her body taught with trepidation.

I'd turned to my sister, hoping for an explanation. 'Liz?' I began, but the only response was an angry outburst. 'The malicious old bag; I'm glad she's dead!'

The price of the ticket from Manchester to Torquay was expensive. I mean really expensive. I consoled myself with a mixture of thoughts; firstly that the journey was direct with none of the usual tight connections, a forward facing seat and the fact that I had recently become the proud owner of a country cottage with an additional, as yet undisclosed, sum of money. So despite the heavy cost of the return rail ticket, I was not about to bitch over the price of travel to secure the ownership.

I'd phoned Andy the previous evening, giving him a brief rundown of the letter, my telephone conversation with the solicitor and my plan for the weekend, with a promise to phone each evening with news of further developments. After conveying his condolences for Aunt Winifred, his reaction to my good fortune was naturally positive. When I asked how the course was going, he gave his predictable, 'It's OK'. With Andy, nothing was ever good or bad, it was always just, OK.

With my suitcase stacked on the shelf above my head and the seat beside me conveniently empty, I opened the novel I had previously taken with me to Blackpool but had only read the one chapter. The first chapter was so convoluting in covering a gruesome death that I knew for sure that once I attempted to read it again, it wouldn't be long before I'd be catching up on sleep I had lost the night before.

* * *

The train finally screeched to a halt after a stop-start limping into Birmingham New Street Station, drawing me out of my semi-conscious state. I'd slept deeply but felt groggy as I opened my eyes to a mass of travellers searching for seats and somewhere to park their luggage. I badly needed a coffee but was loathed to risk losing my seat in a frenzy that oozed, everyman-for-himself.

The train began to move again, not forwards but backwards, and the seat beside me was now occupied by an overweight Pakistani woman who constantly gave orders to a younger Pakistani woman three rows behind, using language that was alien to me. I was only halfway through my five-hour journey and wondered how long this purgatory would last. Again the thought of my recent good fortune came to my aid but after ten minutes of trying to rekindle the feel-good factor, I reached for the discarded novel and read for the umpteenth time, the marked page.

Eventually, overriding the gabble of noise, the voice of an angel. Coming from the above Tannoy system, a clear English voice declaring that a trolley loaded with all manner of refreshments, including coffee, was about to enter this very carriage.

Along with the caffeine, my new status as property-owner was having a positive effect on me. After eating my fill of egg and cress sandwiches, a packet of crisps and a Kit Kat, washed down with the energy-pumping liquid, I indicated to my fellow passenger that I needed to use the toilet so she needed to move to let me out. She turned to the younger woman behind and fired off a volley of words, their meaning unmistakable. She remained where she was, looking straight ahead as though nothing had been said. 'Excuse me,' I said, in a louder, bolder voice, 'I really do need to visit the toilet!'

A return volley of words, this time from the younger woman behind, and this time spoken in English. 'Mother, stand up and let the lady out, please!'

On reaching Bristol and three more chapters into my novel, there was a mass exodus from the train. My neighbouring seat was once again vacant, but so too were many others. Just a few yards ahead, I spied a pair of vacant seats that allowed me to see where I was heading, not where I'd just been. As a child, travelling backwards always affected my stomach, sometimes to the point of being physically sick. The memory of those embarrassing incidents had left its mark on my resolve to always choose a seat facing the direction of travel.

Once the carriage had cleared and before anyone else had the chance to foil my intention, I grabbed my suitcase and shot forward to carry out my plan. Lifting the separating arm of the two seats, I spread myself across them before closing my eyes and pretending to be asleep; inwardly vowing to do the same thing at every stopping station between here and Torquay.

I gave up on the novel at the end of the next chapter. It was probably due to my lack of concentration rather than the lack of pull and grip of the tale. Even so, I'd long since made up my mind to leave the book on the train, an offering to a more tenacious reader. Instead, I allowed my eyes to take in the rolling beauty of England's south-west countryside.

As I relaxed comfortably in my newly positioned seating, I began to wonder how often and for how long I could spend time in this beautiful part of the world. As kids, Liz and I came here often with Dad, Mum choosing to stay home keeping a watchful eye on the small hairdressing business she ran with our neighbour, Jill. I liked Torquay but Cockington, I found especially fascinating. It was like stepping back in time. The anomaly of a quaint old village – its cottages still crowned with thatch – just a five minute drive from the hustle and bustle of the seaside resort. When Liz reached her early teens and boys became the number one attraction, she was forever whining to go to the beach, or the town centre and would often go on her own. Dad and I would accompany Great Aunt Winifred on walks around Cockington, stopping at one of the cafe's for ice cream, or a cream tea.

Once Exeter was reached, the landscape began to change. Soon, all eyes in the carriage were turned left, feasting on the delightful views of river, estuary and open sea. Why, I asked myself, had I not been down here in over three years? The answer was there, lurking in the depths.

I clearly remember now, on my last visit to Cockington. We were expecting our first child. A proud couple at long last having reached beyond the danger zone of miscarriage after miscarriage. I wore my bump with pride, and especially proud was Aunt Winifred who knew how we'd longed for a child of our own.

We'd managed to secure a room at the Chelston Manor Hotel for the four-night stay, which meant we could spend a good deal of that time in the company of the old lady whose eyesight was already beginning to fail. Fortunately, her mind and her memory were still razor sharp. Thinking back, I recall that the weather was kind except for one day when it showered on and off all day – the day of the Cockington Fayre. But even on that day, it was fun, pleasurable and relaxing. On leaving, Aunt Winifred had laid her hand on my belly, saying "God Bless you child for coming and God Bless you for bringing me this wonderful news."

Sadly, seven weeks before our little girl was due, I was rushed into hospital with bleeding and horrendous pain, I knew without being told, our daughter had died! After the devastation and the disappointment, hope of ever having a child of our own seeped away. We became resigned to the fact we weren't meant to be parents.

I suppose if I'm really honest, I hadn't wanted to tell Aunt Winifred of my failure, and I used the excuse of her failing eyesight, not to keep in touch by letter. From then on the holidays we had were more exotic. Expensive destinations around the world to help fill a gaping hole in our lives.

Chapter 3

Torquay Central Railway Station

It was three-thirty-five when the train finally rolled into Torquay's Central Station. Fifteen minutes later than predicted. I'd texted the solicitor, as promised, an hour before my expected time of arrival but the train was held up near Newton Abbot due to a signal failure. I hated being late and even though it wasn't my fault, the calm anticipation of meeting Samantha Devreau had developed into a panic-stricken frenzy of pushing through bodies and frantically searching for a face I'd never clapped eyes on before.

Four minutes later and seeing the last available taxi, I fumbled in my bag for the phone, praying that she would be available to answer and not on the road driving away from the station. Then a voice from behind put paid to my frustration.

'Excuse me! Are you Kate Radcliffe?'

I recognised the voice from our telephone call of yesterday, but as I turned, I found the lively, youthful-sounding articulation, belonged to a woman of late middle-age. I had actually caught sight of her a minute or two earlier waiting at the edge of the car park and assumed she was… To be honest, in my stressed state I wasn't sure what I assumed but I didn't think for one second it could be

Samantha Devreau. 'I'm so sorry I kept you waiting,' I said, dropping my baggage and taking hold of the offered hand, noticing that two of her fingers were arthritic.

'Unavoidable, Kate, but at least I was warned of the delay on the information screen, so I took myself off to the little cafe on the platform for a mug of tea and a read of today's newspaper; something I rarely get to do these days and I'm afraid I lingered over a particularly interesting article. Still, we're here now and I hope you don't mind if we head straight to my office and get the paperwork out of the way.'

Without waiting for a response, the solicitor turned and marched swiftly into the car park. From a short distance, a Mini Cooper in cream and black, signalled that it had been unlocked and on reaching it, the boot was opened for my luggage and Samantha Devreau slid into the drivers seat, more lithesome than I'd thought possible for a woman of her years.

Neither of us spoke as we followed a number 12 bus along the beautiful coastline of The English Riviera which to my mind is superior to any in Europe.

After turning left into Belgrave Road, taking a few twists and turns along roads lined with hotels and guest houses of varying size, we took a sharp left and stopped on a short gravelled drive in Abbey Road – the premises of Devreau & Wilkes Solicitors.

* * *

Within the hour, I was back in the smart-looking Mini Cooper. I had been fully prepared for ringing a taxi to take me to Wisteria House in Walnut Road Chelston, but Samantha had insisted on dropping me there; a small guest house in walking distance to the cottage I now legally owned – along with everything in it and an approximate sum of one hundred and forty thousand pounds, hitherto held in Aunt Winifred's Coop Building Society Savings Account. Samantha explained that she couldn't be accurate on the final sum due to ongoing charges linked to the cottage and maintenance of the garden. But it was as near as damn it (her words not mine) and she was anxious that the maintenance didn't increase too much, hinting that the cottage was a very saleable asset for someone looking for a refurbishment project and would be best sold before the onset of winter. She also hinted even more strongly that Devreau and Wilkes would be happy to handle such a sale.

I'd said very little in response. My mind still trying to assimilate something that had been said yesterday. And now seemed a better time than any to ask. 'What did you mean when you said, I was Great Aunt Winifred's only living relative?'

Her answer sounded matter-of-fact. 'Your father was sole beneficiary. After his death, Winifred simply wanted it to pass to the next in line.'

'But I have an older sister,' I argued, somehow aware that I was poking at a hornet's nest.

'You mean half-sister, Kate. You are the only issue registered to your father. We always make sure of such things. And here we are at Wisteria house. Mrs Evan's will take good care of you. You are very fortunate to get booked in here, there was a last minute cancellation, otherwise it would have been The Premier Inn.'

I thanked her, removed my luggage and wished her a happy holiday.

'I'll be in touch after a few weeks, Kate. And remember what I said about the cottage, I've retained a set of keys so there'll be no problem dealing with the sale from here. I know a very reliable estate agent. Goodbye!' A roar of the engine and she was gone.

It was all a bit overwhelming. The journey had tired me, although for the life of me I couldn't think why? I'd only sat and slept. I was grateful to the solicitor for finding me a suitable place to stay at this busy time of the year, and as I walked up the path to the pretty, red-brick villa, all I wanted to do, was close the door to my room, lie on the bed and allow all that had happened in the last twenty-four hours to sink in.

I'd got as far as the closing of my room door, having been made welcome by Mrs Evans, when my phone rang. 'Shit!' as I looked at the screen I realized I hadn't rung Andy. 'Hi darling, sorry I haven't phoned yet, the train was late and the solicitor was in a hurry to get the paperwork done. How's the course going?'

'It's OK. Yea, it's going OK. How's the cottage?'

'I haven't been there yet. I've got the keys and everything, but I'm not sure I feel up to going this evening. The landlady is going to make me a light supper and I might have an early night. I feel shattered, I don't know why?'

'It's probably the shock, as surprising news, whether good or bad will have an effect but feel free to ring me later. I'm not doing much this evening and most of the lads are going out on the town; treating their time away as a holiday from the wife and kids. I'll probably get the paperwork side of it done, leave a clear run for the last two days.'

That was typical of my Andy. Always liked to keep ahead of the game. 'I'll check over the cottage tomorrow. Oh yea, and I need to pick up Aunt Winifred's ashes from the crematorium, apparently it was written in her will that she wanted her remains returned to Chelston. Anyway, if I don't ring later, I'll definitely give you a bell tomorrow evening. Take care, love you!'

I'd put the phone down before realizing I hadn't mentioned the money, nor had I mentioned the fact that Liz was my half-sister. Five years can make a lot of difference when you're kids, but even as we grew older the gap never seemed to close. We certainly didn't look alike and we had little in common. But she was the image of Mum, while I certainly took after Dad. Not only physically – dark, coarse hair that had the annoying tendency to frizz – but also in mental attitude. Our surnames were the same, always had been, so I naturally presumed... Why, the hell wasn't I told! I felt angry and I knew now wasn't a good time but I decided to ring Mum. Mainly to find out if the cats had settled down again. She picked up on the second ring.

'Is that you Kate? You've taken your time ringing. Is everything all right?'

'I've just got back from the solicitor's, Mum. Are Sheba and Minx OK? I mean, they're not playing up because I've left them again, are they?'

'They're not kids, Kate. They're animals for God's sake, and like all animals, all they care about is getting fed. They've eaten their dinner and now they're doing what cats do best, sleeping.'

A long pause as each reigned in frustration with the other. Then Mum cleared her throat and asked, 'How much did the old girl leave?'

The bluntness of the question took me by surprise. 'I...I'm not sure yet. There are still ongoing expenses and stuff. Samantha... The solicitor said she'd keep me informed.'

'Aye, I bet she will and no doubt her fee will be a big chunk of those expenses! Well I hope you do the right thing and share it with your sister. Your Dad would have wanted that.'

'It wasn't Dad who left it to me.' For a split second I wanted to bite off my tongue, but the words were out and they carried the truth, and thinking of truth and bluntness, I felt I had the right to have been told the truth years ago. 'Why didn't you tell me, Mum? Why didn't you tell me that Liz was only my half-sister?'

A heard the intake of breath then silence as she held it, seeing in my minds-eye the tightly pressed lips, that giveaway clue to her inner indignation. I was expecting the receiver to be put down on me any second.

'What does it matter, Kate? Why should it matter? Your Dad loved Liz as much as he loved you.'

'I know he did, Mum. But do you love me as much as you love Liz?'

The receiver was put down on me with a loud clatter.

* * *

The ham omelette and salad, accompanied by a glass of chilled Prosecco, had revived me and Mrs Evan's had been very kind in bringing the food to my room after observing my shattered state. It wasn't yet seven-thirty and although I had meant what I said to Andy about having an early night, I was beginning to feel restless and in need of fresh air and exercise. Grabbing my bag and the room key, I stepped out into the mild evening and headed towards Old Mill Road.

The cottage wasn't far but there was a steep climb to it and I was soon panting for breath before it even came into view. When it did, I halted, allowing the reality of my new situation to sink in and take hold. *This property is now mine. No rental or mortgage payments. I own every square inch of it. Everything growing in the garden outside the cottage and every piece of furniture and china crockery inside of it.*

The wooden gate, encroached on by the dog rose hedge that surrounded the garden, sagged on its hinges and would only open halfway. I squeezed through its gap unable to resist bending my nose to one of the few rose blooms left – protected in a shady nook on the cottage side. Immediately, the delicate aroma transported me back to the time when I first visited this place. A time when I had to stand on tip-toe to gain the delight of this aroma. A time when I learned the hard lesson that roses should never be picked, they should always be carefully cut, wise words from Aunt Winifred as she wiped my tears, washed the blood from my best frock and bandaged the deep scratch that ran down my forearm.

I stood before the sturdy front door, the brass fittings on it looking tired and pitted with verdigris, remembering that back during my tip-toe days they shone like gold. There was no number on the front door. There had never been a number. 'Rose Cottage' of Old Mill Rd, Chelston, had always been a sufficient address for cards and letters to find their way. I recall Aunt Winifred telling me that before she was born, the previous owner had named the cottage *Apple Cottage,* which was strange because there was no evidence of a single apple tree but Aunt Winifred was never wrong about things of the past.

Pulling the small bunch of keys from my bag, tagged with an incongruously large label marked Winifred Fletcher, I inserted the Yale key into the lock. It turned easily but my push on the door soon came to an abrupt halt. Mail had piled up behind it. Pushing the door back and forth several times dispersed the pile and allowed me to enter.

Deathly silence engulfed me, as did the gloom and drop in temperature. Instinctively, I reached to the light switch, remembering at the same time the solicitor's warning that all services to the cottage were switched off at the mains. I pulled my cardigan tight about my shoulders, reminding myself this was a very old cottage, thick-walled and built in a way that retained heat in the winter while remaining cool in the summer. I also reminded myself I had every right to be here. This was my place now, to do with as I liked. But in spite of my strong resolve, I couldn't banish the feeling that I was invading another's territory.

Leaving my bag and the keys on the small side table, I walked slowly into the sitting room. The curtains were haphazardly pulled together, allowing a slither of light to bleed through, giving me sufficient light to see where Aunt Winifred had slept in her later years and where she would have preferred to have died. It looked so different now to how it did when Andy and I had last visited. Three years ago this was the cosy sitting room I remembered as a child. The colourful cushions, vases of scented flowers and a table that converted to a single bed for Dad to sleep in at bedtime, had all vanished except for the bed. That same bed was before me now, clinical-looking with an off-white, cellular blanket tucked tightly around the three-foot-wide mattress, precise envelope corners speaking volumes. I doubted the bed had been converted back to a table in years. Although everything was neat and tidy, I noticed cobwebs and a thick layer of dust everywhere. Aunt Winifred would have hated to see it, and even though she was totally blind at the end, she would have known. She would have known that like her body, the place she had called home for more than seventy years, was gradually crumbling and decaying.

The light was beginning to fade outside, deepening the gloom within and magnifying my sadness. I told myself that I should be making my way back to Wisteria House and return back tomorrow when I, and the day would be fresher and brighter. Suddenly, a double creak from above. My eyes shot upwards, my mind focusing on the rooms above as I headed for the door. Holding my breath, I listened. Nothing. Nothing except the thumping of my heartbeat. Nothing, but an emerging memory that was rising up and filling my head like water from a punctured dam. But instead of returning to the front door, I turned and crept slowly to the door that led upstairs and lifted the latch, the sound of it echoing loudly in the room's hollow silence. A strong urge to return to the cosiness of Wisteria House and leave any further inspection of the cottage until tomorrow morning was now quickly forgotten. I was here now and it had to be done. It had to be faced. Now or tomorrow, it was going to be difficult. As my weight came to bear on the third step up, I flinched at the loud creak even though it was expected. I was being reminded that I was about to take a look. Just a look, I wouldn't dream of entering, not at this time of day. Not until I was able to flick a switch and flood the room with light. I Just needed to satisfy my curiosity, that the creaks heard were just the beams of the cottage shifting in the cooling temperature.

There were two rooms above. The main bedroom, which as children, we shared with Aunt Winifred, Liz sleeping in one of the twin beds alongside our aunt and I sleeping on an upholstered daybed positioned along the opposite wall. The opposite room was smaller and entering it was prohibited. It was during my first visit, when most things were reached on tip-toe, that I first became aware of the word, *prohibited*, and what it meant. The smaller room, opposite, was kept locked, at least while we were there, and when asked why? Aunt Winifred said it was her private space and prohibited to children. Innocently, I'd asked what *prohibited* meant. Liz, loudly answering for me, had said, "It means you are forbidden to go in there, stupid!" I'd assumed it to be a room where old cast off things were stored and Christmas presents were hidden waiting to be wrapped, just like our box room at home. Liz however, being older and wiser, had been convinced it held something far more sinister.

I'd reached the top stair by the time the reminiscing lost its hold. Lifting the latch gently I pushed. The door held firm. It was locked and the small bunch of keys were downstairs placed near my bag. Another creak from inside the room, the sound less hollow from up here. I pressed my ear to the wooden panelling of the door, again hearing nothing but my own heartbeat. Suddenly, a loud knocking reverberated through the place from below. I screamed with fright and bounded down the stairs. Then more knocking, followed by Samantha Devreau's shrouded voice.

'Kate? Kate, are you in there?'

I yanked the door open, her fist frozen in mid air, stalling her attempt at another battering. 'Sorry, you gave me a fright!' I said, trying to calm my panting. 'Is anything wrong? I mean, it is all right for me to be here isn't it?'

'Yes of course it is, Kate. It's your place now. It's just that I wanted to let you know where the main switch is for the electricity and the stopcock for the water. I tried ringing you on your mobile but you didn't answer so I rang Mrs Evans. She said you'd gone for a walk but hadn't taken your phone – she could hear it ringing in your room. I guessed you'd be here. The office will be closed over the weekend and as you know I'll be unavailable from Monday onwards, hence the reason I'm here is to show you how to switch on the power and water but also to recommend that they be switched off before you return back home. Like I said, if you do decide to sell straight away, ring the office on Monday and my secretary will get straight onto the agent. It really is advisable to get the ball rolling straight away.

I declined the offered lift back to Wisteria House as the evening was still warm despite the darkening sky. I also felt the need for a walk to calm my frazzled nerves.

Chapter 4

Wisteria House – Saturday Morning

I opened my eyes to bars of bright sunlight striped across the ceiling and angled down the opposite wall, reminding me of the dream that had woken me during the night. The reminder was subliminal, my dream was about imprisonment; imprisonment within the cottage I now owned. As with most dreams, there were some recognisable elements but for the most part the dream did not make sense.

Turning onto my back I stretched my whole body, hearing clicks in my knees and ankles warning me that I needed to unwind and take more exercise. I sat up and swung my legs from the bed, noticing a pen and paper on the bedside cabinet and the reason behind it being there, came flooding back. I am a great believer in recording one's dreams, especially dreams that are loaded with emotion. I reached for the paper and squinted at the short hand scribbling of the half-asleep state I was in. All that could be gleaned from the scribbling on the reverse of Mrs Evans' menu, were four decipherable words amongst the illegible squiggling lines – *prohibited room, Elizabeth* and *photo*. For the life of me I could no longer recall the dream, only that it was linked to my evening visit to the cottage and the incident when I was five years old.

Hunger made itself felt, reminding me that the here and now and the needs of the body were more important than fantasy. I flipped over the menu, eager to see what was on offer for breakfast, recalling Mrs Evans' suggestion that if I placed my order before retiring to bed, she would arrive with a tray at a stipulated time. Alternatively, breakfast was served in the dining-room between eight o'clock and nine o'clock. I checked my phone and found it showed the time of seven-thirty-six.

The dining-room was a glass conservatory on the northern side of the early twentieth-century-villa. Ferns, orchids and other exotic plant life were thriving here, adding colour and naturalness to a space that would otherwise be boxy and uninteresting. I sat at a small table set for one, assuming it was mine because the other tables were all set for couples. It was almost eight o'clock and no sooner had I parked my backside on the willow-woven chair, Mrs Evans was at my side, notepad in hand and finger pointing to where I could help myself to orange juice, cereals and croissants. I ordered coffee and a Full English Breakfast, mindful of the walking I intended to do and how the Devon air always increases my appetite. From childhood to the last visit three years ago, the effect was always the same; by the second or third day, I felt ravenously hungry by mealtimes and at bedtime I slept like a log.

The breakfast was delicious, really delicious. Not only did it satisfy my hunger, it brought to mind how much I'd forgotten about the pleasures of food. I hadn't eaten a fry-up in ages, choosing instead to travel a healthier route of fruit, yogurt, skinny latte and brown toast with a thin scraping of margarine – my weight still a stone heavier than it ought to be.

Resisting the urge to head straight to the cottage, I turned in the opposite direction, soon finding myself on Seaway Lane, a hint of ozone in the air. Within minutes, the splendour of Torbay lay before me. The traffic was light, considering the time of year, as I sprinted across the road to Corbyn Head, a place I loved to sit and think.

I hadn't been sitting long when the short ping of my phone brought me from a reverie of thoughts. It was a text from Jenny, one of my teacher colleagues, apologizing for the fact that she couldn't make it that evening. It was a relief really, even if I'd been at home, I'd have chickened out. Drinking upwards of a bottle of wine over a period of two to three hours, piled on more calories than any food, and, after just spending four days away doing just that, I needed a break from it. A typed quick reply giving no excuses or reasons why I couldn't make it either, was sent to the three of them. I didn't want to go so why lie and I certainly didn't want to inform them of my good fortune. Not yet anyway.

* * *

The water meadows that led to Cockington Village showed no sign of rain having fallen for some time and several walkers were enjoying a morning stroll. They were all heading in the same direction. The clip-clop sound of horses hooves on the nearby road, the chuckle of the running waters and the herby scent of my surroundings brought about a feeling that I'd been transported back in time, or more precisely that time had halted. The rush and stress of life back in Halifax now seemed a million miles away.

The familiarity of thatched dwellings dotted here and there, came into view as I climbed over the style back onto the road. A short distance further and there it was – the Old Forge – reputedly dating to the fourteenth century and standing at the south-western corner of Cockington Square. Back at five years of age, this was the most fascinating place for me. The flames that changed black iron to white heat, the hissing steam as the metal was cooled and the clatter of the hammer reshaping that metal, held me spellbound on every visit. Dad responding fully to all my questions. Today, this historical building was mainly functioning as a gift shop, but the very site of the place with its stout tree trunks, still supporting the shoeing area at the front, brought on a nostalgic feeling of wonder and excitement.

After a slow meander around the village, I headed up to the Court, sitting awhile on one of the many bequeathed benches overlooking the cricket pitch and pavilion. Memories came flooding back of sunny afternoons spent picnicking here. Me and Liz, running up the slopes to roly-poly down again, while Dad and Aunt Winifred watched the game – the whack of bat hitting ball followed by cheering voices, provided background sounds to our childish fun.

The Temperature had risen steadily and by the time I reached Cockington Court Tea Rooms, I was hot and in need of a drink. An outdoor table had become available in a quiet and shaded corner, which allowed panoramic views across acres of rolling beauty. I chose, without guilt, a good-sized slice of homemade shortcake to accompany the large pot of tea. I was in holiday mode and this is what you did whilst holidaying in Devon. Besides, the walk back to Chelston would surely burn off the extra calories.

* * *

Once again I stood at the gate of *my cottage*. In contrast to the tiredness and uncertainty of yesterday, I felt relaxed with a strong sense of well-being coursing through my veins. I lifted the gate instead of pushing it and it moved easily to a fully-opened position. With keys already in my hand, I marched purposefully through it, eager to enter the cottage, turn on the power and water, throw open all the windows and carefully inspect each room. Especially the one that was locked.

The mains electricity box was alongside the meter at the back of the utility room – always referred to by Aunt Winifred as the scullery, a word which conjured up in my mind, a place for skulduggery – and on the opposite wall, below a deep ceramic sink, was the stop-cock for the water. It took only seconds to turn and flick, as shown by Samantha, and bring the cottage into full use. Admittedly, it needed a good airing and a fair amount of TLC, but on the whole, it was in a liveable state.

The first room to check out was the bathroom, because I was close to it and I needed to pee. It wasn't ideally positioned, this flat-roofed add-on leading from one corner of the utility room – a long way to walk if you woke in the night bursting to go. When the cottage was built there was no such luxury as bathrooms, well, not for the commoners. It was an outdoor privy and a zinc bath that had to be filled with pans of heated water. I remember Dad telling us that the bathroom was added at some point in the nineteen-fifties, and was long overdue for replacement decades ago, but Aunt Winifred was a stickler for keeping the cottage as original as possible. It was mainly Liz doing the complaining but after listening to Aunt Winifred's tales of lifestyles of bygone days we soon settled into our new regime for the length of our holidays.

I opened the door and peered down the lavatory pan – I was phobic about spiders – finding the standing water discoloured by time but otherwise the pan was clean. My eyes wandered around the six-foot by ten-foot space whilst I sat relieving the pressure from my bladder. Changes had been made since I was last in here. Several changes. Grip bars had been added to either side of the original bath and there was a newly installed shower, looking incongruous as it peeped out from behind a blue and white polka dot curtain. The toilet I was perched on and the sink opposite me were also original but there were more chips than I recalled and the taps were encrusted around the bases, in need of a good dose of Mr Muscle Bathroom Cleaner. Fortunately, the chain flushed, a loud resounding gush followed by the system filling up a lot quicker than the one in our modern semi in Halifax. I turned on the taps and after an initial cough and splutter of air, a steady stream of clean water flowed from each one. My eyes kept returning to the saddest addition in the room; a walking-aid with a carrier bag suspended from the crossbar, was positioned next to the sink. Not wanting to linger upon how my aunt had to cope with her failing sight, her disappearing independence and the need to have carers invading her private space, and her body, I opened the window as wide as it would go and headed for the kitchen.

I believe that in most houses the kitchen is the hub of the home and that the table is the hub of the kitchen. This particular table was made from oak, was both very old and very heavy. I think it must have taken root where it stood because I'd never seen anyone move it. Come to think of it, the table must have been constructed in this very room because there was no way it could fit through any of the doors of this cottage, and it certainly wasn't of flat-pack construction. Two shallow drawers were set into opposite sides of the table, just below the top. One was segmented and used for cutlery. The other, according to Aunt Winifred, was for bits and bobs. The bits and bobs drawer used to hold crayons and colouring books when I was little. Later it was drawing books and reading books, board games like scrabble and monopoly. Things to keep us occupied on rainy days when we weren't eating, singing or listening to the radio.

I sat on one of the two kitchen chairs (briefly wondering where the other pair might be) stroking a hand over the silken, textured surface of the tabletop. Without thinking, I brought my nose close to its surface, the evocative scent of it filling my nostrils. Years of polishing, decades of spillages upon it and over a century of human activity pressed against it, and yet, it was the wood from the original oak that dominated that evocative scent.

Reminding myself that time was ticking away, I continued my rounds of the remainder of the cottage, throwing back the curtains and opening wide the windows, the circulating fresh air seeming to breathe new life into the place. I'd purposely left the locked room till last, not because I was nervous, for some strange reason I felt that I'd never be nervous again, such was the power of the mood I was in. I'd left it till last because looking at the size of the door's key hole, I could see at a glance that none of the three keys on the ring would fit this door lock.

Suddenly, a memory of long ago filled my head. As in the dream, I was five and Liz was ten. It was our first holiday here and we'd been told that this room was prohibited to us. On one of the days during that first holiday, while Aunt Winifred and Dad were gardening, Liz had whispered that she knew where the key to the room was and she needed my help to get it. At first I'd refused, knowing we'd be punished if caught, but her persuading convinced me everything would be OK. Through the gap in the bedroom door, Liz had seen Aunt Winifred enter the room early that morning. Minutes later, she'd come out of the room, and Liz was back at the gap watching as Aunt Winifred locked the door behind her and placed the key on the doorframe above the door – out of the reach of inquisitive children. My help was needed to keep watch whilst Liz carried a stool upstairs to reach that key and take a look inside.

I'd sat on the bottom step of the stairs, my orders being to cough out loud if either of the grown ups came into the house. I can still clearly remember the chop, chop, chopping sound as Aunt Winifred trimmed the hedge and the strong smell of cut grass as Dad pushed the mower back and forth the length of the garden. Then there was a clatter from above my head. Followed by a crash and an almighty thud and this was followed by Liz's screaming.

Bringing myself back to the moment, I reached up and ran my fingers along the length of the frame and sure enough the four-inch-long iron key was there, coated in dust on top of the door frame. No stool was needed to reach it. No risk of the stool toppling on the uneven floor and sending me crashing down, spraining my ankle due to an awkward landing. I smiled recounting the severe telling off we got from Dad. Aunt Winifred said very little about the incident, I think she realized we'd learned a valuable lesson. Neither Liz nor I ever gave another thought to entering that room.

I turned the key, a satisfying sound of the mechanism shifting and allowing me entry. Moving straight to the window, I pulled back the heavy curtains and opened the window wide, sunshine and light breezes pushing into the room, a room that had been denied both in God knows how long? Sitting on the wooden window seat I gazed with wonder and amazement at the secret, prohibited room. Along the wall opposite the window, was the daybed I'd slept on as a child, the upholstery fabric matching the box-like cushion I was sitting on; the daybed was obviously moved from here to the main bedroom whenever we visited. The only other furniture in the room was a desk and chair and a sturdy open-fronted bookcase, rammed tight with books and gaping folders of paperwork, except for the top shelf which was clear apart from three silver-framed black and white photographs standing in line and inviting closer inspection. An ancient typewriter, covered with clear polythene, sat on the desk. There were no ornaments or pictures on the wall; although something had at one time hung above the bookcase because a hook, still visible in spite of being painted over, seemed to be waiting expectantly to be used again.

There was nothing untoward about the room, nothing that gave any credence to the scary goings on that Liz envisaged and planted into my receptive mind – usually at bedtime. From what I could now see it was evident that the room was used as an office by Aunt Winifred. It was conducive to study. It was understandable that she wanted to keep it private and away from children's prying eyes.

Chapter 5

Rose Cottage – Saturday Afternoon

I was physically exhausted and starving hungry as I made my way back to Wisteria House. Mentally, I felt on top of the world. I'd cleaned the cottage from top to bottom, grateful that I had found a sufficient amount of cleaning products in the utility room. I was also grateful that the ancient, upright carpet cleaner was still in good working order. There were no fitted carpets in the cottage but there were several rugs and I have to say, I would have shied away from hanging them over the garden line and beating them with a hefty piece of wood; something I'd seen Aunt Winifred do when a summer storm had caused a power cut.

Once I'd made the place "ship shape and Bristol fashion" (one of Aunt Winifred's many quotes) I was reluctant to leave. In fact, if I hadn't arranged with Mrs Evans to have a meal back at Wisteria House at seven o'clock, I would have picked up a takeaway or fish and chips and taken it back to the cottage, content to eat alone at my lovely, freshly-polished kitchen table.

After checking my watch for the second time, I realized I had only ten minutes to get back, have a shower and change. Instead of putting on a spurt, I marvelled at my changed, relaxed attitude at the likelihood of me being late.

Suddenly my phone rang, 'Speak of the devil', I said out loud, assuming it to be Mrs Evans wondering where I'd got to and also regretting giving her my mobile number.

'Hello, this is Kate Radcliffe and I'm on my way back now. So sorry for the delay; I hope my lateness hasn't inconvenienced you?'

A long silence before 'Kate? Is that you?'

'Andy? Sorry love I thought it was Mrs Evans, the landlady where I'm staying.'

'I tried to phone you several times, is everything all right?'

'Yea, things couldn't be better. I spent the morning walking around Cockington Village and the Court. The rest of the time I've been up to my elbows in hot soapy water cleaning the cottage from top to bottom. I noticed I couldn't get a signal in the cottage, so I switched off my phone. Was it something urgent? I had planned on phoning you later after I'd eaten dinner.'

'The course is all but over. The paperwork side of it I'll get finished this evening so I can get an early start back tomorrow. I'll call in on your mum on the way back and pick up the cats. Get the earliest train you can and I'll pick you up at the station and we'll go out somewhere for a nice meal. Anywhere you fancy.'

Without a seconds thought, I said, 'Why don't you drive down here, Andy? We're both in need of a break and we've got the cottage. Our very own cottage and it's so lovely, especially now it's spruced up.'

'I thought…I mean, I assumed you'd be selling the cottage. Your mum and Liz both gave the impression you would be. Besides, Kate, I can't just drop everything and travel to Devon.'

'Why not, you said yourself you have time owing to you. Just take it, lets relax and have some fun. Incidentally, I haven't said a word to Mum or Liz about my intentions regarding the cottage. When were you talking to them?'

'When I couldn't get through, I phoned them both to see if they'd heard from you and when did they expect you back? I'd assumed you were on the train and that was why I couldn't get through to you. Your mum sounded a bit put-out over having the cats for this long and I promised I'd pick them up tomorrow.'

'Sheba and Minx will love it here. I know it's a long journey for them, but if they're wearing their pheromones collars they'll sleep for most of the journey. Oh come on, Andy, I'm sure you can wangle a few days off, it's August for God's sake, the weather's beautiful and Torquay is rammed with people enjoying themselves! I have to go now, love, I'm ten minutes late for dinner and I haven't even showered yet. Think it over. I'll phone you later. Bye!'

* * *

Wisteria House

Mrs Evans was darting back and forth between the kitchen and the crowded dining room as I entered and headed towards my room. I was stopped in my tracks by her stern voice.

'Mrs Radcliffe. Goodness me I was beginning to worry about you,' she exclaimed, veering towards me, breathless with the exertion of carrying a tray of drinks for six. 'I know you showed an interest in my Vegetable Lasagne but I'm afraid orders have been placed and there isn't any left. Everything is homemade you see, and being a small, select establishment it can get difficult...'

'That's not a problem, Mrs Evans,' I interrupted. 'It's my own fault for being late and not placing a definite order as you suggested. Besides, right now I feel as though I could eat a horse. Can I give you my order before having a shower and changing?'

I'd flummoxed her. She half-turned one way then the other looking for a surface to put down the heavy tray. Settling for a nearby hall table, she lay down her load, pulled her pad from her apron pocket, removed the pencil that had been discretely positioned behind her right ear and stood poised, a look of impatience on her face.

Fortunately, my memory was good and the list of what was on offer I'd seen pinned on the dining room noticeboard that morning, came easily to mind. 'I'd like the sirloin steak – done medium-rare – with chips and whatever veg are on offer. I'll be down in less than twenty minutes.' Before she had a chance to argue the point, I turned and shot off in the direction of my room.

Within fifteen minutes, I was comfortably sipping on a glass of particularly smooth Spanish Rioja at the same table I was having my breakfast earlier in the day, allowing the aroma of food wafting in from the kitchen, to heighten my anticipation.

Considering every table in the place was occupied, I didn't have long to wait; it had to be said, Mrs Evans' stickler for punctuality had to be admired even if it wasn't always adhered to.

The steak was delicious and cooked to perfection and I told her so, showing my appreciation by leaving a generous tip, before informing her that I'd be checking out after breakfast the next morning. I had hinted that I might well be staying until Monday, but now the cottage was habitable, there was no point in wasting money.

Back in my room, I stretched out on the bed, the vague sound of the dining-room chatter distant enough not to impinge on my own thoughts.

My thoughts were of the next day and the next day after that and the next. All I could think about was the cottage and the changes I wanted to make to it. And how quickly I wanted to make those changes. I checked the time, eager to ring Andy but unsure that I'd allowed enough time for him to make that all-important telephone call to his superintendent. On cue and as if by magic, the phone gave a shudder and began to ring. It was Andy.

'Hi darling, how did it go?' I asked, sitting up in anticipation of good news.

'How did what go?' he said, knowing what I meant but teasingly holding back on any news.

'You've got the time off, right?'

'Yes and no. I've managed to squeeze three days after telling a half-truth.' Andy then waited for the expected whinging, which he had become accustomed to lately. As much as he loved his wife, he felt lately she had become negative and easily found fault, which was beginning to get him down.

'Oh that's wonderful, Andy! Three days are better than nothing. What do you mean by a half-truth?'

'I told the super there was a death in the family and the funeral was in Devon. If I get an early start tomorrow, by the time I've picked up the cats I should be able to get there by just after lunch. But, I'm back on shift by Thursday, Kate, and there's no getting around that.'

'I can't wait to see you, sweetheart! If you have a problem remembering where the cottage is, just give me a bell when you're nearly here and I'll give you the postcode to punch into the *sat nav*. Bye! Love you!'

* * *

Sunday Morning

I woke to another gloriously sunny morning; church bells were ringing merrily in the distance calling the faithful to an early service. I was reminded that I hadn't yet collected Aunt Winifred's ashes from the crematorium, mentally adding it to the list of what needed to be done this morning. Andy wouldn't be too pleased about spending part of our precious three days doing such a morbid task but on the other hand, I felt obliged to carry out her last wishes as soon as possible, wondering for the first time, why she hadn't opted for a burial in the local church. Mind you, neither of us were religious and the last time I was inside a church was for Dad's funeral. Even the following year when we were married, I was the one to insist on the registry office ceremony.

When I was eleven years old, I had a good friend who happened to be a staunch catholic. Every Sunday Teresa attended mass, not because she really wanted to, she told me on several occasions how she hated missing out on picnics and all-day-outings that other kids took for granted. She was my best friend – in fact, she was my only friend when I first moved up to Burton Road Comprehensive – so on occasion I'd keep her company by going to her church. I'd follow and mimic all the little rituals, right down to dropping a few pennies in the collection box. The smells of the incense, the chanting voice of the priest and the general atmosphere of the place, I'd found calming, reassuring and comforting.

Liz had left Burton Road Comprehensive the same year as I'd moved up and I was being bullied something terrible by a couple of girls in year two. Having Teresa as a friend and the occasional visit to the church, helped me to cope with that distressing time. One day Mum invited Teresa over for tea and a sleepover. Teresa's mum refused, saying she had too much homework and too many domestic chores to get through. Mum feeling slighted, never made the offer again.

Then there came the time when Teresa fell sick; she was hardly ever at school, and on the days she was, she looked pale and thin. One particular Monday morning at assembly, the headmistress announced that Teresa wouldn't be returning to school, explaining that she was suffering from an illness called *Leukaemia*. She requested that we all focus on her during the morning prayers and ask God to assist in her recovery. Unfortunately the prayers didn't help and Teresa died a month before her thirteenth birthday. I had not once been allowed to see her to say goodbye. For a few moments, anger rose like poisoned bile from the pit of my gut, forcing me to realize just how much I'd hated Teresa's mother.

Determined not to allow the past to colour my future, I took a long shower, washing my hair and also washing the few tops I had with me, ready to dry at the cottage.

Again, I was first down for breakfast, finding my table already laid for one. Mrs Evans heard me enter and following a bright "Good Morning!" took my order of scrambled eggs with smoked salmon. I'd barely returned from the breakfast bar, clutching orange juice and cereals, when a pot of steaming coffee and a rack of toast was placed in front of me with a promise that the rest would follow shortly. This was indeed a well-run guesthouse and I would have no qualms about recommending it to anyone.

After settling up with Mrs Evans, declining her offer of ringing for a taxi, I said my farewells to Wisteria House. My suitcase wasn't large and the strength that powered my body was sufficient for the short walk ahead. Chelston seemed quiet and lazy, exuding that Sunday morning feeling of calm and tranquility that would be replicated in most villages throughout the UK. Looking about me I understood why Aunt Winifred had lived here for so long. There was everything she needed within short walking distance. Buses ran regularly and the railway station was just a five minutes ride away.

I arrived at the cottage in time to see a rabbit hop into the wild undergrowth as I lifted and pushed the gate open, sending a childlike thrill of expectancy at the thought of clearing away the months of rampant growth. But first things first, after hanging out my washing, the first port of call was the village store and then my trip to the crematorium.

* * *

It was well past eleven-thirty when the taxi dropped me back at the cottage clutching the cardboard box that contained the ashes of Aunt Winifred. At the crematorium, it had taken such a long time seeking out the appropriate person who dealt with such matters; even longer for the illusive Mr Cleave to return with, what to me seemed the most irreverent of containers. I'd expected an elegant urn in stone or pottery, maybe even a wooden miniature casket; but when I'd been handed the cardboard box, marked in felt tip pen with, *The Remains of Mrs Winifred Rose Fletcher,* I'd looked at him aghast.

Reading my expression, he'd responded curtly. 'It's a temporary container. The deceased obviously preferred something other than the norm for her ashes. The solicitor dealing with the estate should have a letter giving details, although sometimes it's been arranged that the letter be placed in the container,' Mr Cleave tapped twice on the plain lid that had been taped securely all round. 'This insures that there's no ambiguity as to the wishes of the deceased.'

In need of a cuppa, I opened the newly bought pack of teabags and tossed one in one of the two china mugs that Aunt Winfred kept for tradesmen – all others were served properly with cup and saucer and tea from the teapot. I flicked on the kettle and sat staring at the box, wondering if there was a letter of instruction inside. I pulled open the cutlery drawer in the table and choosing a stubby vegetable knife, slit the tape around the lid of the box. Unsure of what to expect, I carefully lifted the lid, poised ready to replace it quickly if fine dust escaped onto the freshly polished table. A brief sigh of relief, not only were the ashes contained in a strong opaque polythene bag, there was also a sealed envelope addressed to me.

My mug was empty by the time I opened the letter. I'd sat with tea in one hand while the other rested on the opaque bag, not just dust but boney lumps beneath my hand. Between sips and through closed eyes, I said my goodbyes to my Great Aunt Winifred, a lady whom I'd loved but known very little about.

The letter was brief and to the point, poignant yet disturbing. Aunt Winifred wanted her remains to be raked into the soil around the roots of the rose hedge. To go back to the earth were other loved ones lay, to help nourish the ground to aid beauty to thrive.

Who were the other loved ones? Thinking back, Dad had told me that she first came to live in Chelston during the Second World War. She'd married a pilot in the RAF who'd been pronounced missing presumed dead after his plane didn't return from an assault, and moving out of London helped her to feel safe and rebuild her life alone. She never remarried, so the loved ones she was referring to must be pets, although I'd never seen any on my visits.

The phone rang putting paid to my wonderings. I could see it was Andy and it wasn't yet noon. 'Hi darling, you got here pretty quickly!'

A lot of crackling before, 'I'm stuck in a massive queue on the M4. There's been an accident up ahead and until the services clear the road I'm trapped here. I can't say when I'll get there but I'll ring again once we get moving.'

Although Andy was known as Mr Patience, to his friends and colleagues, I could tell when something was frustrating him, and he was frustrated now.

'Can't you put the blue flasher on and sail through it?'

'I'm off duty, Kate,' he fired back, impatience obvious in his voice.

'I know you are, love, I was only joking, but it's not unheard of. Even a couple of your own mates have boasted about doing it when they get held up.' Changing the subject, I mentioned that I couldn't hear the cats and said I assumed they were sleeping before adding, "I'll see you later, darling and don't worry, I'll make it up to you…' I rang off wondering why I'd ended on such a suggestive comment.

Chapter 6

Sunday Afternoon

The washing was dry and put away, the beds were made and the shopping for provisions was done, but I still hadn't heard from Andy. With time on my hands and figuring that the smallest key on the ring fitted a padlock on the outside building, I slipped my phone into my jeans pocket and walked round to the back of the cottage to find out. My instincts were spot on. The old brick building, which had a corrugated iron roof, added in more recent times, was about the size of the average garage, but I knew for sure that Aunt Winifred had never owned a car. The building had one window, a tired-looking Venetian blind in closed position preventing a peek to what was inside. The door was solid oak with a strong hasp and staple padlock fixing – this too looking more recent than the main structure.

Once inside I pulled on the lop-sided blind and looked about me. Like Dad, Aunt Winifred enjoyed gardening. A selection of tools hung neatly along the right wall, ending with the lawn mower. The same lawn mower that had been in use back when I was five years of age, although the paintwork on it much faded and chipped. I clearly remember it because at the time it had my full attention, as Dad bellowed his angry words at me and Liz for abusing Aunt Winifred's hospitality. I didn't need to have the big words explained to me, I knew we'd done wrong. Forcing my eyes from the mower and the memory of Dad's disappointment in us, I looked to the back of the building. It was narrow and a wall to wall bench had been erected there with shelving beneath and tool cabinets on top – probably housing nails and screws and all the bits and pieces that accumulate over the years – more like a man's domain to me. I flicked on the light switch and a florescent strip stuttered into life, making little difference to the gloom at the bench end. I saw lengths of timber, gardening paraphernalia, various empty boxes and flower pots; all gathered along the left-hand side wall. There was also a folded table and chairs leaning into the corner.

Before I flicked off the light, I armed myself with a spade, fork and rake, before headed to where I thought would be the best place to conceal Aunt Winfred's remains – better this job was done before Andy's arrival – but the out of control growth of the hedge, prevented me from getting anywhere near its root base. As requested, I wanted to bury the ashes "where other loved ones lay", but how was I expected to know where along this long, thirty-yard hedge that was? My inspection of Aunt Winfred's office had been scant; I'd had enough to do cleaning and freshening the place in readiness for Andy's arrival; it was becoming obvious that the answer to my dilemma lay in that room.

Deciding to kill two birds with one stone, I grabbed an empty cardboard box from the tool store and headed for the locked room, my intension being to sort through the paperwork and then dump it in the box ready for burning. Who knows, by the time Andy arrives, the office could be cleared of all unnecessaries?

Within an hour the box was full. Full of household receipts going back over a decade. In the earlier years they'd been neatly filed in order of date but during the last three or four years, they'd been shoved together in a chaotic mass. Nothing had come to light regarding my aunt's deceased loved ones or receipts of vet's bills indicating any pets had been owned. The only items left in the bookcase were books and I've never had the heart to dispose of books, although I do have every intention of sorting through them at a later date.

Resting back on my heels and arching my neck backwards, hearing the clicks of strain in my shoulders, I then looked straight ahead, my eyes locking onto the three photographs on the uppermost shelf of the bookcase, silver frames encasing black and white images. I reached for the central one. A photograph of Aunt Winifred with her RAF husband, who went missing and believed dead during the war. Obviously, his remains could not be lying beneath the rose hedge.

The photograph on the left was more recent and appeared more *grainy*, with Aunt Winifred looking older and standing between a boy of about eight years old and a middle-aged man. I could tell the boy was Dad, the way he cocked his head slightly to one side. A characteristic I recognised, whenever he was being focused on and a habit that remained with him throughout his life. Yes, it was definitely Dad and it made my heart skip a beat to see it. But who was the guy on the right? He looked to be in his late forties or fifties, but then again he could have been younger; everyone seemed to look older than their years in past generations. It wasn't Dad's father, he was tall and heavily built. I have a framed photo of him in Halifax.

I turned the frame over eager for knowledge but was faced with a blank wall of purple velvet. A strongly built mechanism allowed the photo to be easily removed and within a minute I was reading the back of the photograph, neatly inscribed with Aunt Winifred's perfect scroll:

James, Winifred and Drew 1948.

Everybody knew Dad as Jimmy and it always felt a little strange to me whilst here on holiday, hearing him referred to as James. Aunt Winifred always insisted on calling you by your proper name. Liz was addressed as Elizabeth and she hated it. Mum named me Kate, plain and simple, to avoid anybody shortening my name, and I hated that. But who was Drew? And what kind of a name was that for a man? The only Drew I'd ever come across was Drew Barrymore, the American, female actress.

Intrigued, I reached for the third frame. This was a photo of Aunt Winifred holding, what appeared to be, a newborn child, swaddled in white with a lace shoal cascading to Aunt Winifred's knees as she cradled the baby lovingly in her arms; the peak of a snub nose and the front of a knitted bonnet the only indication that a baby was lying within the folds. Again, I assaulted the mechanism of the frame, eager to ascertain the identity of the child; fully expecting the photograph to be a record of Aunt Winifred's role as God-mother to someone's child. The wording however was brief, poignant and shocking!

Our sweet little Rose, who sadly died after three short days.
Dying before record of her birth was registered. 1949

I heard ringing close by and it took me a few seconds to realise it was the phone in my pocket. It also took me a few seconds to realise that tears were rolling down my cheeks. 'Hello…Hello Andy, is that you?'

'Of course it's me, how many guys named Andy do you know? Are you OK, you sound…you sound different.'

'I'm fine, really. I was having a bit of a nap that's all. It's made me feel groggy. So, where are you now?'

'I'm just about to fill up at Exeter services. I should be in Torquay within the hour. See you soon, Babe.'

* * *

I'd managed to cut the grass and give the hedge a bit of a trim before Andy arrived. I'd decided against dealing with Aunt Winifred's ashes for now and had placed the box under the day bed in the locked room. I wanted the next few days to be perfect and it was important that Andy felt the same way about the place as I did and I didn't want anything to scupper that.

Feeling nervous and excited I rushed out to meet him, congratulating him on successfully finding his own way and having Sheba and Minx safely here – looking non the worse for their long journey. I hadn't seen him in nearly a week and as we kissed and held each other close, an animalistic passion rose within me. He pulled back, looking into my eyes.

'The Devon air suits you, Kate, you've got a healthy glow about you, but I'm dying for a cuppa, Babe.'

The cats couldn't wait to explore outside so we drank tea and ate cake sitting at a folding table placed in the shade of the hedge, laughing as they stretched their limbs and frolicked about. Then came the nitty gritty of my inheritance. After the second piece of cake, washed down by a top up of tea, Andy asked, what I intended to do with the cottage, adding that Liz and Mum seemed pretty certain that I'd sell it because it would cost a bomb to make it anywhere near habitable.

'What does Mum know?' I cut in, 'She's hasn't even been here, she never once came to the cottage when Dad brought us on holiday. I really don't want to sell it!' I fired back, surprised by the determination in my own voice.

Andy lifted both hands in a gesture suggesting I calm down. 'Hey, I'm not saying what you should or shouldn't do. I'm just relaying what your mother and your sister expect you to do and I think they're annoyed that you're the only one mentioned in your Great Aunt's will.'

'Yea well, I'm sure Aunt Winifred knew well enough that the cottage would be straight on the market if Mum and Liz had a say in the matter. Thankfully they don't and I love the place, always have and always will. You like it too don't you, love?'

Without saying a word, Andy got to his feet. He was observant – had to be, it was a requirement of his job, and I'd watched his eyes roaming over the kitchen the minute he'd walked into it. Now he wandered back into the cottage and I sat tight, knowing he would scrutinise every room in turn. We'd popped in on Aunt Winifred several times whilst visiting Andy's friend in Totnes, a colleague also in the police force. As we'd been staying bed and breakfast on these visits, Andy hadn't seen much of the inside of the cottage.

It seemed he'd been gone for ages. I carried the tray into the kitchen and sat at the table. Waiting. Waiting for his approval.

'What's with the locked door upstairs?' he asked as he reached the creaking third stair from the bottom.

'Oh that, that was Aunt Winifred's private office, which she always kept locked when we were kids. Didn't want us messing up her private papers.'

'You haven't been a child in years, why keep it locked now?'

'Well, I suppose her carers were coming in on a regular basis in the last years of her life. Her eyesight was poor and she must have been slow on her feet, she probably didn't want anyone snooping around up there. I'd feel the same, Andy, wouldn't you?' I felt myself growing annoyed that I had to justify the actions of an old lady who had been very dear to me.

'Hey, I'm just trying to get a feel for the place. Work out its potential as a holiday-let. It needs money spent modernising the place and I'm sure that can be done within the constraints of preservation orders. But yes, you're a lucky lady, this cottage could prove to be a decent addition to our pension-pot.'

I clamped my lips tightly, preventing certain words gushing from them. I had three whole days to bring him round to my way of thinking, so instead of arguing the point, I announced, 'To celebrate, we'll have a Champagne dinner at one of the best restaurants in Torquay. My treat, darling, and when we get back, I'm gonna show you just how much I've missed you.'

* * *

Sunday Evening

The evening was still warm when the taxi dropped us back at the cottage and the Champaign and lobster dinner well settled, following the hand-in-hand stroll around the harbour and along the sea front to the Grand Hotel. Waiting outside the station, we'd spotted an available taxi and looking at each other we'd smiled, our thoughts combining, hungry for the same thing. It would take at least half an hour to walk back and neither wanted to wait.

I felt Andy's hand on my upper thigh as I mounted the stairs ahead of him. I'd chosen to wear the skimpy summer dress I'd bought in Blackpool (at the time thinking, like many other impulsive buys, it would never get worn). All I wanted was to tear every inch of clothing from our bodies, allowing our flesh to meld into one as soon as possible. Andy's needs were different to mine and I gave way to his domination of patience, allowing him to very slowly and very deliberately remove first the skimpy dress, then the equally skimpy bra and panties. The fact that I'd moved from being a size 10 when we'd first met to a borderline size 14, was immaterial, I felt beautiful and sexy and I sensed my husband felt the same.

With the window thrown wide open, the warm breeze carrying scents of newly cut grass and wild rose blossom, we made passionate love, reaching heights of ecstasy I'd never experienced before. Finally, relaxed with satisfaction and without saying a word, we chose to stay bonded together in the one bed – in readiness for whatever our mood demanded in the early hours.

With a feeling of absolute contentment, my arms wrapped around Andy's waist as he snored softly into the night, I realized for certain, I could never go back to the life I had before.

Chapter 7

Rose Cottage – Monday Morning

I had slept till well after nine, and at some point in the night Andy had moved to the other bed. He was a big guy, over six feet and heavily built, not fat, just heavily built and after a while, he must have woken and felt cramped sharing a three-foot-wide bed. Outside, someone was whistling and the gate was being pushed open, the grating of it disturbing the morning tranquility as it stopped halfway. I rushed to the open window and leaned out, just as the young postman looked up – two faces locked in surprise and embarrassment. I grabbed at the curtain to cover my nudity and we both smiled dispelling the fluster.

'Good morning! You must be…' He scrutinized the letter he was holding then looked up again, 'Ms Kate Radcliffe?'

Frankly, I was amazed that a letter addressed to me could have found its way here so soon. 'Yes that's me', I said cautiously, 'although I'm a Mrs not a Ms.'

'Oh, that's a pity,' he said wearing a cheeky grin, 'do you want to collect it personally or shall I just push it in?'

Thankfully, Andy was still dead to the world. 'Please, just deliver the letter in the normal way.'

I moved back from the sill, allowing the curtain to pull free and heard him say, in a fake American accent, 'Yes mam, it sure is nice to see a young face in this neck o' the woods.'

Hearing the slap of the letter hitting the tiled floor, I shot down the stairs, eager to see who knew of my changed circumstances. Sheba and Minx came running to the door, rubbing and twining their bodies about my legs and meowing to be let outside. I opened the door for them and without hesitation they bounded out of sight as if they'd lived here for years. The letter was from Samantha Devreau and was reiterating what she had told me in person, mainly that *Devreau & Wilkes* would be happy to oversee the sale of Rose Cottage. Included with the letter was a brochure from the local agent that Samantha had recommended I use. I tore both in half and dropped them in the waste bin.

Carrying a tray of tea and toast, I headed back upstairs, feeling the freedom of fresh air circulating my naked body. The tray overlapped the small bedside table between the two beds and I made a mental note that after the bathroom, the bedroom was next in line for changes.

'My God! Is that the time?' Andy's voice was thick with sleep as he eyed the tray. 'I certainly need that cuppa.'

'I've always slept well here,' I said, offering him a slice of toast with his mug of tea. 'There are no streetlights so the nights are completely dark and the air is really pure. All you really need for good sleep and overall good health.'

'Yea well, I'm not so sure I agree with the quiet bit. Twice I got up in the night thinking I heard someone in that locked room. Tonight I want it unlocked and the door left wide open.'

'Come now, Andy; don't tell me the tough copper is getting spooked by creaking floorboards. It's only the cottage cooling down after the heat of the day. It's always done that and I don't notice it anymore. I have noticed a few floorboards that creak and they probably need replacing but don't worry it'll all get done eventually.'

Neither of us spoke while we munched through the toast and drank the tea. Andy then turned to me and asked, 'Was I dreaming or what? I thought I heard the gate being pushed open.'

I told him it was the postman delivering junk mail. Then asked, 'What would you like to do today?'

'Well, I was thinking we could have a drive over to Totnes today or tomorrow and maybe catch up with Pete, it's been awhile since I've seen him.'

'I was hoping you were going to say, lets have a lazy day today, after all we haven't seen much of each other either and you need to catch up on your sleep.' I slipped in beside him, the warmth of his body touching mine making me tingle with anticipation.

An hour later and we were sharing the bathroom, both in agreement that any thought of renting would have to wait until at least the bathroom was sorted. Whilst the agreeable mood persisted, I suggested again that we stay put for the day, trying one of the local pubs for dinner that evening. The provisions I'd bought were for breakfasts and snacks only, and knowing how healthy our appetites would be by the end of the day, a sandwich just wouldn't satisfy the hunger. Andy nodded his agreement but stated firmly that Tuesday would be his last chance to see Pete.

'You go, love. Catch up with your buddy. I've got a dozen and one things I can get on with here. Besides, it wouldn't really be fair leaving Sheba and Minx shut up for the day after the long journey confined to their baskets. You know they really love the freedom of being here. At Mum's they couldn't go out because of that bloody dog opposite and even at home, as you know Sheba was always nervous about going out. Here, it's a job getting either of them to come inside.'

'We'll decide this evening, OK? See how today develops and what we get done. I think you should phone your mum though, let her know what's happening and when you'll be back.'

'I was going to phone her today anyway. She needs to be clear on the fact that I intend to keep the cottage and the money aunt Winifred left me will pay for the refurbishments.'

* * *

Monday Afternoon

We lay on our backs in the shade of the hedge feeling the soft blanket of grass beneath us, our arms and legs tingling from the criss-crossing of scratches. Working together we'd managed to bring the garden back into some semblance of order. The most arduous task had been tackling the overgrown hedge. Unlike yesterday, when I'd made a tentative go at snipping here and there, we'd done the job properly; cutting out thorny tendrils that snaked in all directions, robbing the lawn of light and nutrients and encroaching on beds where weaker perennials were being choked to death. It had been hard work but well worth the effort and although Andy would never admit it, I could see he was enjoying having a 'proper' garden once more.

Back home in Halifax, when we first got married we rented a flat on the ground floor of an Edwardian house. For me, its best feature was the large garden. There were no hard and fast rules to the garden's maintenance but all the tenants just pitched in and kept it nice because it was a delight to have it. Having the facility to dry the washing outdoors, having get togethers with neighbours at spontaneous barbecues or just simply sitting in the fresh air at the end of a hard day was most enjoyable. After a couple of years however, we realized that paying rent was just pouring money down the drain. We felt that our best option was to buy a place nearer to town and large enough to accommodate the family we both wanted. The postage-stamp of a garden that came with the newly built, three bedroomed house, was concreted over before we even moved in. The house didn't come with a garage nor any off-road parking and the garden was the only place we could squeeze in our cars. At the time it didn't seem to matter, there was a park five minutes walk away, we didn't have the cats and we certainly didn't have the time to spend cutting grass and trimming hedges – the mortgage-lender saw to that.

I rolled onto my belly, head resting on elbows ready to voice the question I'd been aching to ask my husband. 'Andy?'

Without opening his eyes, or his mouth, he emitted a long, slow, 'mmmm.'

'What are you thinking?'

He opened one eye and turned it on me, the slightest hint of a smile on his lips. 'I'm not thinking anything. I'm just feeling totally relaxed for the first time in ages. Why? Surely, you're not angling for another round of love-making after all the work we've just done?'

I leaned into him and brushed my lips lightly on his cheek, whispering, 'I suppose I can wait till this evening.' He opened his eyes fully and I smiled saying, 'We could improve our lives you know and have this all the time. Shall we move in here?'

I watched as his facial expression changed from languid to serious thoughtfulness then it broke into a dismissive laugh. 'Come on,

Kate, we've got responsibilities. We've got careers, a mortgage to pay. You can't just up-sticks and walk away from that, we're not kids fresh out of college.'

'Surely our first responsibility is to ourselves? We've been given a rare opportunity to enhance our lives. We can move in here and rent the house out in Halifax. Believe me we'll easily cover the mortgage and even make a profit because the annual income from a permanently rented three bedroomed house, close to schools and in a thriving built up area will be easier to obtain than a short term holiday let cottage which will need an agent to manage because we are too far away.'

'And our careers, Babe, the pensions we've paid into?'

'You can apply for a transfer to the Devon and Cornwall Constabulary. Look at the times when you've attended national conferences, you always maintain that policing in this area is less stressful and the coppers are much more laid back and happier because of it. Pete's a prime example, he loves his job but he always has time for the important things in life.'

'What about your teaching, Kate, I know there's been a lot of changes in the education system, not all of them good but…'

'I hate it!' I fired back, annoyed that he hadn't even been aware of my changing attitude towards my job over the last few years. 'Every year there are more changes, more pressures and less time for adjustment. I'm starting to resent the job I once loved. Teachers, especially those like me who are involved with kids with special needs, are just throwing in the towel. All I ask, is that you give it some serious thought and talk it over with Pete tomorrow.'

Suddenly, Minx came bounding over, a mouse dangling from her jaws and Sheba hot on her tail. They ran towards the open door of the cottage and we shot after them, calling for them to stop. By the time we caught up, the prey had been dropped and Minx was batting it with one paw, eager to continue the game of cat chasing mouse. I grabbed the two cats as Andy bent to pick up the seemingly dead creature, but quick as a flash it came to life and shot into the gaping cottage door. More scratches were added to my arms as the cats squirmed and squealed to be set free.

'Shall I let the cats find it?' I asked, 'I don't like the thought of mice indoors.'

'It's a bank vole, not a mouse. We must have disturbed it when we were clearing the brambles on the sloping edge of the garden. The cats will kill it for no good reason apart from, well that's what cats do. Don't worry, It won't stay indoors for long, it'll find a way to get back to it's natural habitat. We'll just leave the door open and keep an eye on the cats. I'm ready for a cuppa aren't you?'

'Yep, I sure am.' What I was also sure of, now was not the time to continue our discussion on the merits of moving to Devon. Although I knew with every fibre of my being that it was the best thing for us, Andy's way was to spend plenty of time mulling things over without being pressured.

* * *

Monday Evening

A stiff breeze ruffled the trees and hedgerows, as we headed back from the Drum Inn, a popular eating place in Cockington village. The food had been wholesome and delicious, the atmosphere laid-back and friendly. By the time we'd walked there, we had both been ravenous and had easily managed a three-course dinner, washed down with a bottle of Merlot and finished off with brandy and coffee.

There was little said as hand-in hand we strolled along the unlit narrow lanes towards Chelston. Every now and then we commented on a certain building or a certain garden when the shy moon, peeping out from the gathering cloud, allowed us to see. Twice we stopped for a long lingering kiss, neither of us saying a word, but I knew Andy was thinking the same as me; it felt as though the clocks had been turned back to our courting days and we were falling in love all over again!

No sooner had we turned the key in the cottage door, the cats were there, scratching and mewling to get outside, haughty with indignation that they'd been confined to the kitchen for the evening with litter-trays in case of need. They shot between us and disappeared in the dark gloom of the undergrowth and we both knew, no matter how long we called and no matter how much we searched, there'd be no getting them indoors tonight.

'Do you think the vole will have found it's way out?' I asked, 'I don't want to be sharing the bedroom with any other beast but my husband.'

Andy smiled, 'I feel sure that the vole is long gone and that Minx and Sheba have done their best in rooting it out. It'll be aware now that they are about and will probably have moved it's nesting place further down the bank. Anyway I'm more concerned with the creaking in the smaller bedroom but like I said earlier, I'll leave the door open to equalize the temperatures tonight. I think the weather forecast is for rain tomorrow. That's just my luck after arranging to see Pete.'

Eventually we climbed into the same bed, a given that another session of lovemaking was on the cards. Somewhere between the kisses becoming more ardent and giving myself up to the pleasures of the flesh, Andy asked me if I'd remembered to phone Mum?

I paused. Everything stopped. Even my breathing was put on

hold. 'What? What do you mean did I remember to phone Mum?' My mind was desperately trying to retrieve back the energy that had been allocated to my intimate parts.

'I just thought you might have phoned her to let her know I'd arrived OK and that we were staying for a few days, that's all.'

'I doubt whether she's interested one way or the other, and if she is, well the phone line runs both ways.'

We both knew it; the magic of the moment had passed and was replaced by tiredness, as Andy left my side with the excuse of opening the door of the room opposite but I knew for sure, he wouldn't be returning to my bed.

Chapter 8

Tuesday Morning – Rose Cottage

I was standing at the window of the prohibited room clutching one of Aunt Winifred's diaries in my hands. Outside the sky was bleak with bloated, black rain clouds. I held in my hands the written knowledge that I'd been searching for and a great relief was washing over me.

Andy had been the first to wake that morning. He'd arrived at my bedside holding a tray loaded with teapot, cereals and toast, an apologetic smile on his face. The apology was for letting me sleep in for so long. I remember grabbing my watch and gasping in disbelief at the length of time I'd slept – it was gone ten o'clock.

As I attacked the breakfast, eating as though half-starved, Andy ran through all that he'd done in the time he'd been up and about; expected sound bites of our daily lives: he'd showered, had breakfast, fed the cats, scrutinized the other bedroom…

Almost choking on my toast, I blurted out, 'What do you mean, scrutinized the other bedroom?' For some reason I'd felt appalled that he'd been in there rummaging around whilst I'd been sleeping.

Again in brief sound bites, as he'd already made it clear that he was anxious to get on the road to Totnes before the holiday traffic built up, I was to learn that the wooden window seat in the room, was in fact a seventeenth century chest. It's giveaway features of hasps and lock were turned to the wall and the top, as I already knew, was covered with a made-to-measure boxed cushion. Inside the chest, he'd continued, stopping my interruption by raising his hand, he'd found a mound of paperwork and a collection of diaries dating back to the nineteen-forties. He ended his revelations on a positive note, saying the chest itself is quite valuable and the paper contents would come in handy for burning the huge pile of hedge cuttings we had created in the garden.

* * *

Fat drops of rain spattered my bare arms, as I raked and clawed at the dark earth that lay beneath the rose hedge where it abutted the wall to the left of the cottage. The spade had been the most useful tool for gaining depth, slicing through roots that I knew nature would heal and replace, but once the corner of the tiny casket became visible, I knew that I needed to take more care. After a time, and I have no knowledge of how much time that was, such was my concentration on the task in hand, the top of the casket was cleared. Reaching for the watering can, which I had placed nearby in readiness for sprinkling on Aunt Winifred's ashes to allow them to blend easily with the soil, I ran a steady stream of water over the riveted plaque which had been secured in the centre of the casket, washing dirt from the letters and laying bare words that were few and heart-rending.

Rose
Child of Three Days
Angel Forever
1949

Tears competed with the steady flow of rain that ran down my face and soaked my clothing. I couldn't have got more wet if I'd jumped in the river, so I dragged the soggy cardboard box to my side, relieved that the ashes held within were contained in a polythene bag, and continued to carry out my Aunt's wishes – spreading and mingling her ashes with the soil that surrounded the casket. The pounding rain and the replacing of the mound of soil, assisted in completing the task and I was soon feeling a deep sense of satisfaction.

Somewhere in the depths of the cottage, I heard my mobile phone ringing. It was probably in the bedroom for that's where I intended to use it to phone Mum, following Andy's reminder whilst kissing me goodbye earlier. It was the second time I'd heard it whilst working under the hedge and I figured it must be Mum. I made a mental note to respond later, as I was sodden and filthy with soil and I wasn't about to spread that soil through the freshly-cleaned cottage. So before anything else, I needed to take a shower.

After rinsing off the worst of the dirt from my hair and arms, I decided to run a warm bath; partially to confirm the efficient working of the water heater and the tank but mainly to relax my back muscles after being bent for so long under the hedge. I didn't want our final evening to be spoilt by an aching back.

The sound of the overhead pounding rain muted as I slid the whole of my body beneath the lavender-scented water. A feeling of utter peace and weightlessness came over me as my breathing ceased and my heart beat strongly in my chest. In those precious, stilled moments, I knew without a shadow of doubt that this was the place I was meant to be. The place where my deepest desires could be fulfilled. I surfaced with a splutter to find the rain easing off and then stopping. In the suddenness of the quiet, another sound could be heard, a scratching sound in the wall, low down near the sink. Then there was a shrieking meow from Minx, followed by a howl from Sheba. I'd shut them in the scullery earlier with their food and dirt tray, the last thing I needed was a game of *hunt the cats* in the pouring rain. They were blatantly showing their displeasure at being confined.

With Andy's huge bathrobe wrapped around me, I padded through to the adjoining room, stopping dead, flabbergasted at the scene before me. The cats had clawed their way through a hole in the bottom of the wall, pulling clear the piece of rotting skirting board that had covered it. Minx, the slimmer of the two had managed to squeeze through the hole and Sheba, anxious to follow, had become stuck half in and half out of the jagged opening. Looking around in panic, I dragged open a drawer, which I knew held a variety of household paraphernalia. I tugged at a claw hammer, and frustratingly untangled it from an unravelled ball of string. There'd been water seeping in from somewhere and it took no time at all to wrench the remaining skirting from the wall. This didn't help the fact that Sheba was still stuck and was becoming more distressed.

'Shush, sweetheart, I'll soon have you free,' I said soothingly, stroking her rump and trying my best to flatten the fur and pull her out. Her response told me that it was too painful and that I'd have to think again. I ran back into the bathroom, found the area on the wall that corresponded to the hole in the scullery and prised off a panel of wood that was fixed underneath the sink. That also came away easily, revealing a large damp patch on the wall. This was where the leaking had occurred. Probably Aunt Winifred had accidentally allowed the sink to overflow on more than one occasion.

With both cats now wailing in unison, I had no choice but to hammer away like a person possessed, grateful that the rot was now exposed and that the piping was surface mounted. I was sure that all would be put to right once a new bathroom was installed and gave the crumpling wall one last almighty thump with the blunt end of the hammer. That did it. I pulled away the rubble and Minx walked calmly out of the opening, her fur covered in dust and cobwebs. From the bathroom side, I set to work widening the hole for Sheba and within minutes she too was free, seeming none the worse for her ordeal.

Above my head the phone rang again and I realized I didn't have a clue what time of day it was. My watch was upstairs with my phone, the clock in the sitting room stilled and quiet, as it no doubt had been in months. My stomach told me it was way past lunchtime and soon Andy would be back, and the place looked a mess. Still in his bathrobe and with my hair hanging like wet rats' tails I began clearing up, frantically sweeping the rubble onto the panel of wood I'd prised from below the sink. Suddenly, I stopped. Was I seeing things…? There, in the rubble, reflecting the dim light from the ceiling, was a ring. A ring of shiny gold and glossy black enamel. A ring with a skeleton engraved around its shank. In a trancelike state I slipped it in turn on my fingers, it fitting perfectly on the third finger of my right hand. Inside the ring I could see engraved words and numbers but needing a brighter light to read them, I ran towards the kitchen.

Suddenly, I heard the sound of a car stopping outside the cottage, then I heard the gate being pushed open to a grinding halt, followed by footsteps walking up the path to the front door. I pulled open the door, expecting to see Andy, happy and excited to show off my find. Confusion descended. Before me stood a uniformed policewoman, a comical look of surprise on her face.

'Yes, can I help you?' I asked, my mind still in a turmoil following all the activity. Erroneously thinking she'd come to claim the ring from me.

'Good afternoon, are you Mrs Kate Radcliffe, wife of Sergeant Andrew Radcliffe?'

'Yes...yes, why? He'll be back soon. He's a policeman too you know.' I was babbling. I knew something was wrong but I didn't want to hear it. I twisted the ring around and around on my finger plucking up the courage to ask. 'What's happened?'

'May I come in please, Mrs Radcliffe?'

The cats shot out between us, as if unable to cope with the delivery of bad news. I wanted to follow them and hide in one of the bushes until everything returned to normal. I held the door open wide, whilst closing the bathrobe tight about my waist. With the creeping numbness of reality filling my head, I led the policewoman to the kitchen table.

Chapter 9

I was lost in a world of disbelief as Francis, Pete's wife, sat beside me looking perfectly turned out, as usual. She was trying her best to make conversation but gave up as it dawned on her that I hadn't yet come to terms with the fact that my husband was fighting for his life. Somewhere in the depths of the hospital, Andy was stretched out and unconscious. I still hadn't been allowed to see him.

The policewoman, I can't recall her name, who had delivered the tragic news to my door, had long-since left. On the drive to the hospital, she'd tried her best to explain what had happened, according to several witnesses. *Andrew* had been involved in a terrible road incident. I didn't correct her on *Andy's* name, I remained staring blankly at the passing traffic, piecing together the horrific scenario as she explained what had happened. He was returning back to me when somewhere near Berry Pomeroy on the Totnes Road, he'd apparently signalled a right turn for the junction ahead. Moving in tandem with him was an articulated lorry, laden with felled pine logs. It seems that the lorry driver's intention was to go straight ahead but as it rounded the curve of the roundabout, it swayed and skidded out of control, jack-knifing and spilling its load in the process. Andy just happened to be in the wrong place at the wrong time. It was just a freak road accident and no one was really to blame. These words, just as the earlier ones, had been spoken gently but without pity or emotion. I'd turned to her, my confused, horror-struck expression prompting her to explain further. The downpour after the long period of hot, dry weather had made the road slippery with grease and it was a miracle more people weren't hurt. When the words *hurt* and *rushed to hospital,* penetrated into my numbed brain, I turned on her demanding, 'So he is alive?'

'Yes, Kate, that's why I'm driving you to the hospital,' she'd said, with a look that read, *has this woman understood a single word I've just said.*

Without realizing it, I'd been twisting the newly-found ring around and around on my finger. The policewoman's assurance that Andy was still alive had filled me with hope. But that hope was diminishing with each passing hour.

Francis returned with yet another cup of tea – the last one, barely touched, stood abandoned and cold in its paper cup on a narrow shelf behind us. She smiled as she handed over the steaming brown liquid, and once again tried to assure me that Andy would come through this. 'He's a fighter!' she exclaimed 'He has a lot to live for!'

The worry and frustration of being left to sit around without any information caused my anger to flare. 'Francis, he's unconscious and completely unaware of anything; how can he bloody fight, for all I know he could already be dead!' Heads turned in our direction and Francis bowed her head with embarrassment.

'I'm sorry, I'm so sorry, Francis,' I said, 'I know you mean well, but why won't they let me see him? I've been here for ages, I just need to see him and hold his hand and maybe then he'll wake up. I just don't know what else I can do.' I dropped my head in my hands, ashamed of my lack of control.

'I'll ring Pete, see if he can find out any news and when you're likely to be able to see Andy. I know he's keeping in touch directly with the Neurology Department. I'll have to slip outside to make the call, drink the tea, love, it will help, I've loaded it with plenty of sugar.'

I hadn't taken sugar in tea since I was a teenager, but I did as I was told, slowly sipping the vile-tasting liquid and waiting for the effect of its help.

Suddenly I remembered that Sheba and Minx were still in the garden. Yes, the tea was a great help, I had even more to be concerned about now. My nerves were shot to pieces, and unconsciously, I swivelled the newly-found ring on my finger, only now seeming to notice that it was there. I slipped it off and walked over to a stark-white fluorescent light, to read the inscription within the ring.

Absent but for a Tyme ob AR 3 Feb 1707

My mind was adjusting to what my eyes were seeing. A R – Andrew Radcliffe? *Absent but for a tyme*. Was the ring trying to tell me something? Was it letting me know that all would be well? That this nightmare would soon end and life would return to normal.

The automatic door swung open and Francis entered looking flustered. I braced myself for more bad news as I slipped the ring back on my finger.

'I doubt very much you'll get to see him until the morning, Kate. There's a whole raft of tests that have to be done before he can be admitted to the ICU ward. Apparently, the trauma to his head has caused some internal bleeding and swelling, but the injuries to the rest of his body are superficial. But as I say, there are more tests to be done. I suggest you stay with us tonight, love, get some sleep and I'll run you back here tomorrow morning.'

'Thank you for the offer, Francis. I really do appreciate all the help that you and Pete are giving me but I need to get back to the cottage. Sheba and Minx are in the garden and there's no way they can get back inside the cottage. Reception have taken my mobile number. If I hear any more news to add to what Pete's already been given, I'll let you know. I'll return to the hospital tomorrow morning using the bus service from the village.'

Francis, took both my hands in hers. 'Well if you're quite sure, Kate, but at least let me drop you off at the cottage before I head back to Totnes.'

***

Rose Cottage

The rain had stopped by the time I was dropped off at the cottage. Sheba and Minx emerged from the hedge, purring and rubbing their damp fur against my legs as I rummaged in my bag for the door key. Once inside, it was though a comfort blanket had been thrown around me. It was after midnight, the day had been physically hard and mentally torturous, but along with the tiredness, a calmness had settled which allowed me to feel that I could deal with anything. Anything at all.

On checking, I could see that my phone was desperately in need of charging. There were several missed calls to deal with along with two messages – all having to wait until morning when the phone would be fully charged. Making sure of hearing any calls made from the hospital, I unplugged the bedside lamp and used that socket for the charging before slipping under the lightweight cover and closing my eyes.

I must have dropped off in minutes. I don't remember anything until I awoke with a start as pressure on my lower limbs was suddenly lifted and a slight thud, then another, resounded up the right side of the bed. It was pitch dark. I reached for my phone and flipped open the cover, the soft glow of light allowing me to see Sheba's hind quarters as she disappeared out of the bedroom door. The time was five-twenty and the phone was ninety-seven percent charged. I lay down again, waiting for the soft padding of two sets of paws to descend the stairs. Instead, I heard the sound of clawing coming from the room opposite. I was up in a flash, hollering my displeasure as I witnessed the pair tearing at the daybed's upholstery with their front claws.

'Get out of here!' I screamed. 'This room is prohibited to you!' I chased the pair of them down the stairs, dropping the latch on the door at the bottom, such was my anger at their invasion of this most private space. It was my own fault, in my exhausted state I must have left the interior doors open, allowing the cats to wander freely. I'll need to be more careful in the future.

The incident had brought me fully awake. There'd been no calls from the hospital and the buses wouldn't be running for hours yet, so once again I entered the prohibited room and closed the door behind me. The backward-facing chest beckoned. I removed the cushion and lifted the lid, staring down at the row of spine-labelled-diaries. The one I'd flipped through yesterday was dated 1949/50. It hadn't taken me long to find the information I needed, the location *for the burial of my aunt's ashes*. But now, my curiosity was burning to discover more; a strong need to learn more about the woman who had left me her home and all her worldly possessions; dismissing outright Andy's suggestion that I burn the paperwork. I slid out the very first volume, a fatter and more thumbed through version than the others. The date on the spine showed 1940/42, and as I fanned through, I could see that this one had obviously been used more regularly and for longer periods. Remembering to lock the door, I carried it back with me to bed. After unplugging the phone and reinserted the bedside lamp, I had enough light to see the words written seventy-four years ago.

November 1940

I've just received the most terrible news. Charles is missing and presumed dead after a planned assault that went terribly wrong. I can't bear the thought of it; my adorable husband lying in a God-forsaken foreign land, dead or dying of his injuries.

London has become like hell on earth. Night after night bombs are raining down from the sky, destroying everything in their path. To cap it all, Oliver has agreed to join the ranks. No doubt he'll be lost to me also before this war is over. Thank God that John and Ethel are in the relative safety of the countryside.

I've decided to leave London and run far away from the noise, dust, death and the uncertainty of life. I have found a position advertised in the Daily Mail, and, on finishing this entry, I intend to write for an appointment and apply for an interview.

Lifting my eyes from the page I felt a deep empathy for the loss and suffering that my aunt was describing, voicing the feelings, 'Poor Aunt Winifred, she couldn't have been married for more than a few months.'

Needing to read more, I feverishly turned to the next page and out slipped a neatly folded newspaper cutting. It was a brief two liner advertisement from the classified section of the newspaper my aunt had alluded to.

Housekeeper / Secretary required. Reply to: Mr D Grimshaw
Apple Cottage, Old Mill Road, Chelston, Torquay, Devon.

The diary was not a diary in the truest sense – each page printed with the given date – it was simply a hard-backed note book containing faintly lined pages. The only wording, was that of Aunt Winifred's hand.

The next entry was a week before Christmas of the same year. The interview must have gone well because Aunt Winifred was arriving at Apple Cottage with all she owned in a single suitcase. Before settling in to read fully the half page of writing, I decided to go down to the kitchen and make a pot of tea to ease the onset of a growing thirst. Halfway down the stairs I was halted by the ringing of my phone, breaking my mental connection to the past and dragging me back to my own personal tragedy of the present.

It was Pete, apologising for the early call, but wanting to assure me that Andy was on the ICU ward and that I could now visit him.

'Has he regained consciousness?' I asked, forgetting my manners and failing to thank him for all he'd done.

A short silence. 'No. I'm sorry, Kate. The doctor, who is also senior consultant of the Neurological Department' – I heard the sound of papers being shuffled, – 'yes here we are a Dr Murray will advise on the prognosis and how long Andy is expected to be in his current comatose state. I think it's only fair to warn you though, Kate, that he'll be needing intensive care for some time, which means he'll be grounded in Torbay indefinitely.'

Chapter 10

Torbay Hospital – Wednesday Morning

After a twenty minute wait in the corridor, whilst two nurses and a consultant carried out their procedural duties on Andy, I was allowed to see him. I wasn't sure what to expect. Images of cuts, bruises, bandages and tubes had all passed through my imagination, sea-sawing between horrific to bearable, but as I looked down on the man I loved with all my heart, an overriding impression dominated; an impression that *Andy* was no longer here. The apparatus's rhythmic noises were hypnotic and the complexity of the given information, awe-inspiring, it was just as I'd seen in many a film. But this was no film, this was real and I had to accept the fact that our lives could be dramatically changed forever. My fingers fumbled and twisted the ring on my right hand, the words of the inscription uppermost in my mind, *Absent but for a tyme.* Five simple words that gave immeasurable hope.

After some time, I've no idea how long, I'd been mentally flitting here and there imagining different scenarios, a nurse popped her head around the door of the small ward and asked cheerfully if everything was all right? I know she meant well and for her own sake she needed to keep an emotional distance from her patients, but her choice of words were insensitive to say the least and I had to hold back from saying so, asking instead when it would be possible to speak with Dr Murray?

She checked the bright orange, rubberised fob watch suspended from her tunic, 'I'm afraid Dr Murray won't be available for about an hour. When he's finished his rounds, I'll point out that you're here and would like a word.'

Not sure what to do for the next hour, but in desperate need to fill the time positively, I wandered outside and found a wooden bench well away from the traffic noise of cars looking desperately for somewhere to park. I couldn't put it off any longer. I had to phone Mum.

The ringing went on for ages, and I was caught between relief and disappointment, resigned to moving on to the next call that needed to be made. Then a breathless voice, Liz's not Mum's. 'Yes?', she asked in that commanding way she always used when answering the phone.

'Hi Liz, it's Kate. Is Mum there?'

'Course she's here where else would she be? And she's worried sick about you, expecting me to drive all the way to bloody Devon to find out what's going on. You've got a mobile, Kate, why don't you bloody-well use it?'

I could hear Mum suddenly enter from the garden, calling out, 'Who is it? Is it Kate?' The sound became muffled, Liz had obviously placed a hand over the receiver and told her I was on the other end whilst handing her the phone.

'Why the hell haven't you been answering my calls, young lady? I've been worried sick thinking that something terrible had happened.'

'Something terrible *has* happened Mum. Andy was involved in a road accident yesterday. I'm at the hospital now. He's lying in a coma!'

'Oh no! I'm so sorry to hear that love. What about you? Were you injured?'

'No, I wasn't in the car, Andy was visiting an old friend in Totnes, he was on his way back when…'

'Perhaps if you'd been with him…', she cut in before stopping abruptly.

'Yea, we might both be lying in a coma!'

'That's not what I meant and you know it. I meant that two pairs of eyes can be better that one.'

'Mum, Andy is the safest driver I know. He's a police sergeant and has advanced driving certificates. It was a wet road and a lorry jackknifed on the offside spilling its load. I'm sure if I had been in the car at the time, I wouldn't be talking to you now.'

'So what happens now? I expect they'll have to transfer him to a hospital closer to Halifax, won't they?'

'I'll be speaking with the head neurological doctor soon, but my guess is they won't move him in the immediate future, it's too risky. If that's the case, I'll get the train back to Halifax and load up our personal stuff and drive back in my car. Andy's car is a total write-off.'

'But you could be down there for the whole of the summer holidays, what about your house here? I suppose you could get one of Andy's colleagues to keep an eye on it for you.'

'It's early days yet, Mum, and I'm only just coming to terms with what's happened. I'll keep in touch, OK, but remember, I'll be at the hospital a lot of the time and I'm not allowed to use my mobile phone inside there. Give Gemma a big kiss from me. I'll keep you informed about when I'll be arriving back. Bye Mum.'

Dr Murray, a tall balding man who appeared to be in his mid to late sixties, greeted me with a warm squeeze of my hand and a sincere apology that I'd had to wait for so long on being brought up-to-date on Andy's prognosis.

'The simple fact of the matter,' he responded when asked bluntly what were Andy's chances of a full recovery, 'We don't honestly know as yet.' He went on to say, more or less, what Pete had already told me, adding that they would know more after test results came through and more monitoring was carried out.

I felt helpless, unsure of what to do next. 'Is there anything I can do to help? I know he can't be moved, but can I bring in his own pyjamas, toiletries and help in any other way?'

'It's natural, my dear, for you to want to help any way you can, but my advice would be to allow his nurses to administer their specialist care, and this is made easier with your husband wearing a hospital gown. Nutrients and breathing apparatus will be relied on whilst he's on the ICU ward. Although nobody knows for sure, it is possible that patients in a coma may respond to the presence of loved ones. A familiar voice or touch may have a calming or reassuring effect on the patient, and certainly can't hurt. We encourage as much bedside contact from family members as possible, as long as it doesn't interfere with medical care. Playing a patient's favourite music could also be helpful. The main rule of thumb is to be sure that contact from family members at the bedside does not lead to increased agitation, which can occur if the patient is semi aware and frustrated by their inability to communicate or express themselves.'

We shook hands once more and I returned to the hypnotic sounds of the apparatus. The morning visiting period was almost at an end and I wondered what I was going to do until this evening.

* * *

Wednesday Afternoon – Rose Cottage

I'd arrived back from the hospital in a daze. I automatically fed the cats, made a cup of tea, swept floors; all accomplished on automatic pilot – my mind lost in a darkened place. I needed something to stop me falling deeper and deeper into the pit of despair. I knew only too well where it could lead. After Dad died, the same dark place had held me captive for months. But Andy wasn't dead. Andy was only *absent for a tyme* and I needed to hold on to that fact with all my strength.

Provisions, such as, milk, bread, eggs and the like were now needed. Something to keep me going through the long hours ahead, but the sudden spark of activity, just as suddenly, dwindled and died. My appetite was gone, put on hold along with everything else in my life and the last thing I needed was to be among other women shoppers, happily going about the simplicities of their daily lives.

Instead, I took myself into the prohibited room, removed Andy's pillows from his bed and made myself comfortable on the daybed, breathing in his left-behind aroma. Then I opened my aunt's diary and continued reading from where I'd left off earlier that morning – this entry was made a month later than the previous one.

18th December 1940

I'd replied to the advertisement by letter and had fully expected to have been interviewed by Mr Grimshaw before being accepted, but a response, by letter, had arrived a week later stating the position was mine and that if possible, I could start my new position, the week before Christmas.

To be honest, it was a great relief to be leaving this broken city at such a time. I was in no mood for celebrating and what little family I had left, were too distant to visit. Quite frankly, even if I'd wanted to, I didn't have the funds for gallivanting.

I was met at the station by Mr Grimshaw himself. A man in his middle years, short and slight of build, with a quietness about him that instantly put me at ease, for I was very nervous. He asked if I minded walking the distance to the cottage, which, he stressed wasn't too far. Walking to my new position of work with my employer carrying my suitcase was the last thing I'd expected, but as it turned out, it gave me the chance to unwind from my nervousness and the opportunity to gain knowledge of my surroundings, and I had the distinct feeling that this was what Mr Grimshaw had intended.

On reaching the cottage, I was shown my room and left to unpack, Mr Grimshaw declaring that he would make tea and a light refreshment for me. I tried to argue against this, saying that surely it was my place to be doing for him, but he'd smiled shyly and with a slight shrug of his shoulders, indicated that I first settle into my room.

The room was a small but adequate space, furnished with a single bed, a 3ft hanging robe and a chest below the window which doubled as a seat. There was no sign of a desk for me to carry out my secretarial duties and when I asked about this on my return downstairs, I was informed that the large kitchen table would prove adequate for the task, especially with the use of one of its drawers for paper and pens. It suddenly dawned on me that there was no typewriter. The cottage was indeed small, but once I'd been informed that Mr Grimshaw would be absent from it from Monday morning until Friday evening of each week, I felt reassured, especially when I learned that the whole weekend was mine to do as I pleased.

My duties during his absence were simply to keep the cottage clean and ordered and tend to all paperwork that arrived via post, filing them in a neat and tidy fashion and writing any due cheques for payment of household services, which would be signed by Mr Grimshaw on his return. Provisions would be delivered twice weekly and I was given free reign as to what was needed. The monthly salary I was to be paid was more than generous considering I had no outgoings such as food, rent or meters to feed.

On the surface, all seemed fine and dandy. But, for the next seven days, I would be sharing this same small space with a man who was to all intents and purposes, a total stranger. I knew nothing about him. Nothing of how he earned his living and nothing about his background. In my letter of application, not only had I given a full account of my accomplishments in gaining merits in English and acquiring a post of governess to three children, and the only reason I wasn't currently employed was because the children had been evacuated to a safer part of the country, I'd also written of my circumstances regarding Charles.

Feeling tired from the long journey, lonely and grieving from the loss of my darling Charles and uncertain about what the future held, I began to wonder if I was up to what was expected of me. Then I thought of all the brave young souls that had given up their lives fighting for the freedom of this beautiful land and I knew I would have to lay aside this fearful self-indulgence and soldier on.

Resisting the urge to jump to Aunt Winifred's next entry, I marked the page with a slip of paper from the pad I kept by my bed, and tucked the diary back in the chest. On another slip of paper, I made a list of what I needed to do before my evening visit to the hospital. First on the list was finding someone to feed the cats whilst I was away – travelling back by train wouldn't be fair on me or the cats, should I take them with me. The weather had turned cooler and damper and the clothes I had with me weren't really adequate but I wasn't about to go wasting money on unnecessaries when I had two bulging wardrobes of clothes back in Halifax.

I layered up as best I could, opened the cottage door and allowed the cats to squeeze by me. An elderly man walking by the cottage stopped to watch as they scampered towards their favourite place in the undergrowth. He stayed where he was until I'd closed the gate and then he fell in line with me as I headed towards the small supermarket in Chelston.

We both smiled as he asked if I was on holiday? 'No,' I replied, 'I'm the new owner of the cottage, and I'll be moving in as soon as I can, my name is Kate Radcliffe.'

'Ah, Winifred's great niece. She'll rest easy knowing the cottage isn't being sold off for the sole pleasure of holidaymakers.'

'Did you know Aunt Winifred well?'

'She was a very private person, but we shared a common interest, so you could say I knew her more than anyone else in these parts, anyone still breathing that is. He held out his hand to be shook, 'Fred Wilson, I'm happy to make your acquaintance, Kate.'

'What was the common interest? Was it gardening?'

'No, I can't stand gardening! I do have a bit of a garden but since my Betty died, she was the gardener of the family, a neighbour of mine keeps it tidy through the growing months. Like you, I have two cats and the garden's mainly for their benefit.'

I seized on the opportunity and bold as brass I said, 'I'm looking for someone to keep an eye on my cats for a few days while I take a necessary journey by train. Do you know of anybody close by who does that sort of thing. If I put them in a cattery I know they'll hate it and refuse to eat.'

'Ah, I know what you mean. Different with dogs, mind. But when it comes to cats they need their own territory. Better to have someone come in and feed them rather than shift them to the unfamiliar. Besides, I don't care much for such places,' Fred gave a dismissive shake of the head. 'They charge a fortune, even though as you say the animals are distressed and rarely need feeding.'

I could see the small supermarket looming ahead as Fred got into his chatty stride. Interrupting his flow on the merits of the independence of cats verses the dependent needs of dogs, I cut in, 'I'm happy to pay such a person, Fred. I just wondered if there was anyone you could recommend?' He remained silent for a while and I thought I'd ruined the opportunity by being too pushy but then he stopped and turned, wearing the sweetest of smiles.

'The only person I could recommend is myself and I wouldn't dream of charging for such a neighbourly act. Round these parts we have an understanding. We look after our own, and I have a feeling that if ever I needed help, you'd do the same for me.'

We parted company at Fred's front gate but not before promising to let him know my plans just as soon as I'd checked the train times. As I shook his hand once more with gratitude, he asked, 'Aren't you curious about that common interest that me and your great aunt shared?'

'Must be cats, right?'

'No! Oh no, Winifred hated cats, wouldn't have them near the place. What we shared was a love of history. She was a very knowledgable lady you know but when it came to these parts, local history,' he tapped his temple with two fingers, 'I could fill in the gaps of her knowledge.'

In the supermarket I loaded my basket with cat food, milk, bread, eggs and a couple of cartons of soup. The desire for rich food and alcohol had left me, my body obviously aware that such foods would prove burdensome in my present state. Soup with fresh bread would suffice before heading out to the railway station to check the times, thus completing all that was on my written list.

* * *

I was back at the hospital and nothing had changed. The rhythmic, hypnotic sounds of the apparatus helping to keep Andy in the land of the living, giving out the same level of information as earlier. After gently kissing his forehead I sat by the bed and held his hand in both of mine. Again that overriding feeling persisted, *Andy,* wasn't there.

It was embarrassing to begin with and it felt as though I was having a one-way conversation with a mannequin, but remembering Dr Murray's advise, I swallowed hard and persisted with my slow deliberation. I began by telling him how much I loved him and missed him but then the embarrassment took over and I fell silent for a while. Then I began talking again, just regurgitating thoughts that flooded into my head. I found myself relaying all that had taken place that afternoon and what I was planning to do over the coming week. I was part way through telling Andy about Fred and how he'd offered to feed the cats whilst I was in Halifax, when Pete walked into the ward carrying a bunch of flowers.

Ceasing the one-way conversation, I stood to greet him. 'It's nice of you to come, Pete, what lovely flowers. It's a shame that Andy can't appreciate them.'

He kissed my cheek before saying, 'The flowers are for you Kate, Fran's attempt to cheer up the cottage whilst you're there alone. Are you sure you won't come and stay with us for a while? It's no problem bringing the cats. Sheppy, as you know is very docile.'

'Thanks for the offer, Pete, and thank Francis for the flowers. What I really would appreciate however, is for you to visit Andy as much as possible until I return from Halifax. And on your visits could you talk to him? Dr Murray believes that could help. I'm getting the train back to Halifax tomorrow. I need to get more clothes and personal stuff down here as well as my car. Plus, I'm giving in my notice at work and I'd prefer to do that in person. I'll also pop in and see Andy's Superintendent, bring him up to date with what's happening.'

'You don't think you're being a bit hasty, Kate? I don't mean to sound negative but if Andy came out of the coma tomorrow, it's impossible to say when, or even if, he'll be fit enough to return to work. I'd hang onto your career if I were you. They're duty bound to allow you extra time off on compassionate leave.'

'I'm not happy in the job, Pete. I haven't been for ages. Andy and I were considering relocating down here. So regardless of when, or if, Andy is capable of returning to work, we'll be in a better place and a better situation to deal with whatever's in store.'

He placed a hand on my shoulder and squeezed. 'Like I said, Kate, it's early days and I have seen a number of cases like this. Give it a month or so before doing anything drastic. Your family is miles away from here and you may become more dependent on them than you realise. Andy and I have been friends for years and as I was the one he'd been visiting when this tragedy happened, I feel a certain responsibility towards you. To be honest with you, Andy and I talked at length on the *pros and cons* of him transferring to The Devon and Cornwall Constabulary, and he came to the conclusion that it wasn't really the best thing to do.'

I watched as Pete walked slowly from the ward, turning and raising a hand before he disappeared from sight. During the time he'd been speaking my hands had remained holding onto my husband – his hand flaccid beneath my tightening grip. I leant forward and kissed his brow again, whilst promising to visit him immediately I returned from Halifax. I also promised to love and cherish him, no matter what his condition.

Chapter 11

Friday Night – Halifax

In the short time I'd been back, which was less than forty-eight hours disregarded travelling time, I'd succeeded in setting in motion several of the life-changing options that were before me. Top of the list, I'd given in my notice, based on my unforeseen circumstances, I wouldn't be returning to my teaching position. I provided my new address to the administrative bodies for future correspondence, before swiftly moving on to the next in line – contacting Andy's superintendent. It was a great relief to learn that I'd been spared the necessity of making an appointment to see him. The super had been informed, no doubt as soon as it was revealed that the driver of the involved tragedy was one of his sergeants, and was probably as much informed as I was. He'd reassured me that Andy's salary would continue to be paid in the near future, despite the accident taking place whilst he was off duty. Not wanting to probe further into such matters today, I thanked him and moved on to the next issue, which I knew would be time consuming.

Houses in the area of our home sold successfully because the local schools are highly-rated, transport links are efficient, and most importantly, there is a lack of good quality rental properties. My local estate agent beamed with delight as I relayed what I had in mind. I was considering renting our home, fully-furnished with the option of selling to the right tenant at a later date. Mr Samson, was super efficient and it didn't take long before the paperwork was completed and we were shaking hands on the agreed rental.

Fortunately, my Ford Focus car was roomy enough to take all that I needed back to Devon in a single trip. Clothing, both of our laptops, and a variety of other personal items that I felt would be needed, were stacked neatly in our spare room, ready for loading into the car. Two large black bags were filled with unwanted stuff to be dropped at the nearest charity shop.

The entire train journey to the north had been spent reading Aunt Winifred's diaries. I'd taken three with me, which spanned a total period of about six years, not dreaming for a moment that I'd have much time covering such a period, but the more I read, the more fascinated I became. During the last two evenings, television was shunned in favour of the intrigue and snippets of her life. At the end of yesterday, exhausted after the clearing of drawers and the packing of boxes, I took a long soak in the bath and retired early with the third volume, eager to learn more of the true life drama that was unfolding.

Aunt Winifred had recently learned of the bombing of her twin brother, Oliver, who, like her husband was an RAF pilot. Unlike her husband though, the wording on the telegram was distinct and brutal. He was not missing, feared dead. He was killed fighting for his country. Gone forever! I could tell from her writing that this had hit her really hard. Her entries became spasmodic, depressing, oozing with loneliness. *I'd been in that same dark place, I knew exactly how she felt.*

After another large gap of about five weeks, her writing began to change. She started mentioning more about her employer. Mr Grimshaw, whom at this point she started referring to as Drew, was apparently becoming more friendly and more supportive towards her. In spite of their age difference of twenty-five years, I could tell that something was beginning to blossom between them. She began writing one-liners that spoke volumes. *I can hardly wait for Friday evening to arrive. I feel bereft, five whole days without his company.*

I reread the entry that had fascinated me so much the evening before.

The most interesting aspect, from my point of view, was Drew's presentation to my aunt of a chart showing her ancestry going back for many generations.

7th May 1943

It is my twenty-fourth birthday and Drew has given me the most amazing gift imaginable. A beautifully rendered chart showing my ancestry reaching back for many generations. A part-time colleague of his, who happens to be a freelance archivist, kindly researched my family tree; discovering that the Mannerings, and in particular Charles Mannering, were a rich and powerful family back in the early eighteenth century. Drew had the chart drawn up and framed by a calligrapher who specialized in such things. I was fascinated and begged to be told more about Drew's involvement with this archivist. What was the nature of the business that robbed me of his presence for five days a week?

After much badgering on my part and much hesitation on his, Drew confided that he is a member of the staff at Bletchley Park. He is part of a team working on diplomatic codes and ciphers of over 25 countries. He followed this revelation by swearing me to secrecy. I am truly amazed and extremely proud of him. I'd learned some time ago that he suffered from dyslexia, and this was the main reason for my employment. The condition, much associated with being backward, is a total misnomer, especially in Drew's case, him being recruited at Bletchley Park based on his high intelligence. Despite his condition preventing him reading and writing in the usual way, his photographic memory and the skill of pinpointing repeated letters, numbers and symbols in a given document, classifies him as indispensable for the war effort.

There was a card accompanying the chart, which was illustrated with a watercolour drawing of a white rose. The inside was blank except for three xxx. Drew has started to call me Rose, my given middle name, a name he declares as to be far more fitting than Winifred. I'd never regarded myself as beautiful, but I do declare, freely in the knowledge that Drew cannot read these words, that when we are together, I feel as though I am the most beautiful, and the most wanton, woman in the world.

I started to fall asleep with the chart on my mind, as intrigued and as fascinated as my aunt had been. However, other thoughts closer to home overshadowed the intrigue. Tomorrow, I will have to pay a visit to Mum. She regarded Saturday mornings as her free time. Free of housework, free of shopping and most importantly, free of childminding. Tomorrow, I figured, would be the perfect time to reveal our future plans.

* * *

Saturday Morning – Burnley

I'd been at Mum's barely half an hour, hardly enough time to make us a pot of tea, give her the latest news regarding Andy and how it would be some time before the medical team could predict the outcome of his injuries, when Liz's car screeched to a halt outside.

'Oh bloody 'ell, what now?' Grumbled Mum as she jumped up

from the armchair and moved to the window. Gemma was already unloaded onto the path as Liz, leaning into the car's boot, was reaching for a large bag. 'Oh! I'm not having this, I need my free time just as much as anybody else,' Mum said aloud, addressing nobody in particular, but giving me pre-warning that this was not going to be the appropriate time I'd envisaged for my revelations.

On reaching the front door, her arms filled with Gemma's necessities, Liz hollered to be let in. Mum stubbornly stayed put, her arms folded across her chest, lips pressed tightly together in a grimace that could evoke nightmares in a child as young as Gemma. So I did the honours of opening the door. Liz brushed passed me, saying, 'What you doing here?' But didn't wait for me to answer. Gemma smiled up at me, briefly brightening the darkened atmosphere of the semi-detached house.

Saturdays were usually Liz's day off from the salon, and she would spend the day at home taking care of her granddaughter while her daughter, Tracey, managed the salon and the three girls that worked there on a self-employed basis. Tracey and two of the self-employed girls had been out celebrating the night before – a hen party that had gone on till past three in the morning. Having drunk too much, danced too much and who could say whatever else was overindulged in, none of them were in any fit state for cutting, colouring or perming and the salon had several appointments for all three. Needless to say, Liz and now Mum, were non too pleased at having their days off ruined. And Mum wasn't about to play ball. She refused point blank and that refusal started an almighty row. Liz was first in the firing line as Mum drove home the fact that when she passed over the salon to Liz, it was on the proviso that she would look after Gemma three day's a week but not on a Saturday. Saturday was her free day.

Before Liz had a chance to retaliate, more accusations were thrown her way. Mum reminded her of the many warnings against the introducing of self-employed stylists and cutters, as this would only lead to them doing what they pleased, and when they pleased. The constant shouting brought on a fit of coughing, forcing Mum to stop and gasp for air. Liz seized the opportunity and responded with the excuse that self-employed staff was a much cheaper option because salons could no longer afford the overheads of permanent staff.

Then out of the blue, Liz turned and fired a question at me. 'Mum's salon is in desperate need of funds. Have you put Aunt Winifred's cottage on the market yet?'

The question hung in the air, seemingly suspended on an invisible charge of emotion. In the brief stillness, I recalled the time when Mum retired. A time when the business prospered with six staff working flat out. It was handed on a plate to Liz when Tracey left school without any qualifications apart from an introductory course on hairdressing. This thriving, ready-made business that Mum had built up over many years was given freely to them both. And I've never been offered so much as a free hair-do. I looked Liz straight in the eye, the answer coming easily. 'We're not selling the cottage. We've decided to move to Devon and rent out the house in Halifax. You've already had your inheritance from the family Liz. My turn now. Let's see if I can put it to better use.'

'You selfish little mare,' screamed Mum. 'You've only ever had yourself to think about, maybe if you'd had children...' She stopped abruptly, the hurtful remark cutting deep but I refused to show it.

Liz joined the fray. 'And what do you think Dad would think about you keeping everything to yourself?'

'I don't know who your Dad is, Liz. I was never given any information on that score. Perhaps you could ask him to help rescue your business, as far as I know, he's never contributed a penny to your upkeep.' I turned on Mum. 'Who is Liz's father, and where is he now?'

'He was a complete tosser, who left me in the lurch as soon as he got wind I was pregnant. I don't know where he is now, but I hope the bastard is rotting in hell!'

'Cheers Mum!' whimpered Liz, trying to stifle the upset of being denied her own way.

The atmosphere was charged with emotion. Liz had already stormed out of the sitting room dragging Gemma in her wake; not wanting her granddaughter to witness the wrath her Nanna was capable of, nor hear the foul language that poured from the mouth of the most senior role model of the family. I remained as calm and as quiet as a cold stone statue. Refusing to have my newly created dreams and wishes smashed to pieces; I'd made up my mind, my future was going to be of my choosing.

Chapter 12

24th September – Rose Cottage

It had been eight weeks since I'd learned of Great Aunt Winifred's death. Just a mere eight weeks and yet my life had changed so much. I was the outright owner of a property with funds to refurbish and upgrade that property. Gone was the plump, overly-stressed teacher that had felt lost and unfulfilled most of the time. I was now involved in a project of my own and for the first time I feel as though I am truly alive.

However, my husband, my Andy, is still lost to the land-of-the-living. No one has said as much at the hospital but from all that I've read, the longer a patient remains in a comatose state, the less chance there is of a full recovery. I know for sure that Andy wouldn't want to continue as he is indefinitely, being kept alive artificially. On the few occasions I'd managed to pin down Dr Murray, the prognosis had become shifting and confusing. The first tests carried out were promising, giving the neurologist hope that an operation to remove pressure from Andy's brain could be carried out quite soon, but as yet, it hasn't happened; and I'm beginning to wonder if the pressure on the funds of the National Health Service is taking priority.

Several well-wishers have informed me that it's necessary to talk things through with Andy's family. They need to share the load when the time comes for difficult decisions to be made, but Andy is an only child, his parents having to wait until their early forties before he was born. Both died in their seventies, before their son married. I didn't get the chance to meet them.

Despite what the future may hold, I find I cannot, or will not, remove the memento mori from my finger, even whilst carrying out chores that could undermine its surface. Whilst gardening, I ensure its protection by wearing thick gardening gloves and during working on lighter household chores, I wear fine latex gloves to maintain the ring's pristine condition. This overpowering need to feel in touch with the ring, to feel linked to it, continues to give me immeasurable comfort.

I am at present painting the spare bedroom, the hitherto *prohibited room,* in a beautiful shade of aqua-blue, (a reminder of the sky-reflected sea on a clear summer's day) and I am wearing a protective pair of fine latex gloves. Thanks to Matt Wilson, a local builder who happens to be the son of Fred, my cat minder, the walls of the scullery and the bathroom have been removed, allowing for better use of the space. I am now the proud owner of a well-equipped office, positioned at the far end of this space. The remaining area has been converted to a more modern, three-piece shower room, leaving space enough for a utility area large enough to house a washing machine, dryer and fridge-freezer. The kitchen and sitting room have been left intact, apart from updating the heating system and modernising the appliances. Matt and his young apprentice are carrying out the heavy building work and I am the painter, decorator and tea maker.

Standing back to admire my work, I wondered, not for the first time, who would get to use this sea-blue room? Mum and Liz had vowed never to visit the cottage, but I'm hopeful the family rift will mend and they'll reconsider once the refurbishments are completed. Moving back towards the wall, I dabbed a little more paint on the vacant picture hook, to help blend it into the wall. I'd been reluctant to pull it out, creating an ugly hole to fill. The bare wall was crying out for something special to hang there but I wasn't about to rush out and buy the first thing that took my fancy.

After reading Aunt Winifred's diaries, I discovered that it was the genealogy chart, which she had received on her twenty-fourth birthday, that had previously hung on the now empty hook. To satisfy my curiosity on its current whereabouts, I sifted through several more volumes of diaries and discovered more than I'd bargained for.

September 1948

I haven't needed to unburden my soul for so long. Life has been good. I have a man who loves me and I love him with every ounce of my being. But my fortune has changed, not necessarily for the worse, Drew and I are still very much in love, but there are complications. I am with child and Drew is insisting we should marry. The fact that I'm already married and my husband one of the deemed 'lost and presumed dead' during the war, – many still turning up years later – doesn't seem to concern him. I, on the other hand, hold grave concerns. Despite my father-in-law still holding a position of power in the military, if Charles did return from the war, nobody would know where to find me but I really don't want to take the risk of committing bigamy, nor do I want to cause a scandal. A scandal could cost Drew his new position in the Home Office. As I write these words, my mind is made clear. We love each other. We will love the child we have formed from that love and nothing else matters.

March 4th 1949

The child came early, three weeks early, and I'm sure in part it was my own doing. Refusing all offer of household help at home whilst Drew was at his office, and not anticipating the weather turning so bitterly cold. Carrying the heavy piles of logs and the constant filling of the coal scuttle, must have bore down heavily and brought on the premature birth – a sweet little girl weighing no more than five pounds but perfectly formed in every way. The child took well to the breast and the midwife assures me that by the summer she will have gained the normal weight for her age.

We intend to name her Rose, Although Drew insists on calling her Rosebud, as a way of lessening the confusion between the two females in his life. I am so blissfully happy!

March 10th

Life can be so cruel! I'm lost in a sea of sorrow and can hardly bear to write the words, for once they are written, I have to concede it's true. Rosebud is dead!

March 11th

I'm in such a sorry state that Drew has been allowed compassionate leave for a few days. He's filling his time by making a tiny casket for Rosebud's remains and digging a burial place near the hedge, where it links to the right of the cottage. Once the gruesome task was completed, he made it clear that he too would like his remains to be scattered at the same spot. He felt that this lovely patch of nature was more holy than any churchyard in the area. Besides, he added, consecrated ground had no guarantee of being left undisturbed in the future.

I had already read this brief entry of March 11th when deciding the final resting place for Aunt Winifred's ashes, but, pressed for time I hadn't read what preceded it or what followed. What I read next chilled me to the bone.

March 18th

I have just returned from walking Drew to the station. I waved him off with a smiling face but inside I was in turmoil, riddled with guilt and shame for not being totally honest with my beloved. Rosebud's death was caused by my incompetence.

Over the harshest of the winter months, I'd taken to feeding a forlorn-looking black cat that frequented the garden. On the 7th of March, the day dawned warm with only a thin scattering of cloud to mar an early start to spring. After her late morning feed, I settled Rosebud in her pram on the front lawn in order to gain benefit from the milder fresh air, whilst I sowed neat rows of vegetable seeds on the small patch of soil prepared by Drew on the previous weekend.

After an hour or so, I went to check on my child. To my horror, as I approached the pram, I could see the black cat curled and asleep on the pillow. I screamed in panic and the cat leapt from the pram and shot into the bushes. I pulled Rosebud to my breast, knowing at once her breathing had stopped, her tiny face waxen and still. Panic took hold of me and before I knew it, I was running down Old Mill Road, Rosebud in my arms wrapped in a blanket, tears streaming from my eyes as I prayed to God for mercy. A car pulled to a halt beside me. It was Doctor Connor and for a moment relief flooded through me. After unhooking my gripping fingers from the tiny bundle, he examined her. His words were gentle and kind, explaining how a high percentage of infants die without apparent cause in the first few weeks after birth. But I knew the truth!

My shame and cowardice prevented me from mentioning the cat to Drew, but inwardly, I vowed never again to allow a cat in or around Rose Cottage.

My life had become a strange mix of three activities. During the hours of daylight, dressed in my oldest clothes, I concentrated on the decorating. When darkness fell and silence reigned once more, I'd take a shower, cook a simple meal before settling down to reading more of Aunt Winifred's revelations. Every now and then, the ritual is broken with a trip to the hospital and a takeaway meal.

I hadn't bothered as yet to buy a television, and if Andy… What I mean is, Andy loves all sports, so naturally once he's home, buying a television will be a must. Aunt Winifred had never owned a television, that was one of the main reasons Liz disliked coming here. We were encouraged to read or play board games during the evenings, both of which Liz hated. I loved reading and found that the more I read about my aunt, the more I realized how alike we were.

One of my greatest discoveries, apart from the memento mori ring, was coming upon the framed genealogy chart. It had been wrapped carefully in brown paper and slid down the inside of the chest, held in position by the bulk of the other paperwork. I'd carefully unwrapped it and discovered the reason behind its removal from the wall. An ugly crack in the glass ran diagonally from right to left down its whole length. It had obviously been placed in the chest for safekeeping until my aunt got around to having it reglazed. I lay it on the bed and stared at it, enraptured as I followed the chart of my ancestors from the early eighteenth century. It was clear that Aunt Winifred had opened up the back and added recent additions to a dwindling family tree. Dad was there, so too the date of his demise, leaving me alone on the end of a branch until Andy joined me in marriage. A tiny offshoot line was drawn between us, expectancy and readiness drawn on the blankness of the parchment, the crack in the glass cutting straight across this tiny offshoot. Left in no doubt that Aunt Winifred had been as bereft as we were at the miscarriage of our child, I'd rewrapped the chart and placed it back in the chest, out of sight and out of mind; I had no inclination for revisiting old wounds, I had enough emotional stuff to contend with.

From time to time, Fred would pop in for a cup of tea and a chat with Matt, making sure all was going well with the alterations. He'd become a good friend to me and was more than happy to look after Minx and Sheba, whilst the worst of the upheaval was going on. The cats didn't like the smell of the new paint and showed their disapproval by clawing at it. On the other hand, Fred was glad of their lively company; he'd recently lost one of his feline companions to old age and the other, suffering from a cancerous growth would probably soon follow. He refused payment for taking care of Sheba and Minx, so each Sunday I cooked us a roast and we'd sit and chat about what I'd read in the diaries and he'd enlarge and enlighten me further about the lives of past owners' of Rose Cottage.

Fred had first met my aunt when he was a teenager in need of coaching with reading and writing to enable him to secure work. Her knowledge of the written word and how the learning of it was the basis of acquiring many other skills, was key to his future love of local history. After the death of Drew Grimshaw, whom Fred vaguely remembered but had no idea he was in a relationship with his housekeeper, they spent many a day comparing notes on past events, leaving Fred to believe that Winifred was considering writing a book on *The History of Rose Cottage*.

Chapter 13

15th October – Torbay Hospital

As already stated, my visits to the hospital have become less frequent and the refurbishments of the cottage a perfect excuse for not facing up to the inevitable. Autumn is blending into winter, the days are shrinking and the evenings are dark, long and lonely; a taste of what my life is to become.

I arrived at the hospital to find that Andy had been moved to a bed in a small room where he was connected to less medical paraphernalia but given more privacy. I wasn't sure if this relocation indicated an improvement but leaning close and kissing his brow, whilst taking his hand in mine, it was clear to me that I was losing him. It had been eight days since my last visit, and in that small amount of time I saw a marked difference in his appearance.

Tentatively, I began relaying what I'd been up to. Giving Andy a run down on the progress regarding his car insurers and the games they were playing to delay paying out. In the next breath, I apologised, I didn't want him to think (just in case he could hear me) that I was anxious to get my hands on his money; far from it. With the final cheque arriving from Aunt Winifred's estate, coupled with the rent from the Halifax house, I'd never been so well off. But money is no substitute for happiness.

Running short of what to say next, I fleshed out my own lacking by reiterating what I had recently learned from one of Aunt Winifred's diaries. I removed the diary from my bag, opened it at the marked page, cleared my throat and began.

June 15th 1954

Drew, my best friend, my lover and the father of my child of three days, is dying! The unfairness of it; he'd been retired from the Home Office for less than a year and already he is confined to his bed, such is the debilitating effect of his illness. As ever, this remarkable man remains untouched by the experience. He displays neither sadness nor fear, recounting, and summarizing that his life has been fulfilling in every way and what more could we possibly ask for during our brief visit on earth. He can sense my returning depression at the thought of his departure and begs of me to expand my thoughts to encompass the future. "War is behind us," he announces, as he squeezes my hand, "And thanks to the sacrifice of many young lives, the future looks more promising for the next generation. You are still a relatively young woman, Rose, with means to remain independent if you so wish, but my hope for you, is that you find someone to share your life, someone to share your love with."

Drew had signed the cottage over to me, along with the contents of his banking account, both of which I'd have gladly swapped to keep him by my side for a while longer.

After the loss of Rosebud, I'd sunk into a deep state of depression; gradually lifting as Drew's ongoing encouragement inspired me to continue writing my diaries and update the family chart, as the future generations emerge. I'd relayed to him every branch of my current family still in existence but I knew nothing of his family, neither past nor present.

June 16th 1954

The birdsong had woken us early and instead of slipping back into sleep as we normally did, we began to chat. Talking of the past and making the most of what time we had left together. It took a minute or two before I realized that Drew was actually beginning to reveal his life as a child growing up. I halted his words, begging him to wait until I had my pen and short hand pad to hand, for I wasn't about to waste this opportunity.

The next entry of the diary was two months later but I couldn't bear to go on reading it. Not here. Not in this room of the *near-dead and the non-conversing*. I was amazed at the similarities of our lives and began to wonder if I was being influenced by my Great Aunt Winifred and the atmosphere of Rose Cottage.

A light cough and the rustle of paper behind me brought me back to the present. Turning around I saw Francis in the doorway holding a bunch of blood-red Dahlias and looking apologetic. 'Sorry for the intrusion, Kate, your reading was so interesting, so beautifully carried out, who is the author?'

'Oh! Thank you, Francis, for the flowers, the compliment and your visit. I was reading my great aunt's diaries and I was just...'

Before I realized what was happening, Francis had her arms around me; patting my back and gently rocking me, as sobbing racked my body and tears streamed down my face. I pulled from her, searching out a tissue. 'Sorry about that, Francis. I suppose it's the shock of what's to come. Has Pete managed to speak with Dr Murray lately? I've heard nothing about the operation they were hoping to carry out.'

'From what Pete understands from discussions with Dr Murray, who is not the easiest of men to pin down, the swelling needs to be substantially diminished before they can operate. Unfortunately, that hasn't happened. Come on, love, I'll give you a lift back. I'd love to see the improvements you've made to the cottage.'

* * *

16th October – Rose Cottage

The only interruption today will be the electrician and he isn't due until eleven thirty. I'd been out for my morning walk, a new regime I'd incorporated at the start of each day to counteract my threatening depression and my burgeoning weight. Hopefully, it would be successful because there wasn't a great deal left to do in the cottage and the garden didn't need any heavy work at this time of year. Walking would be the only means to help burn off the calories. Also, once the electrician has finished, I'll be rescued from boredom by having access to WIFI and the use of my laptop once again.

From what I had read so far from Aunt Winifred's diaries, and also from the reams of papers she'd typed over the years, I could see she had started to write, *The History of Rose Cottage*, using the old typewriter that sat on her desk. That desk is now positioned in my new downstairs office space, my laptop taking pride of place where the typewriter used to sit. Fred was happy to relieve me of the typewriter, it reminded him of happier times in the company of a lady who taught him the creative possibilities of the written word.

I was beginning to be captivated by the same urge that had taken over my aunt, when she stood on the precipice of her own dark and destructive place. Why shouldn't I continue where she left off? Most of the research had been done, and what had happened over the past weeks, I felt would be helpful if I wrote it all down.

Yes, I would do it! I had more than two hours before the electrician was due. Time enough to read the next instalment of the diary and hopefully, strong enough to endure the emotional onset of Drew's demise.

August 20th 1954

For approximately an hour of each morning over the past eight days, I have listened, without interruption, to Drew's account of his childhood years, whilst my pen scribbled across the pages of the notebook, capturing for posterity all of the salient points. Although his delivery was unemotional, unhurried and, I have no doubt completely true, the effort of more than an hour of talking, leaves him feeling weak. It was my suggestion that we set this regular time of one hour and at the end of that hour, I would leave him to rest up, whilst I transcribed my shorthand notes into legible typed sheets.

Rose Cottage was previously named Apple Cottage. I suppose it was due in part to me that the name was changed. I'd remarked on several occasions how unfitting the name was considering there wasn't a single apple tree in sight. As our friendship deepened and a meaningful relationship developed, Drew, unknown to me at the time, had paid a visit to his solicitor and arranged for the ownership of the cottage to be transferred to me, whilst at the same time, having the deeds altered to reflect the cottage's new title. I remember well, the Friday he returned home for the weekend, brandishing the gift of the newly-carved, wooden house sign. It was a sunny weekend and we'd spent all of the Saturday sprucing up the garden and attaching the new sign; without him giving the slightest hint that the property was now in my name.

Drew's memory of what he'd been told as a child was remarkably clear. Long before he was born, Apple Cottage was better known as Apple Cottages, because there were two cottages linked together, both of them belonging to the Grimshaw family, along with several hectares of orchards and a piece of scrubland large enough to accommodate two barns, a cider press and a storehouse for salted fish. Put simply, the Grimshaw's were quite well off.

However, by the time Drew came on the scene, the Grimshaw family fortune was much diminished. This was due in part to a natural disaster, causing the loss of men and fishing boats out at sea, but in the main the downward spiral of their fortunes were triggered by Digory Grimshaw. He was the eldest child and the only son of Ma Grimshaw Senior, and was found guilty of theft in 1867. He was shipped out to New South Wales, Australia, to serve seven years hard labour.

No one in the family believed he could have done such a thing. To them, he had simply taken a train journey to London town, to sell unneeded curios and to purchase a perambulator for his expected first child. The journey became a nightmare and the nightmare resulted in a multitude of negative consequences that reverberated down the years.

Due to the shock of her only son being snatched away from her, Old Ma Grimshaw's health deteriorated rapidly and within the year she was dead; leaving her daughter-in-law, Bridget, with a fatherless child to rear alone. The impact on Bridget was overwhelming and she was driven to find what solace she could from the cider keg.

By the time Digory junior had reached the age of eighteen, ashamed and frustrated by the poverty brought on by his mother's dependence on cider, he headed for Australia, hungry for truth and knowledge about a father he had never known. Drew was only four years old when his half-brother left Apple cottage but even at that tender age, he was concerned how this would affect his mother. But unlike Old Ma Grimshaw, Bridget was made of sterner stuff. The shock of Digory declaring he was leaving, thus cutting off her main supply of funds, focused Ma's mind into thinking more positively about her position, her options and her previous skills which she had neglected.

Before two years had passed, Ma had turned their fortunes around and Grimshaw's Game Pies were popular throughout the area; giving full time employment to herself, her twin nieces and Drew. Throughout the area, Grimshaw's Pies satisfied the demands of alehouses, hostelries and the growing number of guest houses.

During the third year of their growing prosperity and one week before Christmas Day, when Apple cottage was permeated from top to bottom with the delicious aroma of festive pies, two well-dressed gentlemen walked into the pie shop, and then without invitation strolled casually into the kitchen as though they owned the place. Due to the strange, large-brimmed leather hats they were wearing, it was difficult to determine their identities. Drew had sensed at once who they were but kept quiet in order for the surprise to take its course. It was the return of the two Digorys and when their hats were flung merrily into the air, there was instant recognition and squeals of delight filled the air.

It was soon made clear that this was a visit only and in two months hence, they would be sailing back to the 'tropical land of opportunity', which is how they described the continent of Australia to Ma. They talked much of the opportunities there and, as usual, Drew overheard everything.

Both of the men had wives awaiting their return. In the case of Digory senior, he also had five children. He'd married into a family of sheep farmers the same year as he was released from the bonds of the law; neither he nor his bride caring that he was already married. He'd felt justified in grasping this fresh opportunity on account of what had happened to him. On that fateful train journey to London, he'd shared a carriage for a brief time with his friend, Albert Wilson, who gave him the gift of a silver fob watch to sell and to use the money for whatever was needed for the expected babe. Before leaving the train at Torre however, his friend confided something to him that shook Digory to the core. Albert claimed that Baldwin, a close acquaintance of theirs, had been secretly carrying on with Bridget for a long time and that it was Baldwin's child she was carrying; choosing to keep quite because of the lure of the Grimshaw's wealth. The final sealing of Digory's fate was when Albert volunteered to visit the London magistrate, supposedly to uphold Digory's good character, when in truth, he was there as witness to the stealing of the watch from a high-born gentleman of Cockington Court.

Albert had always desired Bridget for himself. With Digory out of the way, he felt he now had a clear path to fulfilling that desire. It was only after father and son finally came face to face that the truth became obvious. Such was the revelation of their reunion, the NSW Herald newspaper ran the story, including printed photographs as proof of the likeness of father and son.

It was Ma who Drew held the most concern for at this time. Digory and his father wanted to settle the score with Albert Wilson but Ma lied to them by saying that he had died. When the time came for their return to their, adopted new land of never-ending sunshine, they pleaded with us all to join them. They offered to build houses for us all, such was their wealth and the availability of land. Drew's cousins, Eme and Constance, snatched the opportunity, but Ma wasn't interested in going and Drew refused to leave his Ma on her own.

Without a hint of her intentions to anyone, the next delivery of rabbit and mushroom pie to Albert Wilson, probably tasted slightly different in flavour. Nevertheless, the whole of the individual pie was consumed by him. Within three days he lay dead in his coffin.

Drew distinctly remembers standing by his graveside gripping his Ma's hand, whilst the small band of mourners cast forth a handful of earth on his coffin before departing. When they were alone, Ma had released Drew's hand, stepped forward to the open grave and spat on the coffin before saying, "May you rot in hell, Albert Wilson!"

Someone knocking on the cottage door broke the imaginary picture in my head of the young Drew, fully aware of what his Ma had done. Marking the page in the diary, I reluctantly dragged myself to the door; yes, I really do mean dragged, because my lower back was giving me such pain. On reaching the door I hesitated, hoping it wasn't Fred returning Minx and Sheba, because I was in no fit state for frolicking about with them on the floor and in no mood for Fred's idle chit-chatting.

The knocking continued, this time with the accompaniment of an impatient voice. 'Hello? Mrs Radcliffe? It's Mike the electrician. I'm here to install your broadband and…'

I yanked open the door, amused by the shock on his face. 'Sorry, sorry I didn't mean to startle you; I wasn't expecting you for another half an hour or so.'

'We can never time it exactly, love, believe me, half an hour early is as good as it gets; one to two hours late is more commonplace especially when the previous job is a tricky one. I was told an old biddy lives here, that's why I was doing the reassuring bit through the door.'

His manner annoyed me and my aching back prevented me from holding my tongue. 'The old biddy you're referring to was my dear aunt who died a few months ago. Come in please, I'll show you what needs doing.'

After giving Mike instructions of what was required regarding electrical sockets for the office area and the setting up of the wifi router, I wandered out into the garden and left him to it. Like I said, I was in no mood for idle chatter and tea-making; there was a pile of old timber and hedge clippings waiting to be burned at the back of the cottage and my back felt most at ease when I was upright. The day was dry with hardly a breath of wind and I felt it might well be the last opportunity before winter to get the job done.

The fire crackled and grey smoke curled and rose into a pale sky, lit by a weak, watery sun. The smell of burning wood reminded me of bonfire nights when I was a child. Dad was anchored in the memory making sure we celebrated this traditional event of the autumn. Mum never felt the same way about traditions; since Dad died, the only time we celebrate, apart from birthdays, is Christmas and New Year.

Taking care in keeping my back straight, I pulled out the next length of wood to feed the fire when I noticed numbers and wording engraved into its surface. On closer inspection, I could hardly believe what I was seeing; the numerals and words marked in the wood, matched exactly the inscription on the memento mori ring that was now held fast on my finger. What a strange coincidence! I'd found the ring in the hole behind the rotting skirting board. In fact, this *was* the rotting skirting board, the face of it turned toward the wall had fared better than the water-splashed outer surface.

I pulled off my right-hand gardening glove and tugged at the ring, but no matter how hard I pulled, no matter how much I sucked on it, it wouldn't budge. I knew it would take ice-cold water and plenty of liquid soap to remove it from my finger. Resisting the urge to bend and pull off my wellies, inflaming my back even more, I placed the length of skirting inside the brick store for safe keeping, before returning to the job of forking the rest of the clippings onto the fire. Standing well back, I gazed upon the bellowing black smoke as it curled and drifted skyward, leaving in its wake the evocative scent of November 5th.

Chapter 14

10th December – Rose Cottage

In the past two months I've visited the hospital seven times. Two of the visits were arranged meetings with Dr Murray; meetings, which were described by him as *informal discussions on how to move forward.* During my first meeting, his manner had been kind, sympathetic and respectful, whilst his words were brutally blunt. He'd informed me that the swelling causing the pressure to Andy's brain had barely diminished and that his main organs were gradually showing signs of deterioration, meaning, his chances of surviving an operation were slim. As if this wasn't shocking enough, he adding that, Torbay Hospital didn't have the facilities nor the resources for the long term care of patients in a comatose state. He didn't say as much, but I took this to mean that Andy would have to be moved to a facility either further north or further east of the country.

For the second meeting, Dr Murray had arranged for Pete to be present, addressing him in the main and reiterating all that was said in the previous meeting. His manner seemed brusquer than before and once again my input during this, *informal discussion,* was not encouraged. I was feeling numb and I totally resented the pressure

I was under but couldn't find the right words to express it. After the frustrated Dr Murray checked his watch for the umpteenth time, he hurriedly arranged for a third meeting to take place on the twelfth of December, asking Pete if he'd mind attending once again; I think he was concerned I might later accuse him of brow beating a decision out of me. Nevertheless, whether Pete was there or not, I got the strong feeling that this next meeting was my last chance for prevaricating. I was being directed down a path I wasn't yet ready to tread. I simply needed more time to adjust to the inevitable.

Looking at the calendar, I realize it is now only two weeks before Christmas Eve. I haven't bought a single present nor written any cards and I have never felt so lonely. There's been no contact from Mum, and even if she had invited me for Christmas, I would have refused the offer. I don't want anyone, especially family members, to see the state I'm in. I've piled on the pounds, I'm not sleeping well, I'm tearful and moody and my back is still giving me problems, in spite of completing all of the decorating and finishing the reading of Aunt Winifred's diaries – the excuse I'd used for the ongoing back pain. It is becoming obvious that I need medical help. I have not yet registered with a local doctor because until now there had been no need. I'd felt strong and well, positive about the future; but now... Now I realize if I don't get help soon, the downward spiral of depression will have an unbreakable hold on me.

I googled the contact details of the nearest doctor's surgery and jotted down the only number given. The telephone was picked up on the third ring with a polite female voice announcing she was Sandra, receptionist for The Chelston Manor Doctor's Surgery. I explained my situation regarding the recent move to the area and the need to register with a doctor. Within minutes, Sandra had my name, address, telephone number and particulars of my previous doctor. Before I had the opportunity to say anything about my present state of health, I was booked for an appointment that evening at six-thirty to see Doctor Payne. Before replacing the receiver, Sandra explained that all new patients were appointed to one of the doctors, following a thorough examination with one of the practice's nurses, and I would need to bring a urine sample with me. Despite Sandra's friendly and efficient manner, I was feeling more than a little concerned. To be completely honest, I was feeling frightened!

I had hours ahead of me and nothing to fill those hours with, regretting, not for the first time, that I hadn't bought a television to help ease the boredom of the long, dark winter nights ahead. I switched on the radio and tuned in to a classical music channel, stretched out on the sofa, closed my eyes and allowed my mind to revisit the inspirational way my great aunt had dealt with the many traumas in her life.

From what I had gathered, it was facing the loss of her beloved Drew that ranked as the most heart breaking period my aunt had had to face. She was only thirty-five, whilst Drew was heading towards his sixty-first birthday. He had already paved the way for lessoning the grief of loss, she was still young enough to build a new life with someone else and she must never allow guilt to get in the way of that. She never did of course, writing on several occasions that Drew, despite the age difference, was her true *soulmate* and she could never love another.

Once Drew had begun to open up and talked more about his childhood and his family, it was revealed what a remarkable person he really was. When my aunt had queried why he hadn't taken advantage of sailing to Australia for a much easier life with Digory.

He simply answered that he knew Ma wouldn't go, and who could blame her. Digory Senior had remarried and now had five children with his new wife. He'd added that if his Ma had been left to live alone, who could say what mischief would befall her. Drew loved his half-brother dearly but the great distance would do nothing to diminish that love. In his opinion, Individual lives could only be fulfilled if they were lived independently. Besides, it was noted in Aunt Winfred's entry and I could almost visualize him saying it with a wry smile on his face, if he had been persuaded into going to Australia, he would not have met the love of his life.

That was the final entry Aunt Winifred had made that month. It was during her next entry four weeks later that I was to learn that Drew had died that night, wrapped in the arms of the love of his life.

According to my aunt, Drew was not a religious man but he did support the theory of the collective consciousness and believed that the soul, the innermost essence of man, survived the body. During those weeks of the diary's silence, I can only Imagine and sympathize with what she must have been going through, especially as she raked the soil to absorb Drew's ashes in the vicinity of Rosebud's remains. My aunt and I, have indeed much in common, and it is deeply concerning that I am heading towards a similar fate; living a life alone and only gaining fulfilment from delving into the lives of those who have gone before.

Growing weary from the depressive turn of my thoughts, I moved to my laptop and opened the folder, titled *ancestry.co.uk*, focusing my mind on the research I'd started into my own family history. The Genealogy Chart already held the names in question; a jumping off point for finding out what I could about the lives behind the names, their occupations, the ups and downs and the traumas they'd encountered. I had pages and pages of information in relation to the Grimshaws of Apple Cottage, but barely anything on the owners of Rose Cottage, there was just me and Aunt Winifred. Both of us were named on the Mannering genealogy chart, but no characteristic details were shown.

Over the last hundred years many Mannering lives were cut short because of the two world wars. These were well-documented and I'd copied and pasted all the relevant details into my folder for future use when I felt more inclined to tackling the mammoth task of turning those records into a book. Impatient for knowledge of those marked in the earlier period of the chart, I entered the name *Charles Mannering*, the earliest name on the chart, and described as a gentleman born in the late seventeenth century.

* * *

6.30pm – Chelston Manor Surgery

I'd almost missed my appointment, such was the captivation and concentration concerning my distant ancestor, Sir Charles Mannering. There were pages of dossiers on him. He was a highly influential politician and a landowner of vast swathes of Cheshire. However, on reaching old age and with his political career faltering, the likelihood of his fortune remaining in the family was slim. It seemed more likely that it would pass to cousins of ill repute because of the inability of his wife to produce an heir. However, Charles Mannering was thrown a literal life-line. Out of the blue, or so it seemed from the dossiers on my laptop, there was much celebration as a fifteen-year-old boy named Percival Glover, arrives at the Cheshire manor claiming to be Mannering's illegitimate son. Apparently, Percival's mother, Agnes Rowe, died giving birth to him during the year 1705 and he was adopted by a childless couple in Newton Abbot. On reaching maturity, Percival's adoptive parents revealed to him his true parentage. Without hesitation, or any regard for the couple who had reared him, the lad travelled north to seek out his rightful place in the world.

It gave Charles Mannering great joy to gaze upon his son. The likeness to his natural father was unmistakable and Percival was soon welcomed into the Mannering fold and became heir to the wealth and lands of the Cheshire manor. Three years later at the tender age of eighteen, gaining the title, *Lord of the Manor*. Unfortunately, the sudden wealth and power bestowed on one so young, turned the young man wayward, and this, coupled with the onset of Civil War, diminished the wealth Charles Mannering had worked so hard to accumulate. Before the turning of the next century, the few Mannerings remaining, were as poor as church mice.

Sitting back to mull over the dramatic decline in the Mannering's fortunes, I glimpsed the time on my laptop screen, telling me I only had fifteen minutes to get to the doctor's surgery. I quickly saved everything I'd collected, before switching off my laptop, grabbing my coat and heading straight out of the door.

I arrived only five minutes late for my appointment, my lower back aching like mad, only to be informed that Dr Payne was running late by as much as twenty minutes.

Eventually, my name is called to undergo an examination from the nurse named Beth, who immediately asked me for my urine sample. Oh no! In my rush I'd forgotten the sample and my expression gave me away.

'Not to worry', said Beth pushing a plastic bottle into my hand, 'take this and and see what you can produce, most women only have to look at a toilet to encourage them to pee. Through that door on the left.'

Fortunately I managed to go, in fact lately I needed to go more often, and I felt sure this was connected with the dull ache in my lower back. Kidney stones and even kidney-failure was prevalent on Mum's side of the family and deep down I felt that this family trait could be the cause of my problem. On returning with the sample, Beth took it from me, stuck an identifying label on it and passed it to another nurse for analysis. She then measured my height, weighed me and checked my blood pressure, before wafting a form at me to be completed whilst waiting for the attention of Dr Payne. The form contained the usual questions relating to name, address, age etc.

By the time I was called in to see the doctor, I'd completed the form and handed it to him. Dr Payne, a tall, wiry man of about fifty years old, greeted me with a warm shake of the hand. His examination of me, both verbal and physical was thorough, checking through what was written in the form and the information that Beth had placed before him. His diagnosis, as to the cause of my malady shocked and startled me! He placed a hand on my shoulder, adding that I should undergo a scan to be absolutely sure, but that a scan, unless paid for privately, may take some time to arrange through the NHS.

I walked out of the surgery in total shock, clutching the slip of paper that confirmed an arranged scan for eleven-thirty the next morning, with instruction to make sure my bladder was full at the time of undergoing the scan.

* * *

11th December – Private Section of Torbay Hospital

By the time I'd retired to my bed the night before, I was exhausted, falling into a fitful sleep, continuously disturbed by several fragmented dreams. I was also emotionally drained and I desperately needed to share what was going around and around in my head. On the point of picking up the phone to call Mum, I thought better of it. It wouldn't be fair to share such news until I was absolutely certain.

I wrote out a cheque for the scan and in return was handed a cup of tea, probably to help top up my bladder as advised by the doctor. Again I was asked a variety of questions, my mind racing off in all directions, as I considered the situation I might find myself in.

The scan was carried out, proving beyond a shadow of doubt, that Dr Payne knew what he was talking about and his diagnosis was correct.

* * *

12th December – Torbay Hospital

I arrived half an hour earlier than the prearranged appointment with Pete and Dr Murray. I felt calm and knew exactly what I was about to do. On entering the small room where Andy lay in a *world-between-worlds*, taking in breath through the aid of complex apparatus, a nurse had just finished attending to him. She smiled and moved further down the corridor, leaving us to our privacy. I kissed his brow and then kissed his mouth before removing the content of the A5 envelope I was holding. It was evidence of the scan from the day before. Evidence of what was growing inside my body. Placing the scan on Andy's chest, I took hold of his right index finger, which was warm from the blood artificially pumping around his body, and traced his finger over the images of two foetuses in the early stages of development. I spoke gently and earnestly of how at last we had a family of our own, conceived in the love we'd shared on the days before his terrible accident. I told him of how I would love and cherish his sons every day of my life. Then I asked, even more earnestly for a sign that my words were registering with him; any sign at all that I was getting through to him that he was now a *father-to-be*.

Time seemed to stand still as I waited and waited...

No matter how much I wanted it to happen and no matter how much I willed it to happen, I could not change the unchangeable. I had to accept that Andy was lost to me. I needed to move forward into the next stage of my life. Our sons depended on it.

Epilogue

Kate Radcliffe gave birth to healthy twin boys on 7th May 2015. Kate's mother, delighted with having the novelty of boys in the family at last, spent a month at Rose Cottage after their birth, helping her daughter to adjust to her new role as a mother.

The once prohibited room, bright in its aqua-blue walls, rang out with the sounds of laughter, lullabies and on occasion crying, altering the dynamics of the space. The floorboards still creaked in the dry months of summer but as the days shortened, and humidity rose, the creaking lessened and eventually disappeared completely. Sheba and Minx took up permanent residence with Fred Wilson in Lower Chelston. They'd enjoyed the openness of the garden surrounding Rose Cottage but had clearly disliked the atmosphere within the confines of its walls.

Kate made sure her sons, Andrew and James, would always be aware of who their father was; his face smiled down on them from an A2-size canvassed photograph, taken when he'd graduated as a young constable and hanging from the vacant hook between their two cots. As to the memento mori ring, Kate continued to wear it. It was a token of her loss and a constant reminder of the hope it had given her, for she had never stopped believing in those five little words *Absent but for a tyme*, and in a way, Andy *had* returned to her in double measure.

When time allowed, Kate continued with the research of her ancestry and with Fred Wilson's help, discovered more information about Agnes Rowe – birth mother to Percival. Kate felt sure she had found the original owner of the memento mori ring. Agnes had died in childbirth, as the young Percival had attested to. However, the date of Agnes' death, didn't quite match the date on the ring.

This deliberate attempt to confound in the early seventeen hundreds, was still confounding today. However, *you*, dear reader, know the truth behind the altering of this all-important date. It was clear Edmund Rowe wanted to take the ring with him to the grave, along with the whereabouts of little Percival, but, maybe the wishes of Agnes Rowe were instilled in the ring… Wishes that it should pass down the family line to the rightful owners rather than be lost forever in the bowels of the earth. You may argue that such thoughts are fanciful or even touched by witchery. But just a mere hundred years ago, who would have thought possible that we'd be conversing in real time, in perfect video linkup to loved ones on the other side of the globe. As a writer and believer of all possibilities, I say, let us keep an open mind!

Much appreciation to:

Brian Read, Author of *Cockington Bygones* – a history of the Manors of Cockington and Chelston and the Parish of Cockington – which provided immeasurable help in my research.

Lilian Murr and Brian Read, for giving their time and effort pointing out and editing my flaws.

Tracey Turner, for bringing to fruition the cover design fixed in my imagination; keeping to my brief, in spite of the difficulties when photographing tiny objects such as a ring.

Elaine Sharples, for promptly, patiently and sympathetically, providing a typesetting service which is second to none.

Barry, as always, for his constant support.